Julie Elizabeth Leto

Dear Reader,

The editors at Harlequin and Silhouette are thrilled to be able to bring you a brand-new featured author program beginning in 2005! Signature Select aims to single out outstanding stories, contemporary themes and oft-requested classics by some of your favorite series authors and present them to you in a variety of formats bound by truly striking covers.

We plan to provide several different types of reading experiences in the new Signature Select program. The Spotlight books will offer a single "big read" by a talented series author, the Collections will present three novellas on a selected theme in one volume, the Sagas will contain sprawling, sometimes multigenerational family tales (often related to a favorite family first introduced in series), and the Miniseries will feature requested, previously published books, with two or, occasionally, three complete stories in one volume. The Signature Select program will offer one book in each of these categories per month, and fans of limited continuity series will also find these continuing stories under the Signature Select umbrella.

In addition, these volumes will bring you bonus features...different in every single book! You may learn more about the author in an extended interview, more about the setting or inspiration for the book, more about subjects related to the theme and, often, a bonus short read will be included.

Watch for new stories from Janelle Denison, Donna Kauffman, Leslie Kelly, Marie Ferrarella, Suzanne Forster, Stephanie Bond, Christine Rimmer and scores more of the brightest talents in romance fiction!

We have an exciting year ahead!

Warm wishes for happy reading,

Marsha Zinberg

Marsha Zinberg
Executive Editor
The Signature Select Program

SPOTLIGHT

Julie Elizabeth Leto

Making Waves

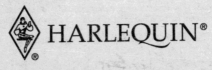

HARLEQUIN®

TORONTO • NEW YORK • LONDON
AMSTERDAM • PARIS • SYDNEY • HAMBURG
STOCKHOLM • ATHENS • TOKYO • MILAN • MADRID
PRAGUE • WARSAW • BUDAPEST • AUCKLAND

ISBN 0-373-83653-8

MAKING WAVES

www.eHarlequin.com

Printed in U.S.A.

Dear Reader,

So this author walks into an agent's office and says, "I have this story I want to write. It's about this woman who wants to live up to her bad reputation in Key West. She meets this handsome journalist. They have really hot sex." The agent is hooked! Tell me more, she says! "Well," the author continues, "there's also this story within the story, set in ancient Greece, starring a young woman who's having an affair with...well, a fish."

Sounds like a joke, right?

Okay, so that's not exactly how it all happened. And Reides isn't really a fish. But sometimes, the wildest ideas can come to fruition when the right team is put together at the right time...and not one second before. That's what happened with this book.

Tessa and Colton first revealed themselves to me back in 1998, shortly after the birth of my daughter. What I didn't know then was that their story wasn't ready to be told yet. Luckily, I had an editor who recognized that and over time, the tale ripened into what it is today. In the meantime, I had twenty books under my belt instead of two, a fabulous agent and an amazing group of writer friends to help me through the rough spots. So here I am, seven years later, and the team and ideas have finally come together. See the dedication page for a scorecard with most of the players—with my deepest thanks.

And hopefully, this story is one my readers will enjoy. If you do, I'd love to hear from you. You can e-mail me at my Web site, www.julieleto.com.

Happy reading,

Julie Elizabeth Leto

For Brenda Chin—
I'll bet you always loved that
"we will buy no wine before its time" commercial, didn't you?
Thanks for being such a connoisseur.

For Marsha Zinberg and Alethea Spiridon—
for seeing the possibilities, giving me freedom and keeping
me on track. Your vision and hard work are appreciated.

For Helen Breitwieser—
here's the book that brought us together!
Already the first of many.

For the Plotmonkeys—
Janelle Denison, Leslie Kelly and Carly Phillips.
I can always count on getting into hot water with you guys
around. Here's to all the fun you can have at 40!

For Susan Kearney and Stephanie Bond—
your encouragement and support mean so much.

CHAPTER ONE

"Is the coast clear?"

Parked a half block away, Tessa Dalton watched her attorney's house, her chest tight. The front window sheers fluttered. Karen stepped into view and waved, then scanned the street outside, lending a second pair of eyes to confirm that Tessa was safe to leave the confines of her rental car. Damn, she resented taking such paranoid precautions, but she hated ambushes even more. Most of the guests had already arrived at Karen's, and if Tessa could just slip inside the house relatively unnoticed, she might actually have a good time.

Switching her cell phone to her other ear, Tessa listened to the tropical Jimmy Buffet beat playing in the background of Karen's party, the perfect sound track for small talk and laughter on a hot Miami night. A mortgage payoff celebration should have been the last place Tessa wanted to be, but with every measure of music, she longed to dash inside. Escape. Enjoy. Relax. Besides, Karen deserved Tessa's support for the long hours her attorney had logged while working on her high-profile divorce, not to mention the even longer hours she'd spent bolstering Tessa's confidence in the human race. Karen had promised an evening of good music, food and laughter with people who had enough class to ignore Tessa's current situation. A night like that could go a long way toward restoring her faith in her fellow man.

Well, maybe not her fellow *man,* but her fellow woman at least had a decent shot. And after nearly six months of self-imposed exile—protection from her world as it unraveled around her—Tessa wasn't about to let an opportunity for some long-deserved fun slip away.

Still, caution couldn't hurt.

Karen's sheers skimmed back into place. "Looks clear to me," her attorney concluded. "I'll send a friend out to meet you. I'm so sorry about today at the courthouse. I don't know what happened to your bodyguards."

Tessa smirked. "Yes, you do. You're just too devoted to that *innocent until proven guilty* credo to say it out loud."

Tessa had no doubt her wily, soon-to-be ex-husband and his powerful father had been behind the defection of her protection. Daniel had likely doubled their salary so they'd leave her vulnerable to the reporters hovering around the Palm Beach County Courthouse. The ravenous swarm couldn't have anticipated that she'd have no more meat to give them. Since she'd announced her separation from the prince of West Palm Beach and then had had the audacity to deny his claim to her wealth, the press had picked her clean.

Which didn't mean the insects didn't return to the carcass every so often, to make sure they hadn't missed a morsel of muscle, a prime cut of cartilage—anything they could twist into another outrageous lie.

Tessa scanned the street one last time, hating that she felt like a prisoner in such a wide-open space. A van caught her attention, causing a prickle along the back of her neck. "Who's catering your party?" she asked, suspicious.

"Lido's from South Beach, why?"

The Lido's logo, complete with palm trees and a setting sun, spanned the side of the van. So much for trusting her instincts. *Hello, paranoia. Glad to meet you.*

"I have a serious craving for strong Cuban coffee," she said to cover her overactive imagination.

"I've got a whole carafe here, just for you. I'll be waiting by the front door," Karen said, her inflexible attorney voice replaced with her more natural, feminine inflection. "I can't believe you came all the way to Miami to celebrate with me. Means a lot."

"Hey, I owe you," Tessa said. "And more than just your retainer and fees, you know?"

"You've paid in full. If you hadn't, I wouldn't have been able to pay off my mortgage," she joked. "Now get in here so we can party."

"I'm on my way."

Tessa disconnected the call, pocketed the phone and pulled the keys out of the ignition. She took a deep breath, exhaled. God, this could be such a mistake. Going out in public, opening herself up to the snide remarks and speculative glances of strangers. She knew that sooner or later, she wouldn't give a damn about what other people thought. That, at least, was her goal.

Besides, she owed Karen, and couldn't blame her attorney for the mess she now faced. It wasn't Karen's fault that Tessa had preferred to bank on love instead of legalities, ignoring her attorney's advice years ago about a prenuptial agreement before her marriage. It also wasn't Karen's fault that Tessa had thought she'd found true love with a rotten, double-dealing son-of-a-bitch who'd sucked the magic out of Tessa's romantic heart just like the pool vacuum hose he'd accused her in court of using as a sex toy.

She had only one more day left until the judge issued a final ruling in her divorce. For over three weeks, she'd sat in the courtroom, listening to Daniel, his family, his attorneys and his lying private investigators paint her as a sexual deviant, an insatiable seductress who'd fucked everyone from the pool boy—emphasis on the word *boy*—to the elderly cook, a woman, no less. They'd used her secret love, the erotic stories she wrote under a pseudonym, as the main evidence against her.

Tessa's editor and agent had come to her defense, but they lived in New York. Daniel's attorney had made a strong case that they couldn't have known about Tessa's sordid life of excess in West Palm Beach. *Of course* they didn't know. No such life existed. Except for the fact that she wrote erotic stories, Daniel's claims had been fabricated, bought and paid for to ensure that Daniel not only got his hands on the money she'd inherited from her filthy-rich father, but that he kept every dime of his own. He wanted everything. Homes, cars, cash—spoils he'd purchased from business deals Tessa had helped arrange through her contacts or had at least supported with her social aptitude.

She'd been the perfect corporate wife, and now she'd become the perfect society pariah. Her so-called West Palm Beach friends had either deserted her long before the trial or they'd bolstered Daniel's salacious tales with misinterpretations of their own.

Vilified and crucified in the courtroom, on the television newsmagazine shows and in the tabloids, Tessa could either run or hide. Or she could say, "screw 'em," and go have a good time. If reporters came after her again, the worst they could do now was slow her progress to her coffee.

She checked her makeup in the rearview mirror under the dome light, unlocked the car and opened the door. No sooner had her foot met the pavement than someone yanked the handle out of her hand and shoved a microphone in her face.

"Mrs. Reese, is it true you're writing a memoir of your sexual exploits? Who is the publisher? Do you have a release date?"

Tessa grabbed for the door, but the reporter placed her body between Tessa and the handle.

"Get out of my way," Tessa demanded. Enough was enough. Pushing out of the car, she swung her purse, only half trying to hide her grin when the heavy leather bag punched the reporter in the gut.

Luckily, the piranha had quick reflexes or Tessa might have knocked her over when she slammed her door. Tessa ducked under the symbiotic cameraman and hurried toward Karen's house, not giving a damn if the woman followed. Or pressed assault charges. Chances were, after tomorrow, she'd have nothing left to be sued for.

A quick glance to her left verified Tessa's earlier suspicions as another cache of reporters rolled out of the Lido's van, armed with lights, cameras and microphones. She had no time to congratulate herself on sensing trouble—or berate herself for not listening to her instincts. She judged the distance to Karen's front gate, but couldn't sprint fast enough. In seconds, she was surrounded. Bulbs blinded her. Microphones poked her in the face, ribs. Questions, accusations and lurid, disgusting suggestions assailed her from all angles, all volumes. She wanted to stand her ground, scream, fight—but she settled for a startled yelp when a strong hand grabbed hers and yanked her out of the melee.

Within moments, she was through Karen's gate and darting to the backyard with her rescuer. Behind them, Karen stood barking above the din, threatening lawsuits if one member of the uninvited press set foot on her private property. Only after they rounded the corner into the quiet backyard did Tessa take a minute to identify her knight in shining armor.

"You!" she said, disbelieving. She'd seen her Galahad in the courtroom, taking notes and weaving his stories with the rest of the media. He was a hard guy to miss. Six foot two, rakish dark hair, pewter eyes that missed nothing. Karen had told her his name. Granger. Colton Granger. With the *Chicago Sun-Times*.

"You okay?" he asked.

Tessa quickly traded one bout of shock for another, but glanced down to find her clothes in place and her body unhurt. Unhurt, but not unaffected. Colton Granger was one fine specimen of male flesh—and her female flesh couldn't help but tingle whenever they shared less than ten feet of space, even in the courtroom. Another woman might have wondered how the heck she could feel anything remotely like sexual interest after what Daniel had put her through, but Tessa was both shocked and pleased to learn that her slimy ex-husband hadn't killed her natural-born passions.

"I'm fine, thanks," she answered. "Why are you here?"

"Karen sent me out to meet you."

"Where's your press pass?" she cracked, slinging her purse over her shoulder. Ready to strike in case her instincts to trust this man—even briefly—were off by a country mile.

He ignored her question and slipped his hands into the front pockets of his loose-fitting khakis. "Karen said you craved coffee."

She couldn't resist. The press had played her up to be the poster girl for fallen women. Why not live up to the reputation a little?

"I crave a lot of things, haven't you heard?"

His eyes narrowed, darkened. When he tightened his jaw, the clench emphasized the rugged, squared shape of his chin, the full curve of his generous mouth. Tessa swallowed and remained silent, no moisture in her throat, her tongue thick.

He wanted her.

Instinctively, she took a half step backward. She'd thought she knew what a man looked like when his concealed desire broke through to the surface. She'd thought her current situation with her divorce and trashed reputation had given her ample armor to protect her from succumbing to even a little hint of want or need for a man.

She'd thought wrong. In a flash, Colton revealed a depth of hunger she'd only dreamed up in her books. Then just as quickly, the look was gone.

She held up her hand and stepped forward, reclaiming the ground she'd nearly lost. "Why are you here again? No, wait. Don't bother answering unless you know why I'm here in this ridiculous situation, too. I'm betting only my therapist can answer that one."

He chuckled; she rolled her eyes. She hated men who found her funny. No, that wasn't true. She simply hated men in general. But she wasn't so possessed with loathing that she'd blindly lump Colton Granger into the whole rotten barrel. He had just pulled her from the throng. And, in truth, he'd been the one reporter to give her a fair shake in the press, questioning the veracity of Daniel's claims in the respected print of the *Chicago Sun-Times*.

This incredibly handsome man had taken her side. Twice now. She could at least produce a civil response. And if he rewarded her with another glimpse of his intense appetite for…what? Her? Her story?

"Thanks for the escort," she said.

"You're welcome."

She waited, but though his jaw clenched again, nothing flashed in his eyes except compassion. "How about you grab a step on the porch and catch your breath? I'll track down your drink of choice."

"I should go in. I promised Karen."

"She'll understand if you take a minute to get yourself together first."

She tugged at the sleeves of her blouse, a sheer purple confection she couldn't resist pairing with tight jeans and ankle boots. Panels of silk hid her bra from view, but revealed her bare tummy through a plum haze. Never in her life had she had the audacity to buy such sexy clothes, much less wear them, but she'd already been publicly pegged as a slut. Why not enjoy some of the benefits?

"Don't I look together?" she asked, wide-eyed with feigned innocence. She smoothed her hands down her sides, emphasizing the curves beneath the blouse, the slim cut of her jeans.

The return of his hunger, so clear in his dark gray gaze, surged through her like electricity. And her reaction—a tiny prickle of heat between her thighs—so unexpected and overwhelming, nearly sent her running. Luckily, Colton seemed to wield great control over his needs, which he once again tamped down just by clearing his throat.

But when he licked his lips seconds before he spoke, he jolted her with another wave of hot awareness.

"You look like you could take on the world," he answered.

She allowed a half smile to quirk through. "Maybe I'll just take you on."

He tilted his head to the left, his expression doubtful. "Promises, promises."

She couldn't help but laugh and the light, tinkling echo sounded so strange coming from her. She had no intention of taking him on, or any other man for that matter, but for the first time in forever, she at least felt comfortable in her skin.

When was the last time she'd allowed herself the freedom to indulge in a round of harmless flirting? When was the last time she'd allowed a man into her personal space at all? Maybe having her life torn to the point where she had nothing to lose and everything to gain wasn't so much a tragedy as an opportunity. For change. For liberation.

She followed Colton up to the gleaming white, wraparound porch of Karen's Cape Cod-style mini-manse and sank to the bottom step. Behind her, the screen door creaked, and she closed her eyes. The sound of the party surged, waned, then surged again less than a minute later, finally dulled by his firm closing of the door.

"This ought to smooth out the rough spots," he offered.

She turned to accept her coffee, but instead, her hand met the cold glass of a longneck beer bottle. Mexican, with lime. She thought she might cry with gratitude.

"You read my mind," she said, swiping lime around the lip of the bottle before taking a long, cold sip. The beer eased down her throat, icing her frazzled nerves into cool submission.

"I have a knack for anticipating what a woman wants."

She laughed, shaking her head. "My turn to say, 'promises, promises.'"

His grin had no hint of contrition or capitulation. "You do that to men, don't you? Incite the natural male instinct to show a woman a good time?"

She smiled. "I'm just sitting here, innocently drinking my beer."

Gray eyes—gray, intense eyes, she amended—cast a glance toward the longneck bottle she dangled suggestively between her knees. Oh, that. Maybe his instincts weren't the only ones rising unbidden to the surface, simply from their shared company. To counteract the effect of her inadvertent sensuality, she lifted the beer to her lips and took a most un-ladylike, unseductive swill.

With a chuckle, he twisted the top off his own brew and matched her swig for swig. The atmosphere alternately crackled between charged and comfortable, and surprisingly, Tessa didn't know which she liked better.

"You've been quite the rescuer tonight."

He tilted his head again, and this time an errant sweep of thick, black hair swung down over one eye much like a pirate's signature patch. He raked the lock back with a strong, long-fingered hand decorated with a gold college ring. Now, who was trying to be seductive?

"Right place, right time." His voice hinted at an accent buried deep within his sultry baritone.

"And I don't suppose you want an exclusive interview for your trouble?" she suggested, unable to tone down the not-so-subtle bite in her question.

"That would be crass."

"Isn't Crass 101 a required course at journalism school?"

He chuckled again, the warm sound inspiring Tessa to take another long, cooling drink from her beer.

"Where I was born, crass is a horrible offense."

She placed the accent. Southern, but carefully hidden beneath a Midwesterner's cadence.

"I'll have to visit your Oz someday," she joked. "Be a nice change of scenery."

They remained silent on the porch, Tessa sitting on the step, Colton standing along the rail. After she'd downed half the bottle, she turned and gave him a good once-over, one last time. As intrigued as she was by Colton Granger, Tessa couldn't allow a foolish dalliance right now—not even with a sexy reporter who seemed to be on her side. She had hard decisions to make about her life, and she needed a clear head to make them. She'd learned the hard way that even the smallest hint of passion tended to muddle her brain worse than San Francisco fog.

The light from the porch sconces rimmed Colton's broad shoulders with a glimmering sheen, casting his face in shadow, causing Tessa to instantly compare him to the mysterious warriors and princes she wrote about in her novels. Or used to write about. Before Daniel blew her cover. Before he decimated her love for her one talent in life.

Tessa took another sip. She knew she'd had too much beer too fast, but she needed the fortification. Under any other circumstances, she would have cut off this interaction with Colton immediately after she'd thanked him for his help. She didn't need strange men in her life. She was having enough trouble with the guys she knew. Better to nip this in the bud. Nothing like a little reality to drown the last of the heat sizzling between them.

"You don't want an interview. Good for me," she said.

"You could ask me a question."

She eyed him skeptically, but his expression remained open, honest.

"Okay," she said. "Why is a Chicago reporter following a divorce case in West Palm Beach? Other than as means to annoy my soon-to-be former father-in-law?"

Martin Reese's company headquarters had recently relocated to the Windy City. He'd spent a good deal of time and money buying whatever political favors he could there. But he was a relative newcomer in a town that prided itself on two mayors from the same political dynasty. Colton's columns about the lurid Reese divorce trial had to have fueled public speculation that old Marty didn't want to deal with. In Florida, he could control the damage. In Illinois, he was out of his element.

Colton didn't answer, but cleared his throat guiltily.

Bingo.

"Well, whatever your reason for sticking up for me, thanks. You got the old man's goat, too." She remembered the scene so clearly—someone shoving the newspaper in Martin's face after a lunch recess, just a few days into the divorce hearing.

Controlled, cool Martin Reese had turned a particularly bright shade of red and barked several interesting expletives at no one in particular. At the time, she hadn't understood her father-in-law's ire, but after she'd found out, she'd considered Colton Granger to be a brave, if not brilliant man.

Now, she could add sexy to the list. Lucky, lucky her.

"I'm surprised he didn't have you fired," she added.

"Oh, he tried."

She raised her bottle. "Kudos to your editor, then."

"Have you read my columns?"

She sighed. "Funny, but I've been avoiding newspapers and television lately."

"My stuff is good. I'll send you copies. Though they would have been better with that exclusive interview."

She swiped her tongue over the lime, closing her eyes and enjoying the tangy bite. "So, that is what this is about, then."

"Nope. Tonight is off-the-record."

Once glance told her he was serious. "Damn, but those fifteen minutes of fame go by quick," she said, snapping her finger. "From the crowd out front, I figured I had at least another five left."

"You have a smart mouth, you know that?"

Too bad she didn't have a smart heart to match. "Betrayal tends to make a woman a little bitchy. I shouldn't take it out on you."

"I can handle justified resentment."

Good, because she had that in spades. "So, tell me, what *do* you want, Colton Granger, defender and rescuer of women in desperate need of privacy and beer?"

He grinned, but didn't hesitate. "Honestly, just one answer to one question. Off-the-record."

She smiled. Of course. A journalistic veteran like him could probably pack one heck of a punch into one question. Oh, well. What did she have to lose? Tessa had had enough of trying to project the right image to the court, of defending herself against Daniel's ludicrous accusations, and mostly, of running from the tabloid press that seemed to follow her everywhere. She'd had fun in these few minutes with Colton when she'd slipped into the role Daniel had created to destroy her—the flirt, the seductress, the insatiable woman with a thousand secret needs. More fun than she'd had in months. And she'd definitely had Colton's interest, which also felt very, very good.

Colton seemed to handle her transformations with aplomb, as if he expected no less than her cold quips one minute, hot innuendos the next. And as a reporter, he was legit. Why not answer his question? Could be a real kick.

"Fire away," she challenged.

He eased down next to her and placed one boot—comfortably worn tanned leather—beside her foot on the lowest step. He watched her squeeze lime juice into the bottle, then stuff in the rind until it floated in the last of the amber lager.

His smile would have been devastating on someone completely sober. Tessa had achieved a light buzz. She blamed her heightened awareness on the beer, the stress. And Colton's irrepressible magnetism.

Yet she wasn't so loopy that she'd forgotten the uncertain life she now faced thanks to her inexperience and naiveté with men—especially the handsome and charming ones. Though what Colton may or may not ask—and what he may or may not print in the paper tomorrow, despite his off-the-record promise—couldn't possibly affect the outcome of her case.

She curled her hair behind her ears, wishing for something to tie the thick tresses away from her neck. The Miami night had cooled to a humid eighty-five degrees. The acrid scent of citronella burned her nostrils, but kept the buzzing swarms of mosquitoes at an impotent distance. Salsa music danced into the air through a newly opened window and she watched Colton's fingers tap a rival beat on the bottle.

"Are you game to discuss Charlene Perrault?"

She shifted in her seat. Her "secret identity" wasn't a favorite topic. For the past month, she'd struggled to convince the court that Charlene Perrault was a writer of fiction, not a crazed nymphomaniac. A task necessary after Daniel had revealed with lascivious glee that Tessa Dalton Reese, socialite, was the force behind Perrault, the author responsible for some of the edgiest erotica published in the mainstream market since Anne Rice donned the pen name A. N. Roquelaure and sent *Sleeping Beauty* into sexual servitude.

As Charlene Perrault, Tessa had taken up the gauntlet where Rice had left off. With a lighter touch and a strong spirit of romance, her carnal fairy tales fired the imaginations of men and women alike. And thanks to her prize Pulitzer-like divorce, the books, produced by a small-press publisher, were selling like proverbial hotcakes on a cold day.

"Is that your *one* question?" she asked.

"Not exactly. What I want to know is, *are* you Charlene Perrault?"

She glanced at him sideways, but when her vantage point proved ineffective, she twisted her entire body. She searched his face, finding his expression blank, cool. She'd expected another glimpse of lascivious undertones and, for an instant, suspected he'd used this opportunity alone with her to see if the nympho-author wanted a quickie on the back porch.

With a sting of disappointment, she realized that wasn't why he'd asked.

"Everyone in the free world knows I'm Perrault, Mr. Granger. Wouldn't you rather ask me why I married Daniel in the first place? Why I didn't sign a prenuptial agreement to protect myself? Why I didn't just pay off the putz when I had a chance with the millions my Daddy left me?"

He shook his head. "I'm not interested in your past. Just your future."

He scooted back on the wooden porch step, his jeans rasping against the painted pine, so confident and comfortable with who he was. Tessa couldn't control the sudden quiver rattling her insides, until she harnessed a flash of anger. How dare he, a perfect stranger, care about her tomorrows when she wasn't yet sure there'd be anything to care about? How dare he ignite fires she had no business burning?

"How about if I ask you another question first?"

"Why not?" He drank a draft from his beer. "I have nothing to hide."

"Everyone has something to hide." She punctuated her insight with a snort, a cynical grunt that she might have contained in the past, simply because it wasn't refined. Too fucking bad. The sound expressed a hard-won wisdom she planned to hold on to for the rest of her life.

"I won't make it too hard. You're a reporter…."

"A columnist," he corrected.

"Even better! You spout opinions, probably hang tight to some single-minded agenda."

He nodded. Tipped back his beer. "You could say that."

"Okay, then. Do you believe every word you write? Every idea? Every judgment?"

"I try."

Honest, but noncommittal. How lucky for him. She took one last drink from her beer, then set it down in the inch-or-so space that separated them. Standing, she rubbed her hands down the front of her jeans, then hooked her thumbs in the empty belt loops.

The anger simmering inside her now shot to the surface in

hot arcs. "You have no secrets and you believe every word you write? Then you're one lucky guy. Either that or you're too good to be true."

She'd meant her words to sting with sarcasm, but he had the cool audacity to drain the rest of his beer without looking the least bit offended. Either he didn't give a damn what other people thought of him, or he was a true master of controlling his reactions.

After tamping down her admiration, she rolled her eyes and headed toward the door. She peeked through the half-moon window on the door and spied the kitchen, relatively empty. She'd go in, exchange the required small talk, then find one of the five bedrooms in Karen's house and crash until court tomorrow, when some self-righteous judge would decide if she'd at least hold on to the legacy her father had left her. She had her hand on the screen-door handle when a business card flicked in front of her.

"For the record," Colton said, "I'm too good to be true just the same as you're too bad to be believed. If you ever want to really answer my question or just set the record straight, get in touch."

Tessa snatched the card, stuffed it in her pocket and forced her gaze forward to the glossy white panels in the door. After she heard those sexy boots of his depart down the steps and across the walkway, she risked a glance over her shoulder. He was just as hot on the flip side, and she was just as determined to stay away.

Hmm. In less than ten minutes, he'd jump-started her libido and had given her food for thought. Either she was drunker than she realized after just one beer, or this Colton Granger knew how to fascinate and entice a woman recently convinced she'd be jaded and lonely for the rest of her life.

With a groan, Tessa opened the door. She couldn't help leaning toward the second theory, even though every fiber of her being hoped like hell for the first.

CHAPTER TWO

One Year Later....

From Son of the Siren

"My, but isn't he delicious?" Aphrodite licked her lips, smoothing a silken hand across Morpheus's chest while they gazed into the enchanted mirror and watched young Reides, bastard son of Poseidon, drop his tunic. Wet from a swim, his body glistened. He was muscled and tanned. Powerful. So unlike Aphrodite's current lover, Morpheus, who flitted between dreams and reality so often that his form rarely attained the stone hardness the goddess of love so craved. This half god, half sea creature, Reides, though...he looked carved from pure marble.

"His mother was a siren, yes?" she asked. "I've never encountered one, but I hear they have amazing powers of seduction."

Morpheus's chuckle prickled her skin. "As if you need seducing."

She kept her curse to herself, more interested in the images in the mirror than the god who nightly invaded her chambers. In the reflective glass, Reides stalked across the room where a young, pretty maid fluffed cush-

ions on his bed, her ample buttocks rocking suggestively. Blind lust turned Reides' sea-green eyes nearly black. His chest tightened, muscles bulged. His hands curled into fists. Lust drove him mad—lust Morpheus had injected into the hapless half god through a series of dreams. Aphrodite had long known the tortuous tale, but seeing the effects for herself made her breath rasp and catch.

Every night, Morpheus implanted Reides' brain with erotic dreams of Alina, a beautiful virgin maiden he could never have, never find, as the goddess Artemis had tucked her far away. Poseidon had conspired with the goddess of the hunt to hide Alina and her sisters away from salacious suitors such as Reides, thwarting Morpheus's scheme to yet again interfere in the lives of mortal lovers. To avenge the slight, Morpheus intended to torment Reides, Poseidon's son, until he was driven mad with unrequited lust. But to amuse herself, Aphrodite had secretly interfered. Not only had she arranged for Alina to experience the same intoxicating dreams, but Aphrodite soon planned to give Reides a clue to his lover's hiding place.

But not today. Not now that she'd seen his frantic cravings with her own eyes. This morning, Reides had turned to the sea, desperate to find relief from the fire burning him from the inside out, enveloping him like a cloak from Medea. Swimming in the cold ocean had done nothing to slake his desire. But the maid billowing his sheets might take the edge from his madness. If he took her now.

From behind, Aphrodite hoped. She wanted to watch him ram his impressive rod into the maiden's slick, pink folds. With no gentleness. No hesitation. She adored how mortals mated, with raw, intoxicating violence.

Morpheus captured Aphrodite's uninterested fingers, then forced her palm around his sex, so much less impressive in comparison to the man in the mirror, even if Morpheus was a full god and Reides only the son of one.

"You can have him for yourself once you do my bidding," Morpheus commanded.

Aphrodite hated Morpheus, god of dreams, but she did owe him a debt for recently conspiring with her to thwart Zeus's plan to marry her to Hera's deformed son, Hephaestus. So dutifully, she stroked him to stiffness, ignoring his grunts and pants, imagining he was Reides, whom she would indeed have when the opportunity arose. She considered asking Morpheus to amuse her by shifting his form so he appeared as Reides. He was adept at the skill, and often aroused her by assuming the likeness of Ares or Apollo. But again, she decided to bide her time, until she could hold Reides' rod in her own hand, until she could hear him beg for access to her gossamer, immortal flesh—until she would show the son of the siren the ultimate rewards for pleasuring the goddess of love.

Morpheus turned away from the glass, tore the golden mesh away from Aphrodite's breasts and suckled her nipples like the thirsty brute he was. Despite her disdain for him, jolts of fire shot through her. Her center throbbed for satisfaction, so she lied about how much she wanted him inside her. Yet when Morpheus buried himself to his hilt, Aphrodite turned her eyes to the mirror—to Reides, who pumped his shaft into his maid like a hungry beast. Aphrodite closed her eyes, listening raptly to the maiden's pleasured cries, her *sweet pleas for him to thrust harder, deeper, lest she die for wanting.*

To have that insanity for herself, Aphrodite would willingly give Morpheus whatever he wanted. He'd come to her this eve with the mirror, to give her a glimpse of Reides in all his lustful glory, to pique her insatiable interests, to curry her fickle favor. He knew well how to manipulate her, and if Reides was her prize when all was done, Aphrodite didn't care.

Alina wandered the shore, invigorated by the storm. The wind whipped shards of spray against the rocks, against her skin. Her clothes clung to her flesh; her hair soaked the skin of her back. The elements buffeted her, but nothing sated the fire burning from deep inside.

For yet another night, she'd endured the carnal dreams. At first, the images, the cravings, the need, had only confused her. Ever since she was a child, she'd grown up on this wandering island, where no man reached the shore alive. But she'd slyly questioned her sisters, whose broken hearts had set them in exile here, the gift of solitude from the goddess Artemis, who protected young maidens such as them. Her sisters had known the cruel love of men bent on seduction. From them, Alina had learned about the ways of men and women. Of coupling, of mating, of hungers that could easily drive a woman mad.

Now, she understood what the images tempted her to do and think and feel. But despite her knowledge, she could do nothing to quench the thirsts of her mind and body. Not, at least, until Artemis set her free and she could find a man to initiate her, with her full and curious consent.

Alina hated the loneliness of the island, but she loved the storms, as she loved the sea, as she had eventually come to love the hot waves of desire coursing through her body during the day—and endlessly torturing her during the night. She opened her mouth and drank in the brackish mixture of fresh rain and sea salt, hoping the stimulation to her sense of taste would somehow alleviate the constant throbbing between her thighs.

"Come inside!" her sister ordered from their cottage on the hillside. "Father's likely riding out the storm at sea. There's no need for you to wait for him in the rain!"

Alina turned away from the sound of her sister's voice, knowing Miri spoke the truth. Her father, a fisherman, had not yet returned with the day's catch, but he had persevered in worse tempests than this one many times. Without her father to impose his overprotective will, Alina had taken this chance to escape the tiny cottage and mingle with the elements, with the sea, with her delicious fantasies.

Artemis's promise of refuge had lasted each and every moment of these ten long years. Nothing could hurt them here. And still, Alina fought hard to feel gratitude. Her sisters had found sanctuary in this haven, but Alina had found nothing but emptiness, frustration— desperation to find the secret lover who haunted her nights.

"I see something," she shouted. "I'm going to the lookout."

Before Miri protested, Alina ran straight into the raging winds, through the swaying palms and prickly bramble, up the slippery rocks to the highest point on the island. She'd lied. She'd seen nothing but white-capped waves, illuminated by the streaks of lightning that slashed through the gray sky. She couldn't go inside. She couldn't face another night trapped in the contented dryness of the cottage. She couldn't bear another night alone in her bed, crazed by visions of a man from the sea, a lover who would take her beneath the waters and show her true pleasure.

Once at the top of the crag above the ocean, Alina raised her arms and dared the wind to cast her into the raging depths. Her thin robe molded to her flesh. Gusts twisted and tightened the folds around her until she was nearly immobile from the binding clothes.

She tore the fabric until she was nude against the elements. Her hair, long and golden, streaked into the wind behind her. At the cold caresses of the sharp rain, her small breasts peaked. Shivers racked her, nearly broke her resolve, until she looked out at the water and caught sight of a human form flailing in the waves.

The man in the surf wasn't her father. This creature's flesh gleamed taut and pearlescent, like the inside of a shell. She gasped. She knew him. From her dreams. Her vision from the gods, she guessed. Punishment from Morpheus, torment because she offered no gratitude to Artemis for casting her family from the civilized world.

In her sleep, she'd learned the fire of her lover's caress, the arousal of his probing, hungry touch. Night upon night, she'd endured sensual torture until her body thrummed with wants she couldn't satisfy, needs she knew not how to name.

A wave surged. The body floated closer. His hair, dark as polished slate, gleamed in the flashes of light from the sky. She knew it was him. Unconscious, unmoving. Had he drowned? Had he been haunted by the same dreams, and come in search of her?

She knew neither his name nor his purpose, but the power of desire overwhelmed her. She had to save him. She had to know who he was, what he wanted. Fortified by need, she dived into the raging ocean.

TESSA STARED at the computer screen. She reread the words, edited a sentence here and there. A little melodramatic at the end, she acknowledged silently, but this was mythology, after all. Mystical. Larger than life. Just like the fairy tales she'd adapted in the past, the stories of gods and goddesses of Greece had lasted through centuries, likely because of the universal truths of greed and lust and passion.

Yet mythology had one thing in abundance that fairy tales lacked—sex. Just like Tessa's life. She shook her head, then grabbed her can of diet soda and sipped. She'd made her celibate bed last year after her divorce, now she had to sleep in it. Alone, just like Alina. Aroused by dreams of a forbidden lover.

Only Tessa's dreams didn't feature the son of the siren, her half god, half fish. Tessa's fantasies featured a certain Chicago journalist she had no business messing with, even in her dreams.

The phone rang and Tessa checked the caller ID. The New York exchange showed up on the LCD—212.

"Hello, Audrey," Tessa answered, not surprised to hear from her agent on a Tuesday morning. They had established this routine years ago and even when Tessa had stopped writing, Audrey still called, cajoled, encouraged and tried to give her client a not-so-gentle kick in the ass.

"Tell me the good news." Audrey's Jersey accent injected her tone with urgency, though Tessa knew Audrey rarely expected good news anymore. Until this morning, Tessa hadn't typed one word into her new state-of-the-art computer, except for fiddling with e-mail or arranging her account spreadsheets, maybe pounding out an occasional letter. Twelve months after the divorce judge had decreed she could exit her marital prison with the fortune she'd brought into it, the earnings her small publisher continued to send her from reprinting and repackaging her erotic fairy tales, provided a steady stream of income for Tessa's literary representative. So Audrey dutifully called, asking about Tessa's works in progress, which until this morning, had not existed.

"I'm writing," Tessa answered simply.

"What are you writing?" Audrey's tone was cautious, but anxious. "Your grocery list? Because if you add a couple of sexy adjectives and maybe one mildly offensive noun, I can probably pull in a six-figure advance."

Tessa laughed. Audrey exaggerated with such flair. "Better than a grocery list."

Audrey's pause brimmed with expectation. "Tell me it's a novel."

"It's a novel."

"Tell me it's a fairy tale."

"No can do. I'm too old for fairy tales now."

"You're thirty-two," Audrey reminded her.

"So call me jaded. Besides, I'm trying something new."

If that confession scared her agent, she didn't let on.

"Is it hot?"

Tessa's mind flashed with images that had aroused her from sleep just after dawn, images that had lured her to the computer like the siren's song had led sailors to crash on jagged rocks. The comparison had struck her immediately, and in the same haste, had solidified a story idea she'd toyed with for weeks. A water myth. Based on the stories she'd read in Mythology 101, but molded to fit the fantasy sprung from the images in her dreams—a man born of the sea, half god, half creature. A lost island, set adrift by the gods to protect the women who lived there from the lusts and cold hearts of men. A woman hungering for the pleasure only an enchanted lover could provide.

Wetness pooled within Tessa even now, courtesy of the smallest details of the liaison she imagined in the surf, on the sand. But before she returned to the fantasy, she had to get off the phone.

"Do I write any other way?" Tessa asked.

"No, and I send you a silent thank-you every day."

Tessa believed her. "When are you coming down?"

"Let's see, I'm in New York, you're in Key West. Think winter is a good time?"

Tessa chuckled. She loved Audrey's not-so-subtle sarcasm. "First cold snap and you book a flight, okay?"

"Only if you promise to have something interesting for me to read. It is physically impossible to lounge beside a turquoise-blue ocean without good reading material."

Tessa scrolled up her computer screen. She'd logged about five pages today, and should manage another two before the dogs begged for their walk. "I think I can manage something substantial by then."

"Good. Then I can finally make you a star based on your work instead of on your notoriety."

Tessa smirked. "Do you really care how or why I'm a star?"

"Not in the least, babycakes. But *you* care."

After a few more minutes of chitchat, Tessa disconnected the call, mulling over Audrey's comment about her becoming a popular writer on her own merits rather than on the infamy of her divorce. Her mouth dried at the prospect. Her heart skipped. God, it had been so long since she'd had a goal. A golden grail to work toward. She'd struggled for an entire year until the idea for her new book had finally solidified. Luckily, she'd had the luxury of time—and money. Thanks to a judge with more sense than she'd ever expected, she'd gotten out of her marriage with all she'd brought in, despite Daniel's grab for the trust fund and properties left to her by her father. And she'd desperately needed the freedom that afforded. To heal. To relax. To undo the damage of her own naive choices.

And try as she had to put her ex-husband out of her mind, he'd been at the crux of her greatest fear. Though Daniel reportedly visited the Florida Keys from time to time, she hadn't heard one peep from him since that last day in court. Unfortunately, his damage had struck deeper than she ever wanted to admit. After such a long bout without a single idea and only a vague desire to write, she'd wondered if the bastard had managed to extract all the romance and sensuality out of her consciousness.

She'd done everything she could to counteract his effect on her life and career. Immediately after the judgment, she'd retreated to the one place on earth where she could find buff bods and sensual living in abundance—Key West. The biggest victory of her divorce settlement had been the deed to her father's house, situated on a private key six miles from the main island. She'd reopened the five-bedroom, five-bath mansion her father had bought in the late sixties, but hadn't sequestered herself by any means. Thanks to some old friends of her father's and a few new ones of her own, she'd jumped right into Conch living. No boundaries, no rules. Hers was now a relaxed Caribbean lifestyle, with a strong dose of "anything goes."

She sampled every restaurant, tested every drink. She shopped every gallery and boutique on a regular rotation, filling the house with an eclectic collection of trinkets and art. She'd even rediscovered the joys of fishing, and had learned all over again how to handle and maintain the powerboats that her father, the notorious Rip Dalton, had designed, raced and man-ufactured—boats that had lead to both his fortune and his death.

Still, Tessa associated "Speed Key," as the locals called her home, with the happiest times of her childhood. Whenever her agoraphobic mother had cloistered herself in her Hampton es-tate, Tessa had been sent to Rip in the islands. At his knee, she'd learned the seduction of dangerous living. Fast boats. Hard drinking. Free love. She admired people like her father and his friends who lived for the moment and died doing what they most enjoyed.

Even after her visits ended and she returned to staid, proper New York State, Tessa had clung to her vicarious interest in hedonistic delights. She'd incorporated her prurient fascina-tions into a secret career she had cherished.

And yet, since setting up shop on Speed Key, she hadn't experienced a strong desire to write again until two months ago, when she'd received one short, concise e-mail from the handsome columnist from the *Chicago Sun-Times*.

What's in the works, Dalton? Can't wait for your next book. C. Granger.

No naughty innuendo, no subtle flirting. Nothing particu-larly charming or seductive. *Nada.* And still, the thrum in her bloodstream had surged and boiled like newly spewed lava, and she'd been brazen in her reply.

Too busy living to write. I'm considering memoirs. Might be too hot for a book, though. Even one of mine. Tessa.

She'd laughed to herself, thinking how she couldn't have lied more in so few words. Yes, she had retreated to the Keys with a vengeance—determined to live up to the bad-girl persona Daniel and his cronies had painted for the press. But even on her wildest nights, she always went home alone. When she'd sworn off men, she'd meant it.

Except for Colton Granger. For him, she could almost be tempted to make an exception. Unfortunately, he only seemed interested in her work.

She'd expected a few hard bouts with loneliness, even in the crowded Keys, but she'd survived solitude in her marriage and could beat it now that she was on her own, commanding her own destiny.

What she hadn't expected was the keen sexual frustration. Hot and bothered came too easily in the Keys, but she wasn't stupid enough to work off that energy with just any lover.

But with Colton? *Hmm.* Now that would be hard to resist. Too bad he wasn't asking.

Since that first volley of communication, they'd e-mailed back and forth, his messages always focused on her work, hers always containing some sassy comeback. He'd even called once, and they'd chatted for hours. She smiled, wondering if she'd ever had more fun giving a guy a hard time, teasing him about her supposedly lusty exploits, inviting him to fly to Key West so she could show him delights he'd never known.

But Colton Granger preferred his women to be "ladies," in the truest sense of the word. He hadn't told her as much, of course. Transplanting a born-and-raised Southern gentleman into the polite Midwest precluded such an admission. But his columns reinforced it. She'd read them online, past and current. His words were the first thing she called up on the Internet every morning. During her divorce, he'd taken up the gauntlet of defending her virtue. Yes, he'd done so to piss off her ex-father-in-law, but she'd learned that Colton truly didn't write anything he didn't believe. She'd been touched, grateful. But she'd also realized that if she had had no virtue to defend, Colton Granger might not have given her the time of day.

Now, she no longer gave two flips about virtue. During her marriage, she'd been the epitome of a society wife and all it got her was a bad reputation. And if a bad reputation was hers for the long run, she might as well have some fun living up to it, even if she did draw the line at bringing a man home. She flirted, kissed, partied and occasionally groped. But going to bed with someone meant letting a man get way too close for comfort.

Which meant no Colton Granger for her, at least, not beyond friendship.

Not that she couldn't yank his chain every so often, just for the pleasure of it.

Determined to inject her already glorious day with more excitement, Tessa finished editing the scene she'd started this morning, then took her dogs, twin Rottweilers prophetically named Artemis and Apollo, out for a quick walk. After grabbing a fresh diet soda and a bowl of pretzels, she sat in front of the computer and continued to work.

By midafternoon, the story flowed, sensual, erotic. Alina had reached her lover, but the weight of his body—injured in a battle with a sea creature sent to avert his invasion of Alina's sanctuary—had dragged her down. She fought the sea, expending all of her strength until the current caught them and threw them onto the shore, where she climbed atop Reides and breathed her last breath into his mouth.

A kiss of life for him, death for her. But then he would return the favor, of course, by making love to her limp body until he revived her.

But Tessa wasn't ready to write that scene yet. Instead, she opened her e-mail program and clicked Colton's address.

He'd wanted her to write again, right? He'd been begging her for months. After several clean pages, she'd done enough work for one day. Besides, she really didn't know where she wanted to take the story next. She'd sketched out the plot, but the characters were still strangers, still entities waiting to be discovered. Writing from the thoughts of the vengeful goddess Aphrodite had been great fun. Alina also came easily to her—they had so much in common. Women struggling to believe in love and romance and sensual discovery, even when the world of men was forbidden. But Reides…who was he, really?

For the purpose of this mythological fantasy, she'd altered her style in so many ways that she wasn't sure what to write next. Her fairy tales always followed the plotline of the original legend. The princess bit into the poisoned apple. The starry-eyed girl learned to fly. With this story, there was no original to mimic. *Son of the Siren* was entirely her own, inspired by the tidbit about the legend of the island Delos, which had floated without roots until inhabited by one of Zeus's many lovers, and spurred by Tessa's own fascination with the meddling ways of the Greek gods.

In the fairy tales she'd written during her marriage, the main character—the virgin princess, the human-obsessed mermaid, the lusty queen—had always narrated. But this story begged to be told differently. She wanted to explore not only the thoughts and needs of Alina, the fisherman's daughter, but also those of her experienced, half-god lover, Reides.

A man's point of view? Tessa wasn't sure how to tackle that one. And while she trusted her writer's instincts enough to know she'd eventually figure it out, she'd have a hell of a lot more fun drawing Colton into the process, if for no other reason than to shock the heck out of him. And if her writing got him all hot and bothered, all the better.

She typed the message, then clicked the appropriate files to attach what she'd written so far, along with the story outline she'd put together for her own use.

Okay, Colton. Here it is. Two scenes and I'm stuck. You said you wanted a sneak peek at my work in progress. You're a writer—tell me what happens next.

After a split second of hesitation, she hit Send. She wasn't accustomed to sharing her work at such an early stage, but if she succeeded in piquing Colton's interest, she might have all the inspiration she needed to move to the next chapter.

In her book. In her life.

CHAPTER THREE

COLTON READ TESSA'S REQUEST one more time, just to make sure he'd understood. Chuckling, he hit the reply key, but hesitated before drafting a response. The woman never ceased to intrigue him. He still remembered that moment four months ago when she'd sent him the first chapter of her new book and asked him what should happen next.

He hadn't told her, of course—he'd shown her.

Colton couldn't believe he'd taken such a chance, writing the next scene of her book. He was a respected, award-winning journalist. He'd crafted a spotless reputation as a harbinger of truth in the two-faced world of local and national politics. Columnists of his caliber—who appeared periodically on the Sunday morning news shows and received personal invitations to press junkets hosted by dignitaries ranging from the mayor to the President—did not dabble in erotica.

But he had. He'd written the next scene of Tessa's book from the perspective of the hero, Reides. He'd stretched creative writing muscles he hadn't tested since college, crafting a scene from her outline as hot as it was brimming with action. At the time, he'd told himself his response was a joke, a lark. Up until then, Tessa had had too much fun at his expense with her cheeky e-mails and outlandish lifestyle. His foray into fiction had only given her a taste of her own brazen medicine.

But the whim had turned into a pet project and the story

had burgeoned into something allegorical, mystical—and steamy. The more of their creation he read and wrote, the more he learned about Tessa. And about himself. Their occasional e-mails had turned into a steady stream of communication, through the chapters and over the phone. When they hit the halfway mark of the book, Colton knew he'd involved himself in a full-fledged obsession with a woman who likely had no idea how much he wanted her.

Her—not the book.

Unfortunately, her priorities were flipped. She seemed committed to their unlikely friendship mainly because of the story they'd created together. Though she acknowledged the sexual attraction sparking between them, running like a sizzling conduit beneath the surface of every word they wrote together, she did so with humor. As if their sensual connection was nothing more than a joke.

Only, he was no longer joking. She now wanted her agent to market the novel to the biggest New York publishers. Since she'd written the book with a partner, she needed his permission before a proposal could make the rounds, even if she had promised to use her pseudonym, Charlene Perrault.

But pen name or not, she needed him.

Interesting.

He considered his response to her e-mail request for a few minutes, then settled on two words.

No way.

He signed his name, hit Send and waited. After months of back-and-forth communication, he knew Tessa hadn't sent her e-mail query and then left the computer. She was waiting for his response. Anxious. Impatient. And *no* wasn't an answer she'd accept. Just how would she attack next? Phone? Fax? Another, more persuasive, e-mail? If Lady Luck smiled his way, Tessa would hop the next flight from Key West to Chicago and proceed to convince him in person.

The trill of his cell phone sounded from within his briefcase. He glanced at his watch. Less than a minute. He loved high-speed connections. Yet after communicating exclusively with Tessa Dalton via the Internet and occasionally by phone, he wanted a little face-to-face.

Ultra, close-up face-to-face. But first, he'd have to get her riled up, break down her interminable wall of defiance. Spark her flames of indignation. He unzipped his briefcase and pulled out the phone, comfortable with his plan. To achieve his goal, he'd take a clue from Morpheus. He'd manipulate her, plain and simple, in the best way he knew how.

You want a woman with a bad reputation, strong ideas and limitless powers of persuasion to do what you want? One strategy had the best chance at success—tell her no.

Now his phone was beeping and her private number glowed on the caller ID.

"What do you mean 'no way'?" she snapped into the phone before he'd finished the second syllable of "hello."

Colton grinned. She was riled, all right. Score one point for him.

"Having trouble interpreting two words, Tessa? You've been on that island too long."

"You haven't even thought about it," she insisted, and Colton imagined her stamping her foot.

"What's to think about? The book has been fun. An interesting way to pass some time, simmer off creative juices."

He paused after his last word, letting it linger, intending to spark that sensual awareness they shared whether she liked it or not. She'd likely fight her natural response with sarcasm, distance. Bravado. Lord, she intrigued him. And Colton took that as a very good sign.

"I never intended to make a career out of writing erotica with you," he added.

Now *living* erotica, that he might consider—had considered—since he'd first met Tessa. Only she had sworn off men, at least those who wanted more than a hot and heavy fling. With his thirty-sixth birthday looming, he didn't have the energy for one-night stands and meaningless liaisons anymore. The dating game no longer interested him, particularly since he hadn't had a stimulating date in months. How could he when his pool of contenders consisted of sweet, educated, ready-to-please-at-any-cost-so-long-as-there-is-a-ring-involved women?

His mother and father would have loved each and every one of them. The heir to the Granger estate in tony Lexington, Kentucky, had been raised to keep an eye toward finding the perfect wife. Gracious, charitable, pretty. Worthy of the centuries-old name. For a while, Colton had actually hoped he might find a woman who possessed all those qualities, and who would fire his passions and inspire his fantasies at the same time.

And so far, he'd come up empty in the perfect woman department—until Tessa. Sassy, smart, seductive Tessa Dalton had occupied his private thoughts since he'd first read her collection of erotic fairy tales just before the trial. A raw earthiness simmered beneath the romanticized sexuality, piquing Colton's male curiosity. Then, after meeting her in person and being on the receiving end of her sharp wit and sensual stare, he'd been enthralled.

Tessa's less-than-virtuous reputation wouldn't go over well with his parents, but as much as Colton loved his family, he was too old to waylay his passions in some misguided bid for their approval. They'd adjust.

He wanted Tessa. And to get her, he'd have to play rough. Starting right now.

"I'm not asking you to change your career, Colton," Tessa insisted. "I'm not even asking you to put your name on the manuscript. Your involvement will be our secret, though I'll pay you half of whatever I earn. Audrey flew in this week. She didn't even wait until winter. She read the first half of the book—and she couldn't put it down."

"So the book is turning out to be a decent first try at a co-written novel," Colton concluded, knowing his assessment was no less than a gross understatement. The book was fire-hot and intriguing. Even if he hadn't penned the scenes from Reides' point of view, he knew he'd still assert that the story had bestseller written all over it. "You don't need your agent to tell you how good it is."

"No, but I do need your permission before she can send a proposal to publishers."

"You have more money than God, Tessa. Why do you need to sell another novel?"

She growled and he was certainly glad she didn't have a phone that allowed her to see his wide grin. They'd argued this point before—that her inherited wealth didn't deter her from having hopes and dreams. The need to survive was not a pre-requisite to worthy ambition. She didn't want to sell the book for more money or more fame. She wanted something so much more elusive—and valuable. She wanted respect, recog-nition. And this book, with its layered characters, mythological allegory and blazing sensual imagery, could be her ticket.

If only he said yes.

"My answer is still no," he said.

"You're yanking my chain, aren't you?"

"You might say that," he admitted.

"Okay." Pause. "What do you want?"

Colton leaned back and kicked the door of his cramped, corner office closed.

"I can't tell you now," he answered.

"Why not?"

"I'm at the paper."

"So leave. Go downstairs to the lobby and call me back."

"I can't share these details in public."

She sighed. "Take your cell phone outside. Chicago is big and noisy. No one will be interested in our conversation."

"Oh, I think this conversation might turn a few heads. The price for my answer has the potential to ruin my reputation."

"Your reputation as a selfish bastard?"

He laughed. "I'll call you tonight. From home."

"Stop jerking me around, Colt. Just tell me what you want and you can have it."

Don't be so sure, Tessa.

"You are an incredibly impatient woman. Has anyone ever told you that?"

"As a matter of fact, no. I've always been the most patient, malleable woman on the planet. Haven't you learned anything by studying my past?"

"I haven't been interested in your past for a long time."

"I'm old news, huh?"

He heard the crack of a smile in her voice. "For the moment. Your father-in-law is making the papers again."

"Thanks to you?" she asked, hopeful.

"I can only take partial credit, I'm afraid. He's being investigated by a grand jury for possible bribery charges."

"Any indictments in the near future?" To anyone else, her question would have seemed natural, emotionless. But Martin Reese and his family had put Tessa through hell. Daniel, Martin's only son, might be a first-class asshole, but he'd been raised by the king of all assholes. Martin had slithered into Chicago politics with his mega bank accounts, West Palm Beach manners and smarmy smile. He'd wasted no time inviting Colton, one of Chicago's most respected columnists, to lunch, hoping to sell him—and subsequently, his readers—on a new revitalization plan of several old neighborhoods already fighting gentrification. At the time, Colton could find little wrong with the plans on paper, but his instincts insisted that he decline to write one word about the project until he'd at least talked to the opposing neighborhood associations.

So Colton had started digging into Reese's background, leading him to discover the circus of a divorce headlining the news in Palm Beach County. And to discover Tessa.

So, in a way, Colton supposed he should be grateful to the man for throwing down the challenge. He'd make sure to send Reese a fruit basket before the man went to prison for ten to twenty-five.

"No telling with grand juries," Colton said, hoping this group of jurists would look beneath the highly educated, suave persona Martin Reese wore for the public and see the creep within. "I'm following it, though. Want updates? I've got a great source for leaks."

Tessa clucked her tongue. "No, thanks. I just used up my 'talk about my ex-husband or anyone related to him' time for the month. Maybe in a few weeks I'll have the stomach for more."

"How much time do you allot?" he asked, amused and curious. Just like Tessa to make another outrageous rule about her life and stick to it like glue.

"Five minutes. Generous, aren't I?"

"Wonderfully generous. Reese doesn't deserve two minutes of your time."

A knock sounded on Colton's door, and then in poked the head of John Nichols. Colton acknowledged his co-worker with a quick nod, then turned away to complete his call in semiprivacy. "Stay by the phone tonight."

"This better be good. I don't like waiting."

"Believe it or not, neither do I."

Colton disconnected the phone, tossed it in his briefcase and turned back to his visitor.

"What's up, Nichols?"

"Sorry to interrupt, but Frank wants you to look over this article I've written about the Reese indictment."

Colton grabbed the manila folder Nichols thrust toward him. "What indictment? The grand jury is supposed to continue hearing testimony until next week, at least."

His co-worker rolled his eyes in that particular way that made Colton want to donate some testosterone.

"*Pending* indictment," John amended.

"You're a writer, Nichols. You'd think you'd be a little more careful with your words."

Colton flipped open the folder and scanned the headline. Nichols was an okay writer. In fact, in his relatively short time with the *Sun-Times,* he'd developed a decent following and a fairly distinctive style. Still, the man had a tendency to shadow Colton, hanging on his every word as if he were some brilliant pundit rather than a hard-working journalist who happened to possess as much talent as luck.

"Why are you writing about Reese? And why does the editor-in-chief want me to look over your work?"

Annoyance brimmed from every crevice of Nichols's put-upon expression, from his eager eyes to his cover-model cheekbones. "He thinks I might be stepping on your toes by addressing the topic before the grand jury makes a decision. And he seems to think you have some sort of dibs on the story. You don't, do you?"

Colton grimaced. Yeah, to him he did, but the basic tenets of freedom of the press said otherwise. "You don't usually write about politics."

As if he'd caught a whiff of something unpleasant, Nichols sniffed and delicately swiped at his nose. "Neighborhood happenings are more my forte, but Reese is all the talk in Lincoln Park. He donated that shelter last year, you know. And playground equipment for the school that had the fire. Not to mention that he bought and upgraded those two condo buildings without so much as upping the association fees."

"So he's a saint to the citizens of Lincoln Park?"

Nichols shook his head, then after a silent request for permission—which Colton granted with a nod—leaned on Colton's dusty credenza. "This is Chicago. Unless you're Catholic, we don't believe in saints. He's been suspect since the moment his foot touched the tarmac at O'Hare. I'm on your side on this one, Granger. Frank just wants to make sure I'm not repeating anything you've already said. Woe to me if I irritate a reader of the *Chicago Sun-Times.*"

"Or an advertiser."

"Precisely."

Colton tossed the folder onto his desk. "When's the deadline?"

"This afternoon is fine."

John Nichols sounded resigned to the situation, but Colton knew otherwise. Had to be a painful insult to have the editor-in-chief request that another columnist look over his work. Colton didn't give a damn if Nichols's work mirrored his—each writer had his own style, and frankly, Colton had the popularity and clout that Nichols lacked. Nonetheless, he agreed to deliver the copy back to Nichols by two o'clock, then packed up his laptop, eager to meet with a source over a greasy burger at the Billy Goat Tavern. He had one more column to write before he could make the final arrangements for his plan to entice Tessa Dalton into becoming his lover.

And if all turned out as he anticipated, they'd give even their ravenous characters a run for their money.

HE WAS UP TO SOMETHING. Something big. Tessa hung up the phone and narrowed her eyes at her computer, as if Colton's secret resided somewhere in the circuitry. Over the past few months of working together, she'd gotten to know him incredibly well. And though they'd only met once and their single, in-person conversation had lasted less than twenty minutes, she suspected that with little effort, she could reconstruct their conversation, word for word.

Colton Granger had a way of making an impression on a woman, even one still smarting from betrayal. Chances were, she knew Colton better than she wanted to admit, and could easily guess what price he'd demand before she could market the book.

Aw, hell. She didn't have to guess. He wanted to have sex with her. Trouble was, she wanted the same, though she wouldn't dare admit it. From the beginning of their friendship, she'd been careful to act coolly unaffected by Colton's magnetism and frank sexual appeal—as if every day of her life she dealt with men who oozed sexuality like he did. Her attitude had provided a barrier between them, a means to protect her foolish heart from involving itself with a man who couldn't possibly love the real Tessa Dalton. The careful woman raised half her life by an agoraphobic mother and the other half by a father who'd invented the word *extrovert.* The uncertain woman who hid first behind a pen name and now behind a bad reputation she'd hardly earned just so she didn't have to delve too deeply into her own crazy psyche.

Tessa smacked herself on the forehead, then cursed her impulsive decision to send him that scene four months ago and challenge him to help. She'd only wanted to shock him, maybe hear his take on the hero's perspective. But had he given her that? Oh, no. Nothing so predictable from Colton Granger. He'd written the next scene. He'd hijacked her characters, her style, her tone—and then injected the story with his personal brand of literary testosterone, transforming Reides into a hero no woman could resist. A half god who lusted after his woman so thoroughly, he made love to her near lifeless body until she gasped again for breath.

Tessa had given him the outline for the scene, but Colton had taken the idea and written it so that his had nearly singed the no-glare coating off her computer screen. She sighed, resigned to the fact that involving him may have started as a cheeky joke, but the outcome had been amazing. They now had the first half of what might be the best book Tessa had ever worked on. Even now, she couldn't reread that first scene he'd written without her skin sizzling like wildfire.

A glutton for punishment, Tessa slipped back into her office chair and called up the chapter on her computer.

> *Reides awoke with the taste of Alina in his mouth. Her flavor, tinged with sweet, essential sea salt—like air to him—lingered on his tongue. How he knew her essence, her texture, her aroma—he didn't know. Aphrodite had only given him her name and an enchanted map to her secret location. Had he found her? Finally? Had he actually won the bloody battle against the Hydra, sent by his father, Poseidon, from the swamp to the sea to keep him from his treasure? What danger did Alina represent that his father would go so far?*
>
> *Reides swallowed, coughed, his throat dry, his skin tight. He shook his head, clearing the cloudiness, banishing the pain. Then he remembered.*
>
> *Momentarily blinded by the bright sun, he reached forward to remove a weight from his chest. Soft, but cold. The creature he'd slain in battle, perhaps? Poseidon may have plotted to stop him, but even a school of*

Hydra wouldn't prevent Reides from finding his Alina. He'd never known a need so powerful, so consuming. The map from Aphrodite likely came with a price, but Reides could think of nothing he wouldn't willingly give to spend one night with Alina. Only after he had her flesh to flesh would he be able to break her haunting spell.

By Zeus, his body ached. He grunted and sat forward, the unknown weight thudding against the sand as he opened his eyes.

Death's kiss drew a pale line around her lips. Her bright blue eyes stared sightless into the sun.

"Alina!"

He grabbed her shoulders, shook her. He forced his ear to her chest, but heard no heartbeat, felt no breath. Horror struck him. Images. Alina dragging him, injured, from the ocean. The sound of her struggles. The taste of her desperation. She had pushed her last breath into his lungs, then died with her body shielding his.

"No!"

Reides sprang to his feet, ignoring the hot rush of blood from the gash in his side. He cursed the gods, his father most of all, then knew what he must do.

Half his blood sprang from Poseidon, an immortal. The other came from his mother, a powerful siren. Like her, sexual power surged through him, marked him. Made him unlike any other creature roaming sea or shore.

Alina had given him her life. Only he could restore her.

He tossed aside his knife, ripped his tattered clothes. He'd have nothing in his way. He lifted Alina into his arms and plunged into the icy water, drawing strength from the world of his father. He floated her into the now calm waves, folded her arms across her chest, cupping her hands just beneath her breasts.

Even in death, her beauty defied the perfection of his dreams. Her legs were slim, her hips curved, her mons feathered with dark curls. Slits of pink flesh pouted from the coiled strands and his tongue ached to taste her, part her, explore the depths of warmth now chilled by mortal death. Her buttocks, round and full in his hands, felt pliant beneath his touch, yet stiff enough to clutch his cock. Her nipples, lax and pink, centered globes of flesh he'd suckle to red ripeness once she lived again. But first, her mouth. First, the kiss.

Then, he'd have what he'd traveled half the world to possess.

CHAPTER FOUR

COLTON DIALED TESSA'S NUMBER, hit the speakerphone button, put the handset on the gleaming marble counter and proceeded to brew a pot of coffee to accompany his Italian takeout, just as he would any evening he intended to work beyond midnight. He acted naturally, on automatic—as if nothing crucial to his love life would occur when Tessa answered the call.

Except for the scents of garlic and tomato wafting from the aluminum containers on the breakfast bar, the kitchen in his Lakeshore Drive apartment smelled like a pine forest stuffed in the middle of Colombian coffee country. His cleaning lady sometimes went a little crazy with the Pine-Sol. He wrinkled his nose, satisfied only when the unnaturally clean scent battled and lost to the nutty aroma of the brew dripping with painful slowness into the glass carafe.

He pulled a mug from the cupboard and counted the rings from the phone. Three. Four. At six, her voice mail would pick up. Either Tessa wasn't as anxious to hear what price he'd demand for his cooperation, or she was attempting to manipulate the game herself by playing nonchalant.

Just after the fifth ring, she picked up, panting. Colt slammed the mug onto the counter and rushed to the phone.

"You okay?" he asked, grabbing the handset.

"Yeah," she assured him, though it took her a better part

of a minute to catch her breath. "I heard the phone. I was… outside."

Colton glanced at the darkness beyond his window. With the time difference, Tessa had toasted the sunset over an hour ago. "What were you doing?"

"The dogs were barking."

The prickle up Colt's spine was all too familiar. He hated that Tessa lived alone on that damned private island of hers. Out in the middle of nowhere, six miles from civilization. He didn't care if she described her canine companions as man-eating monsters or if she had her father's shotgun collection locked up in the library. Anyone with enough determination could overpower two dogs—even big, mean ones. And he'd bet big money she hadn't taken a gun outside with her when she'd gone to check things out.

"I hope they found a snake in the brush," he volunteered.

"Sorry, no snakes on my island. A boat came in a little too close. After dark, if Arty or Apollo see white stern lights or hear an engine that isn't mine, they go a little crazy."

He supposed that should be good news, however, he didn't feel any more relieved. He couldn't tamp down the male protective instincts bred into him since birth.

"Did you think I'd miss your call?" she asked quickly.

He strolled to the coffeemaker. "Are you trying to deflect another of my diatribes on why you have no business living alone?"

"Absolutely."

"Then no, I didn't think you'd miss the call." As strong as his inclination was to lecture her about her unwise living arrangements, they had more important things to discuss. He sprinkled a half teaspoon of sugar into the bottom of his mug, poured the coffee and wandered into the living room.

A bank of floor-to-ceiling windows faced Lake Michigan,

renewing Colton's satisfaction in owning one of the best views in the city. In the distance, white flashes from the top of the water intake cribs two miles offshore blinked like squat lighthouses. He wondered if Tessa could see any lighthouses from her windows. He knew two existed in the vicinity. At least, they used to. He hadn't been to Key West in nearly ten years, long before Tessa retreated there to lick her emotional wounds and reinvent her life. But if all went as planned, he'd soon redeem the round-trip, first-class ticket to paradise he had on hold with the airline.

"Okay," Tessa said. "Name your price."

The offer danced on his tongue, but he drowned his premature enthusiasm with a sip of coffee. "Tell me again why you want this publishing deal. Why our book can't just remain private, between us."

"You know why I want to publish again."

Of course he did. But he wanted her to state her reasons— out loud. One more time. He needed her to hear for herself the determination in her voice, the hope in her tone. Only then might she willingly break her one hard-and-fast rule regarding men—that she wanted nothing to do with the species beyond an occasional fling with someone she'd likely never see again. Tempting as that sounded, he wanted more from her. Much more.

At such a crucial moment, though, he knew he shouldn't ask for anything so drastic—he had a more devious scheme in mind.

"Tell me again," he demanded.

She sighed, and the sound rolled over him like a warm, tropical breeze.

"My fairy tale stories were wonderful, I love them, but they're short, simplistic. Idealistic."

"You've sold hundreds of thousands of copies," he pointed out.

"*After* the divorce, they sold," she countered, argumentative even though they'd had this discussion before. Good. He wanted her on the defense. On edge. "But before that, only a few die-hard readers could find my books, much less like them. The blockbuster sales and the mass distribution didn't come until after Daniel dragged my name through the mud."

"So this is a chance to redeem yourself?" He slid onto his dark leather couch and kicked his bare feet up onto his brushed-steel coffee table.

"Redeem? Have you read what we've written, Colt?" she asked, incredulous. "My stories aren't about redemption."

Aren't they? he wondered.

"Bad word choice," he conceded. He'd hold that argument for another time and place. "What do you want from this book, Tessa? What do you really, really want? When I wrote that next scene, I'd only meant to shock you. When you countered with the next chapter, I thought we were playing a game. Enjoying a private flirtation of sorts."

He paused, waiting for her to acknowledge aloud what had been tacit, yet until now, unspoken—the undercurrent of desire flowing between them. Not surprisingly, she remained stubbornly silent.

"But I don't know," he continued, undeterred. "Publishing what we've written…that's serious. You'll be thrust right back into the spotlight you've been trying so hard to avoid for the past year. And I'll be there with you."

"I don't care about the spotlight and, as I told you, we can keep you anonymous, if that's what you want," she answered. He expected to hear resignation or weariness in her tone, but he heard only enthusiasm, strength and resolve. "This book is good. Damned good. Yes, it's hot. Yes, it's erotic. But it's also a frickin' great story. The best I've ever written. Can't you understand my wanting to shine for something positive, rather than for lies made up by my smarmy ex-husband?"

Oh, yeah. He understood. He knew the power of her desire because her intensity matched his own. Only Colton wanted something infinitely more personal than his name on the cover of a critically acclaimed, bestselling book.

"I'm flying to Key West in the morning," he told her.

Silence sizzled over the phone lines. "You'll do it? You'll sign the agreement with my agent?"

"There's still that matter of what I want in exchange."

"Half of everything. Advance, royalties."

He clucked his tongue. "That isn't what I mean."

"Lay your cards down, Granger. What's this magnanimous gesture going to cost me?"

She talked a good game—strong tone, steady rhythm. But they'd communicated exclusively via phone line too long for him not to recognize the subtle, nearly imperceptible quiver in her voice.

"I want to make love to Alina."

"Excuse me?"

He shifted on the couch, his cock hardening at the slightest possibility of getting what he wanted. "When I read your scenes, I see you as Alina. I don't suppose you'll try and convince me that you don't see me as Reides?"

He could have sworn he heard her swallow with a thick gulp. "No denials from me. It's natural."

"What I want from you is entirely natural, too. I want to reconstruct that first scene between them from the book, where Alina is on the shore and Reides brings her back to life by making love to her." He lowered his volume to a sultry whisper. "You'll have to be very, very still, you know. You'll have to pretend my lips aren't pleasuring you, my tongue isn't exploring every inch of your skin. Will you taste sweet,

Alina? How long will I have to ply my tongue before you blossom back to life?"

This time, he knew he heard her gulp.

"You're crazy."

She laughed, but the hollow sound reverberating across long distance lost any hint of humor.

"Crazy with wanting you, yes."

He heard her slam the phone down, but she didn't disconnect the call. He could hear her dogs whining in the background. Concerned for their owner, perhaps? Unnerved by her pacing? By the string of breathy curses he could only barely hear?

She retrieved the phone. "You're serious?"

"As a heart attack."

"And if I sleep with you, you'll let me market the book?"

"I didn't say that. But if you take the role of Alina to my Reides for one night—and if you enjoy the lovemaking as much as I'm sure you will—then, we can discuss your plans for marketing the book."

This time, she didn't bother to put the phone down before she told him off. "Extortion isn't your style, Colton."

"No, but Reides wouldn't hesitate to resort to blackmail to get what he wanted."

She couldn't argue. They'd written their half god hero with no scruples whatsoever when in pursuit of fulfilling his desires, including freeing Alina from her sea-bound prison. Part of his appeal was his inability to accept any form of denial or defeat. Colton fully understood this trait of the fictional character, since he'd had a heavy hand in creating him.

"Come on, Dalton," he urged. "You've got nothing to lose here. I'm the one with his balls on the line. If word got out that award-winning journalist Colton Granger had written an erotic novel, management of the *Sun-Times* would not be pleased."

"I guess your credibility would take a blow."

"To say the least." Colton refused to think about that scenario. He trusted Tessa's discretion. And his own. He received e-mails from her on his BlackBerry, and he was careful never to download any scenes from the book to his office computer. He left no notes lying around and whenever he could, he limited their phone calls to when he was at home, far from any overly curious ears.

Besides, he wasn't about to let his employer dictate his love life any more than he would his family. Not that he wanted to lose his job or tarnish his reputation, but with all his precautions, there was very little risk.

"As hard as you've been working at cultivating that bad reputation of yours," he promised, "I guarantee I'll be the best you've ever had."

She didn't answer, so he pushed further.

"The heat's been sizzling between us since that first night in Karen's backyard. Now, after taking a peek into each other's sexual fantasies, it's a veritable inferno. If we don't allow ourselves a little relief soon…"

"Stop. Let me think."

"Don't think. Thinking is for real people. I'm talking about a fantasy."

"That's just it, Colton. You've been my fantasy man for a long time. Making it all real…"

"Nothing will be real, I promise."

He waited, knowing her silent hesitation, her failure to deny him outright boded very, very well. His mind raced, trying to formulate a plan B if she denied what he considered to be an offer she couldn't refuse.

"I could meet you at the airport hotel in Miami. We could work off our sexual energy there."

"Bor-ring. This is the deal, Tessa. Take it or leave it."

WILLA LAWSON, Coast Guard Commander and Captain of the cutter *Racine,* strolled down Duval Street, tossing a casual salute at Bangor Bob, who wove palm frond hats on the sidewalk in front of The Bull and Whistle to sell to the tourists. In Willa's estimation, a person had to be drunk to wear something so ridiculous in the daylight, but luckily, in Old Town, finding drunks was as easy as finding bars and cheap booze.

Cutting through an alley across from the Hard Rock Café, she only hoped that her favorite hangout, Brew's Pub, tucked away from the tourists, wasn't too crowded. Lunchtime hadn't yet arrived, but she needed a drink and she wasn't in the mood to wait.

Yet a prickle of warning caused her to stop just outside the swinging panel doors. Inside, Leroy "Roy" Brewster occupied his familiar place behind the bar, pouring a pink mixture into a blender while across from him, fellow regular, Heather Love, fingered her dangling bracelets, waiting somewhat impatiently for, Willa guessed, one of Roy's special Rumrunners.

"So, are you going to tell her?" Heather asked.

"None of my damned business. None of yours, if you ask me."

Willa lingered on the other side of the doors, eavesdropping on a conversation she wasn't sure warranted her intervention or interest. She'd just come off a long, hot duty rescuing a bunch of drunken college boys playing Popeye and Blutus on their rich daddy's yacht. After a beer fight over some skinny chick, one had gone overboard. Unfortunately, it was the one who knew how to pilot the boat. She and her Coast Guard team had fished him out, rescued his scrawny butt, and then turned him and his friend over to the sheriff for drunk and disorderly. And after impounding the vessel, they'd had to endure a verbal dressing-down by the rich daddy—and his team of attorneys. And Willa had thought Olive Oyl would *never* stop crying! So after a quick shower and a change into her civvies, Willa simply wanted a quiet drink at her favorite hangout without any chance of running into the rowdy diaper-wipe kids constantly prowling the Keys.

But while Leroy Brewster allowed most anyone with cash into his establishment, his corner pub, one block off Duval Street, normally attracted an older, semisedate crowd. Locals mostly and no freaks allowed, though in the Keys, defining *freak* was harder than finding snow to make a snowball. Even willowy artist Heather Love, twenty-five at the most, looked out of place, despite her daily appearance for one of Roy's specialty drinks. Willa couldn't think of a better place than Roy's to unwind.

Instead, Willa's buddies were plotting something. And while she wasn't sure just who the "she" in this overheard conversation was, she had two guesses.

"Tessa deserves to know," Heather insisted.

Willa raised her eyebrows. From Roy's determination to remain uninvolved, she would have voted for herself as guess number one. Dodged that bullet.

Roy leaned forward over the bar and attempted a whisper, though he never had perfected that skill. At least, not anywhere outside the bedroom.

"I can't believe you stole the man's credit card receipt," Roy said to Heather. "Not exactly a legitimate business practice."

Heather waved the old-style carbon-copy paper in front of her. Despite her youth, Heather had a thing for nostalgia. She probably thought those inky, black-sided credit card forms were quaint.

"What does it matter? The card was declined. It's not like I can charge anything to his account. And I wouldn't have looked twice at the guy's name if he'd had decent credit."

"So it's his fault?" Roy asked.

Heather arched her eyebrows, but apparently didn't think the question deserved an answer.

Roy threw down a battered cardboard coaster and poured Heather's drink into a plastic cup. "You're asking for trouble."

"Trouble for Tessa if we don't act soon," Heather insisted, leaning across the bar to extract an orange and a cherry from the condiment tray. Roy always had a hard time remembering to dress up the drinks. "I called about his account. Declined for nonpayment. They asked me to retrieve the card and cut it up."

"Did you?"

Heather tsked. "American Express doesn't pay my salary. They can do their own dirty work."

Roy poured a trio of beers and put them on a tray so Sonia, the waitress, could promptly deliver them to a table by the jukebox. Tom Petty & the Heartbreakers crooned about "Free Fallin'." Willa smiled. Roy only played Florida singers and songwriters at the bar. And at home. The more Jimmy Buffett, the better.

"So, you going to tell her he's here?" Roy finally asked.

Heather shook her head, her wispy blond hair brushing against shoulders bared by her cropped tank top. "I don't know Tessa well enough to upset her."

"It's not like you invited him to vacation here," Roy said, his tone surprisingly reasonable. "Better tell her before she runs into him on the street. This ain't a big place."

Willa decided her need for a drink overrode her reluctance to get involved in this drama. Besides, she considered Tessa Dalton to be her best friend, though they'd met only a year ago when the heiress had some uninvited reporters camp out on Speed Key and Willa and her crew had run them off. Since then, the women had shopped together, partied together. Even played poker every Wednesday night that Willa wasn't on duty. Though they had vastly different backgrounds and the gap in their life experiences was best reflected in the contrast between their bank accounts, they liked each other. Trusted each other. So if someone had again arrived on the island to harass Tessa, the news should come from Willa and no one else.

She slapped through the entrance, watching intently for any change in Roy's dour expression. His eyes glimmered with unchecked annoyance.

A shiver raced up her spine. "What trouble are you yahoos brewing and how do I get a piece of the action?"

Heather's grin went from dangling earring to dangling earring. "Willa! I was going to track you down next."

"Best way to find me is to come straight here."

Roy ducked beneath the bar and pulled out his one bottle of tequila. With a grimace, he poured her a shot, neat. Roy hated tequila. The smell reminded him of some as-of-yet undescribed weekend he'd once had in Tijuana. But since Willa had been stationed on Key West, she'd bugged him to carry the stuff in the bar. Then one night out of the blue, he'd pulled out a bottle—worm and all—and poured one for her. When another patron had requested a similar shot, Roy had nearly bit his head off.

That's when their strange and unpredictable affair had started. All on account of tequila.

Andale.

She slid onto a bar stool, threw back the shot and relaxed as the bitter liquor burned down her throat. By the time she opened her eyes, Roy had tossed a plastic plate with salt and lime in front of her. What a guy.

"Hit me again," she directed to Roy, then turned to Heather. "Okay, spill. Who's in Key West who shouldn't be and why is this person capable of hurting Tessa?"

Heather handed her the canceled sales slip. She read the name twice, just to make sure she wasn't mistaken.

Daniel Reese.

"The ex-husband?"

"The jerk," Heather snapped.

"Are you sure? The name Daniel Reese isn't exactly Belvedere MacGillicuddy. Maybe it's not the same guy."

"Will Smith is a common name, but I'd know him if I saw him," Heather assured her.

Who wouldn't? "You know what Reese looks like?"

Heather sipped her drink through her straw, and Willa couldn't help notice how dainty her action was.

"I do read the newspapers, tabloids included," Heather answered. "It was him. He came into the gallery shopping for jewelry. The snake even made sure to mention that his new squeeze is younger than I am. That for all her 'youthful acrobatics,' she deserved something one of a kind. Ew."

Willa nodded. *Ew,* indeed. She'd never met Daniel, but she and Tessa had downed more margaritas and *mojitos* over the man than any male deserved. In the past four months, however, Tessa had rarely mentioned Daniel's name. Something about a statute of limitations. Anyway, since Daniel had ceased to be a topic of dish, Tessa had started writing again. And her friend had some freaky flirtation going with some reporter over the Internet. The last thing she needed now was the ex-husband in the picture.

"What happened after you told him his card didn't go through? Tell me he ran out with his tail between his legs."

Heather frowned. "He paid cash."

"Was the piece expensive?"

She shrugged, took a long sip before answering. "Not particularly. Couple of hundred. But he's here in the Keys, and I don't think it's a day trip."

"Why not?"

"He asked me to have the jewelry delivered. He has a condo that only rents for a month at a time."

Willa grabbed a slice of lime, squeezed it into her mouth, downed her second tequila and then finished the experience with a fingerful of salt.

"What's the address?"

Heather's impossibly big blue eyes widened. "Why?"

Willa puckered, sucking the last of the tequila, lime and salt flavors from the inside of her mouth. Roy knew better than to pour her more than two shots in an hour, but if he wasn't too distracted by his fishing buddies that had just walked in, she might get a chaser.

He loaded up a tray of beer on tap, leaving one in front of her before he handed the brews to Sonia.

Willa toasted him with a wink.

"Why do you think?" she asked.

"You're going to rough him up?"

Willa nearly choked on the smooth, yeasty brew. "I'm a Coast Guard officer, Heather. I do *not* rough people up."

Heather's stare was nothing less than mocking.

Willa conceded. Having grown up the only female smack in the middle of four boys, she'd discovered the subtle degrees of "roughing up" someone, and it had come in handy in her line of work. From what she'd heard, Daniel deserved nothing less than a good, old-fashioned ass-whooping, but as a law enforcement officer—of sorts—she had to gauge the situation first.

"I'll just check things out. Before I go throwing Tessa's peaceful world into a hurricane, I want all the facts."

Heather bit down on her pouty bottom lip, then pulled a card out of her purse. On one side, was the sunny logo of the art gallery she managed, and on the other, she explained, was the address of Daniel's lair-for-rent.

"So you'll clue Tessa in, tell her to watch her back?"

"Don't worry about Tessa," Willa reassured her. "She's perfectly capable of watching her own back."

Heather nodded. "A little help from her friends wouldn't hurt, though, would it?"

Willa licked the froth off the top of her beer, wicked thoughts of sweet revenge dancing in her brain. "Not in the least, honey. Not in the least."

CHAPTER FIVE

AFTER TWEAKING the engine for two hours, changing the oil and scrubbing the deck of her favorite powerboat—chores she'd performed just weeks before—Tessa decided to quit pretending she wasn't wound as tight as the bowline. She gathered the greasy rags, tossed them in the washer, showered and then changed into breezy cutoffs and a tank top, her standard-issue Key West uniform. After slathering herself with sunscreen, she prepared her boat for the trip to Old Town, the social epicenter of the main island. She needed a serious distraction. Colton wouldn't arrive until well after sunset—a good six hours away—so she had plenty of time to rein in her nerves and figure out how either one of them could possibly live up to the sky-high expectations they'd both built up in their minds. And more importantly, in their bodies.

Hours ago, he'd called her from the L train as he'd rolled into O'Hare.

"Until tonight, Tessa," he'd whispered into the cell phone, his voice as deep as the ocean and just as warm and inviting. Ever since he'd offered his delicious deal, one word—any word—from Colton's lips managed to caress her ear, then ooze downward through her bloodstream, inducing a sensual flutter at the juncture of her thighs.

"Or should I say, Alina?"

Despite the eighty-degree breeze tousling the palm trees on Tessa's island, she shivered at the memory.

Until tonight.

She'd taken two days to mull over his proposition. The spontaneity and bravado that had been her mantra since her divorce couldn't carry her through this one. Making love to Colton, not as herself but as the character she'd created with him, would be the ultimate test. She'd worked hard to change her thought processes and emotional vulnerabilities, to fortify her sense of self. Now, because she wanted the book deal and all the success it represented, she had to put her newfound strength under the gun—with a man more than able to shoot her down.

Able to shoot her down, but she had to trust he was neither ready nor willing to hurt her. Not intentionally, anyway. Over and over, she reminded herself that Colton craved only the fantasy woman she presented to him and the rest of the world—the persona she'd embraced after the divorce. Sexually free. Party-all-night wild. Devil-may-care. He wanted the bad girl, the ready-for-anything hellcat who lived on her own island and played by her own rules. But he wanted her while she pretended to be his sweet, innocent ideal—Alina—all to fulfill his fantasy.

It took Tessa two days to work through the psychology on that one, but what she'd deduced had given her permission to pursue a fantasy of her own.

The scenario was ideal for both of them. The real Tessa could remain off-limits, even to Colton. Only her persona would come out to play, and that free-spirited woman could not be hurt. That way, Tessa could have the sensual pleasure she wanted so desperately—and the book deal, too. Everyone would walk away satisfied.

Still, Tessa couldn't totally downplay the inherent risks.

Colton was nothing like Daniel, but that didn't make the man any less dangerous. Instead of a heartless jerk who tore women down as a sport, Colton was smart, strong, handsome. Sexy. Competent and courageous. Did she mention handsome and sexy? Colton Granger and his irresistible charm made a shark like Daniel Reese look like a cuttlefish.

But no matter the potential perils, for just one night, she had a shot at the exact type of man she'd always craved. So as her writing partner had requested, she'd made arrangements to transport him, just after his plane touched down, to Speed Key.

They'd be entirely alone. Strangers who knew the inner workings of each other's most secret fantasies. Lovers who'd met only once, yet were about to step straight into an erotic scene of their own creation.

Tessa stopped untying the line that secured her boat to her dock and squeezed her thighs together, hoping to offset the insistent throbbing. A temporary fix to a delicious dilemma. God, she'd been celibate for too long. Too reliant on her own hand and a varied collection of dildos to ease the pressure of too many sultry nights spent alone.

Tonight, she'd have Colton, a real man, despite his fantasy role. The tryst would be his to control, his to direct, all for her pleasure. She'd agreed to step into the role of the innocent, sensual Alina—forgetting, for one night, all she knew about sex. All she knew about Colton. All she knew about herself. He'd asked her for one night of passion in exchange for his answer to her request.

A small price to pay?

Tessa shook her head, released the line, and then while the engine idled, grabbed a bottled water from the cooler in the galley and wondered what the hell she'd gotten herself into. How could she act, even for one night, innocent and naive after all she'd been through? She had no trouble slipping into Alina's mind while writing, but she wasn't an actress. Still, the idea of remembering the time when she'd trusted a man to care for her, pleasure her, bring her to the limits of her sexual knowledge—the mere possibility jolted her with fire, licking at her with hot tongues of flame from the inside out.

And for this one night, he'd be hers and hers alone.

Or more appropriately, she'd be his.

She inhaled, held the salt-tinged air inside her lungs for a long moment, then exhaled, unable to produce anything steadying or calming with the breath. Tonight could be the chance of a lifetime or one more mistake she'd have to drink too much to forget.

As if forgetting anything about Colton was remotely possible.

The sun, tucked behind white fluffy clouds that dotted the sky like cotton balls in a child's diorama, brightened the water beneath her boat to a sparkling turquoise, reminding her of syrup on a blueberry Sno-Kone. God, she loved this place. Truth be told, with enough time and enough tequila, she could forget anything while surrounded by the tropical lushness of the Florida Keys. She pushed the boat away from the dock and after clearing the shallow water, shoved the throttle full forward, laughing when the wind and spray slashed her face and arms. The combination of speed and salted, sultry air injected Tessa with energy, vitality. Anticipation.

Tonight, the moon would tint the waves to sapphire. She sniffed, but no extra humidity hung in the air to indicate a storm. The clouds were high in the sky and few enough to count. When evening descended, it would be clear and full mooned. As she reclined on the sand, waiting for him, her tight nipples and quivering flesh would be Colton's to see, even from a distance.

As she neared the main island, she adjusted the throttle,

slowing in the no-wake zone so that the currents more than her engines propelled her alongside Mallory Square. She returned greetings to a cluster of tourists snapping pictures of the incredible view and noted the trio of vagrants nestled beneath palm trees, waiting out the heat until sunset, when the bricked square blossomed to life with street vendors, musicians and artists.

Near the city marina, she did a shout-out to the crew of a charter catamaran carting anxious snorklers to the reef for a "once-in-a-lifetime," three-times-a-day chance to swim among some of the most beautiful sea life in the coastal United States. As the sailboat crossed her bow, one of the crewmen blew her a kiss and yelled some unintelligible message Tessa didn't need to hear in order to understand. Her chest clenched, but she responded by tossing back an endearment of her own. He'd likely asked her to marry him. Maybe this time, just to have his baby. Todd, she thought his name was. Maybe Tom. Or Tony? Just last month, after a particularly hot and heavy telephone call from Colton, she'd cooled off by popping down to Sloppy Joe's, indulging in a pitcherful of margaritas and then dancing with the college-aged crewman well into the night. The kid had some moves.

Tony, that was his name—his skill on the dance floor her clue. That night, she'd compared him to Tony Manero, John Travolta's character from *Saturday Night Fever.* Only this young Tony, complete with dark hair and piercing blue eyes, hadn't known who she was talking about until she'd explained. Too comfortable with herself to feel old, Tessa had laughed at the kid's lack of pop-culture knowledge. But what he'd lost in trivia points, he'd gained in kissing prowess. For hips and lips, Tony was the guy to call.

But as always, Tessa had drawn the line at making out. Okay, she was fairly certain he'd copped a few feels, only because she had herself. Thanks to the tequila, she hadn't cared. Still, she'd remained sober enough to know when his hands had dipped too low or held on too tightly. They'd had a good time with no serious repercussions—spontaneous marriage proposals aside. Tony didn't know who she was, who she'd been. Not really. Not like Colton knew.

And once Colton arrived, there would be backlash, no matter how she tried to scheme otherwise. Part of her bristled at the thought that yet again, someone had the power to derail her destiny and control her life. With the book. With her heart. But the other part of her—the basic, intrinsic, elemental part, built from the components of her feminine heart—knew only that she was likely about to have the most thrilling night of her life.

So in light of that, she reacted as any woman would—she sought out a girlfriend so they could dish and obsess until the big event.

Tessa pulled into her slip at the city marina just behind the Hilton, and dialed Willa's cell phone then home phone with no luck. Undeterred, she called Roy.

"Haven't seen her," the barkeep grumbled. Tessa glanced at the clock on her dashboard. At eleven-thirty, she knew the Brew's Pub had opened about an hour ago.

"Well, when you do, could you tell her I'm looking for her?"

"Don't expect to see her today."

Yeah, right, Tessa thought with a silent snort. Though Roy had a good fifteen years on Willa agewise, he and Willa had been secretly setting fire to the sheets for at least a year. If Willa had a respite from rescuing boaters from the tricky Florida currents or chasing down drug runners attempting to deliver their wares, she and Roy would find time to hook up. When Willa was in port, Brew's had a weird way of closing for uncertain periods of time or else Sonia, Roy's most trusted employee, would take over, which the regulars cheered since Sonia loved nothing more than ordering up plates of complimentary nachos for the crowd.

At the thought of the cheese-and-spiced-meat-laden chips, Tessa's stomach growled. "Well if you do, especially before lunch, could you tell her I'm hungry?"

"I got a grouper sandwich special today. Blackened."

Tessa's mouth watered. "I love you, Roy."

"Say that to every guy who feeds you and you're gonna get yourself in trouble."

"The constant state of my life. I'll see you later."

Tessa disconnected the call, disappointed, but wondering if she should intrude on Roy and Willa if they were planning a little afternoon delight. She'd find someone else to hang out with today, just as soon as she secured her boat in the slip, which was reserved for life in memory of her father.

Tessa jumped onto the dock and tied the lines. She'd need every ounce of her father's legacy tonight. Rip Dalton had never met an eyebrow-raising scheme he didn't like, right down to assuming the role of Admiral of the Fleet for the Conch Republic when the tiny Key West community, rebellious to the last, seceded from the United States in 1982 to protest unreasonable search-and-seizure laws. If Rip hadn't died ten years later, flipping his boat after beating his best time in a powerboat competition, Tessa'd bet her entire trust fund he'd be cruising Duval Street right now, picking up women and spending his money showing them an obscenely good time—emphasis on the word *obscene*. After all these years, Tessa finally had her chance to step into Rip's flip-flops, kick back and push her life to the limits.

With a quivering breath, she calculated the hours until Colton's arrival again. God, she'd never make it. Not without something to engage her mind. Tessa beelined toward the Sunrise Gallery just around the corner of Front Street and Simonton, shivering at the blast of cool air that greeted her when she opened the door.

Heather Love was behind the counter, tallying the receipts for the owner.

"Tessa!"

Tessa stopped before the wind chimes over the door had stilled, wondering why her friend looked so surprised to see her. Her round blue eyes teetered on the verge of popping out of her head.

Instinctively, Tessa checked her clothes. Yes, she was completely dressed.

"Thought you might like company for lunch," Tessa explained.

Heather glanced at the clock, a handcrafted mechanism set in the center of a painted tin sun. "Oh, jeez," she exclaimed, the receipts flying from her shaky hands, her bracelets tinkling. "Is it that late already?"

Heather dropped to the floor behind the counter, seemingly to retrieve her paperwork. Heather Love was a lot of things, but clumsy wasn't usually one of them. Willowy, yes. Breezy, too—in an artistic sort of way. Tessa had taken an instant liking to the fresh-faced, barely twenty-five-year-old from the first moment they'd met, likely because the pretty artist was perpetually suspicious of anyone who carried a Y chromosome in their genetic makeup.

Definitely gave them something in common.

Tessa hooked her thumbs in the belt loops on her cutoff denim shorts and squatted, watching through the glass case as Heather shuffled the papers back into order.

"Need help?" she offered.

"Got it!" She popped up and thrust the papers into the cash drawer. "Why are you here, again?"

Tessa squinted, gauging the level of shock on her friend's face, wondering if she'd gone more than two weeks without stopping in. No, she'd come in last week and bought the hand-beaded body scarf she intended to wear tonight, the one she could wrap around and tie in several different sexy configurations.

"I thought you had something big planned tonight," Heather added.

Tessa's birthday wasn't for another three months. The anniversary of her move to the Keys, another holiday Tessa celebrated in style, was even farther off. Why was Heather acting as if Tessa had shown up early for a secret society meeting she hadn't been invited to? Though Tessa had filled Willa in on her plans for tonight, Heather hadn't been brought into the loop just yet.

"Yeah," Tessa acknowledged. "Later."

"Did you want to buy something special?"

"No, I just want lunch."

"Lunch!" Heather exclaimed, as if the concept was somehow brilliant, even if Tessa had mentioned the midday meal all of two minutes ago. "Great idea. Is it already time for lunch?"

Heather's sudden and feigned calm did not dilute the sense of warning coursing through Tessa. Something was definitely up with her friend.

"You're counting your drawer, Heather. Don't you always do that right before Jasper arrives to cover your lunch break?"

Heather glanced at the register, then took one of the deep, calming breaths she'd likely learned in yoga class. "Oh, yeah. Sorry. It's been one of those mornings."

When Heather relaxed, Tessa did, too. The last thing she needed was more stress.

"Lots of customers today?" Tessa asked, hoping for a reasonable explanation for Heather's weird behavior.

"A few bored wives of the lobster crowd." Heather grabbed a half-empty box of beaded bracelets and arranged them on a T-stand. "As the week progresses and the women feel more ignored, I'll sell more stuff. By Sunday, I'll make another windfall with the men feeling guilty if they come home with only crustaceans to be cleaned and cooked." Heather winked. "I love this business."

Now, this was Heather. Chatty, devious, ever-so-slightly resentful about men, though for no reason that Tessa was privy to. She'd arrived in the Keys one spring break and had simply never left. Yet so far as Tessa knew, she'd had no tragic love affairs more memorable than the kind of drive-by make-out sessions Tessa indulged in every so often. Heather's hurt came from somewhere deeper, but even without knowing the details, the ache connected the two women like kindred spirits gliding through life on parallel paths.

"You're so bad, Heather," Tessa said, shaking her head. She stood and leaned on the case, admiring a new offering of bracelets crafted of silver and shell. She recognized these as Heather's work. Delicate, unique. Just like the artist herself.

"Not even remotely," she denied, "but I do enjoy making money."

"I don't doubt your powers of salesmanship. I've succumbed too many times to your sales pitches myself. These are gorgeous." Tessa removed a bracelet she'd soon own, a collection of tightly coiled mollusk shells, all the palest pink, entwined by handcrafted silver. She draped the creation over her wrist. "Are these new or have you been holding out on me?"

Heather bit her bottom lip, uncharacteristically reluctant to push her latest design on Tessa. Without commenting, Tessa reached onto the rack and pulled out a bracelet made of mother-of-pearl. How would the shimmering shell look in the moonlight?

After a full minute *without* Heather claiming how perfect the pink inner shell looked against Tessa's tanned skin, Tessa draped the bracelet back on the display and thrust her hands onto her hips.

"Okay, Heather. Enough is enough. What's going on that you're not telling me about?"

Heather graduated from biting her lip to chewing. "Willa says you won't want to know."

"Willa's MIA."

"I know where she is. Sort of."

When Heather didn't elaborate, Tessa asked, "She doesn't want me to know what she's up to?"

Heather shook her head. "She asked me to call you later and tell you she'd still run that errand for you tonight, no problem."

Errand? Just like Willa—the queen of discretion. She was supposed to pick Colton up at the airport and deliver him to Speed Key.

But throughout their entire tête-à-tête to coordinate the scheme last night, Willa hadn't given Tessa a clue that anything was up that she shouldn't know about. Tessa was the first to admit she'd become somewhat self-absorbed since Colton's offer, but she wasn't usually so wrapped up in herself that she didn't know when a friend like Willa needed help.

"Is Willa doing something particularly dangerous today?" Tessa asked, wondering if her friend had finally followed through on her threats to take up free diving, the sport that required swimmers to submerge to great depths without oxygen tanks. Tessa loved the water and was a certified diver, but to counteract the effects of being the daughter of daredevil Rip Dalton, she had been blessed with antitheti-

cal genes from her mother, Marjorie Hallingsworth, a certified scaredy-cat. The diametric personalities of her parents
had not only made her wonder since age two how Rip and
Marjorie ever hooked up in the first place, but it also injected
Tessa with boundaries. Boundaries her friend Willa constantly tested.

Heather's brow furrowed, denoting her deep thought. "No
more dangerous than when she's on duty," she answered.

That didn't say much for the security of Willa's adventurous hide. Still, Willa loved to tease Tessa mercilessly over her
death-defying exploits, so she couldn't see her friend keeping even a free-diving junket a secret.

But she might keep something more devious to herself.

"Is she checking Colton Granger out or something? Because I told her last night that the guy's legit."

"Who?" Heather asked.

"Colton Granger?"

Heather shook her head. Obviously, this wasn't about Colt.
Okay. So why was a chill chasing up Tessa's arms?

"Heather, why did Willa think I wouldn't want to know
about whatever she's doing today? Willa and I don't usually
keep too many secrets and your worried expression is starting to rub off on me."

Heather turned to study her reflection in a hand-painted
mirror that retailed for four hundred and fifty dollars. Shaped
like a sunflower, the center threw back the stressed expression Heather had worn since the moment Tessa had skipped
into the shop.

"Oh!"

Heather's dangling bracelets jingled as she smacked her
hand just above her heart. "I do look worried, don't I?"

"It causes wrinkles," Tessa teased, encouraging Heather to
unburden her soul before she looked one minute over twenty.

"Willa said you'd already used up your time talking about your ex this month."

Daniel?

"I'll give myself an extension if it's serious. And if Willa is talking about Daniel without my knowing about it, I'm figuring *serious* is an understatement. Is he dead or something?"

Heather swallowed. "Not yet."

Despite her claim, Heather didn't look entirely sure.

"Is he sick?" Tessa asked.

"He looked fine."

Her heart dropped. "You saw him?" Tessa's voice came out in a strangled squawk, not exactly the epitome of cool that she'd been working on since chucking mainland life and moving to the Keys. Still, she had to give herself some credit. The only emotion driving her right now was surprise, not fear or loathing—definitely progress.

Heather twiddled with the carved, shark-tooth necklaces dangling beside her. "Yesterday. He came in the shop to buy a bauble for his latest babe."

Tessa tried to mimic that deep breath she'd seen Heather take earlier. Daniel was in the Keys? This weekend? With Colton just a few hours away?

What were the fucking odds?

Tessa Dalton. Lucky to the last.

She took a second breath, releasing it more as a snort than a sigh.

"Did he say why he was here?"

"Lobster season, just like every other rich boy with a yacht and too much time on his hands."

Tessa smirked. "Sounds just like him. I've known a lot of rich boys in my lifetime, but none quite fit the stereotype like Daniel."

After only about a year of marriage, Tessa had decided

Daniel coveted his quintessential playboy ne'er-do-well image, even if his thick wallet was heavier on plastic than cash. Apart from a trip to Rio de Janeiro to play baccarat with the sons of sultans or jetting to Telluride to swap embellished skiing stories, no event suited Daniel more than the opening of lobster season in the Keys.

She couldn't remember how many excuses she'd had to come up with to keep him from commandeering her father's Speed Key hideaway during the lobster seasons when they'd been married. He'd desperately wanted to impress his buddies with the custom-built structure, though she figured most of his so-called friends could have afforded a half-dozen houses twice as impressive on their weekly allowances alone. But even before she'd had any reason to suspect that her marriage would someday implode, Tessa had protected her father's sanctuary—a sanctuary she'd soon share with Colton.

With Daniel possibly circling her island like a rogue shark sniffing out a meal.

"Do you think he sought me out in particular?" Heather asked. "Because we know each other?"

Tessa shook her head. "He'd have no way of knowing you and I are friends." Daniel's unwelcome appearance in her life had to be no more than a raging case of bad timing. Had to be.

"Not unless he checked you out," Heather added.

It was Tessa's turn to bite her lip. While she couldn't imagine Daniel shelling out one cent to pay a private investigator when he could spend the money elsewhere, his father likely had several P.I.'s on retainer who wouldn't mind an all-expenses paid trip to the Keys to follow her around.

Still, she'd promised herself over a year ago not to expend any more of her spiritual energy on her ex or any member of his family. If Daniel had contacted Heather as an attempt to bait her, she didn't have to snatch the chum like a hungry fish.

"What do you think he's up to?" Heather asked.

Tessa closed her eyes and finally, after spending the morning trying to avoid thinking too long about tonight, surrendered to the sultry image of waves washing over her warm flesh. Her skin tingled in anticipation of stripping down and lying prone on the beach, awaiting Colton's arrival. She would set out the torches to illuminate his quest. Maybe stop by Island Scents for a new blend of herbs-and-citrus essence to perfume her skin.

After a long moment indulging in the possibilities, Tessa smiled. "I don't care."

"What?"

Tessa rolled her shoulders, then her neck, releasing the tension Daniel's name and presence had injected into her. "Willa knows about Daniel?"

"She went to check things out, find out what—"

Tessa cut Heather off with a flat palm. "I don't want to know. Daniel no longer exists in my life. He's nothing more than a notch on my bedpost."

Sculpted blond eyebrows rose over Heather's saucer-shaped blue eyes. "Really?"

Exaggeration aside, the sentiment was true. Tessa didn't give two flips about Daniel. Not anymore. Not ever again.

"Absolutely."

Heather's blue eyes narrowed, nearly enough to make Tessa nervous again—but not quite. "And you don't care what happens to him?"

"I can think of no situation in which Daniel's existence would be of the least interest to me."

Heather pressed her lips together and a twinkle brightened her expression. She imagined a similar sparkle enhanced her own face when she allowed herself to imagine the night of fantasy and pleasure she was only hours away from creating. On her private beach, the sand quivering in the firelight, the waves lapping at her toes while she awaited her hero—her solid, breathing male ideal—born from the deepest spring of her creative soul.

As for Daniel, as far as she was concerned, her friends could do with him whatever they wished. And since she knew her compadres rather well, she allowed one tiny shiver of vengeful glee to shoot through her bloodstream before she pushed the feeling and all thoughts of her ex-husband away.

In just a few hours, she had no doubt that her veins would pump with the more desirable emotions of lust, wonder and release. Colton promised to make her fantasy come true, and she had no reason to doubt him.

Or herself.

CHAPTER SIX

COLTON SAW THE FIRELIGHT FIRST—tiny flashes of orange flame dotting a dark mass of land a half mile off the boat's bow. Torches? Colton drew in a sharp breath and shook his head, trying to avoid a mental comparison between his current situation and a final episode of *Survivor*. But try as he might, he couldn't help but find similarities between his situation and that of the contestants of the reality television show marching up a torch-lit path to receive their judgment. Soon he'd walk the gauntlet to his fate—not for money, but for a once-in-a-lifetime chance at intense, unforgettable pleasure. And if his strategy succeeded, he'd possess the nirvana he craved—and for more than the one night Tessa expected.

Much, much more.

Over the sound of the rushing waves and the drone of the high-powered engines, their position was announced by his guide for the evening, Captain Willa Lawson—a blatantly intimidating woman with enough physical presence to dump his ass overboard if she thought for one minute he was up to no good.

"Grab your duffel, lover boy. We'll be on Speed Key in five."

He did as she commanded, hoping she at least intended to pull up to the dock, which he could now see, thanks to reflective red lights at the edge of the structure. Not that Colton didn't intend to swim tonight, but he'd rather do it after he stripped out of his traveling clothes. Just in case, he kicked off his loafers and tucked them into his bag. Never could trust a woman who wore combat boots on her off-hours.

From the moment his plane landed at the airport, the trip had shifted into truly surreal territory. Willa, wearing cutoff jeans and a much-worn Coast Guard T-shirt, drove up on a battered old Harley and retrieved him with little fanfare and even less conversation—though she'd made time to check him out from head to toe, even going so far as to circle him at baggage claim, her hands clasped behind her back, her Coast Guard ball cap shading her sharp eyes as she hummed her assessment. The sound had denoted neither approval nor disapproval. She clearly hadn't decided if he measured up.

On one hand, he appreciated that Tessa had cultivated strong, protective friendships in her brief time on the island. A woman living alone as she did needed someone to watch her back. On the other hand, he considered coating his skin with tenderizer and maybe smearing on some steak sauce in hopes of making his meat more palatable to the suntanned, buff-to-the-bone woman who eyed him so skeptically. Willa obviously wasn't going to deliver him to the prearranged destination unless she thought he was worth the effort.

The ride to the dock hadn't been much friendlier, though Willa had been gracious enough to point out a few of the sights. Not that Colton cared much about the historic Casa Marina hotel or the Hemingway House, but he appreciated her attempts at hospitality all the same. At the marina, he'd even offered to assist with the boat. She'd declined, though his manners had at least earned him a half smile. Or half smirk. The darkness and Willa's ambiguous snort had kept him from being entirely sure.

But soon this first impression wouldn't matter. Willa obviously intended to bring him to Tessa, despite any misgivings. And she wasn't the only one with doubts. When Tessa had agreed to his terms, she hadn't sounded quite as enthusiastic as he'd hoped. The wary crackle in her voice, the skeptical tone, forced him to consider if he'd asked for too much too soon.

Less than a year and a half had passed since her divorce had become final and despite Tessa's tales of wild living, Colton suspected her scars hadn't completely healed. Unlike other women who might have thrown themselves into their careers or cordoned themselves off from a social life, Tessa had parachuted into living like a daredevil. Thanks to her lifestyle, he'd have to employ extreme measures to impress her. Flowers and serenades wouldn't win him a woman like her. No, for Tessa, he had to push the limits.

As the boat neared the private island's slim dock, Willa pressed on the horn, playing a four-note tune that likely alerted Tessa to their arrival. The engines rumbled as they idled, the water beneath the boat surged, rocking the deck like the floor in a fun house. Colton grinned. Anticipation pumped his blood, tightened his groin. He could practically hear Mr. Roarke's accented greeting, *"Welcome to Fantasy Island."*

Flaming golden-red tiki torches stood in the sand, forming a curved line that led from the end of the dock along a path hidden by a thick expanse of trees. Thin wisps of charcoal smoke curled into the night, teasing his nostrils with the piquant scent of citronella.

And Tessa waited, likely, just beyond the darkness.

With a gentle jostle, Willa eased the boat against the bumpers fastened to the dock, then gestured for him to disembark. She held the boat steady with a tight grip on the line.

Before he stepped completely onto the dock, Willa knocked him on the arm with her fist. Not enough to hurt, but enough to get his attention.

"Tread carefully," she advised simply, then winked.

Colton jumped off the craft. After a skillful U-turn, she disappeared into the darkness.

"Tonight isn't about careful," Colton whispered to himself, unsure about who might be listening beyond the collection of dark green palm fronds. But he was forced to reconsider her advice after he strode to the end of the dock.

Blocking his descent on the half-dozen stairs leading to the beach, an open treasure chest brimmed with gold coins. Luckily, Colton knew his way around a pharmacy well enough to know the glittering doubloons were actually cleverly packaged condoms. Several hundred, all winking at him.

He dropped his duffel bag, his eyes wide. A quick dig revealed that she'd stuffed the box with newspapers, so maybe fifty or sixty prophylactics were in the box. Still, while he was no slouch in the stamina arena, he doubted she meant for him to use more than a few of these babies in one night. Her attempt at intimidation had worked—for a minute.

Colton chuckled, pocketed a few, then after giving the situation some thought, changed his mind and tossed them back. Instead, he glanced quickly over his shoulder to make sure Willa and her pleasure craft had definitely departed and stripped down to nothing. He retrieved his dark swimsuit from his bag, put it on and tucked one condom into the waistband. Then he pulled out the smaller mesh bag he'd tucked into his duffel, glad as all get-out that he hadn't been chosen for a random security search at the airport. Nothing he'd carried with him was dangerous—except in the hands of a man planning a delicious seduction.

Colton would make this night count, since Tessa had warned him that this interlude might very well be all they ever had. He wasn't deterred. When it came to the words he chose for his columns and for the book, he always went for quality, not quantity. And so far, his approach had served him well.

Slinging the mesh bag over his shoulder, he left the rest of his belongings on the dock and followed the tiki torches down the path. The sounds of the tropical night—the rustle of palm fronds in the balmy breeze, the whine of mating crickets, the rhythmic ebb and flow of the cool waves on the shore—enhanced Colton's impatience. God, he hadn't seen Tessa in so long. And their one meeting had been short—fifteen, twenty minutes, tops.

He knew he was taking a risk. He could blow this seduction with one misspoken murmur, one wrong touch. But playing out this fantasy with Tessa tonight was just the beginning—and yet, if she threw him off her island tomorrow, he'd have huge regrets but he'd also have a night to remember. Yes, he wanted more than one night—but if that's all he got, he'd deal.

He broke through the last gate of palm fronds and caught sight of Tessa lying near the water's edge, fire gleaming from a concentrated collection of torches, circling her in a mystical ring. His chest tightened. A thin sheen of sweat broke out over his bare skin and he speared a hand through his hair, amazed. He'd heard her agree to his demands, but until this moment, he hadn't believed she'd throw herself into the sexual role-playing scenario with such verve.

He should have known better. Tessa was all about verve.

Firelight sparkled on her moist skin, wet as if she'd just emerged from the storm and sea. Translucent from the water, the white material of her dress clung tightly to her skin, hiding nothing—not the dark circles of her areolae, not the high, taut peaks of her nipples, not the shadow of downy curls at the juncture of her thighs. Her flesh, tanned to a luscious golden brown, glimmered. He licked his lips, imagining her sweet taste. And even from the distance, with her face turned into the glow from the torches, he could see her lips, pink and slightly parted, waiting for the kiss to bring Alina back to life.

She didn't move a muscle, and yet the air in Colton's lungs rushed out.

Here you go, hotshot. Showtime.

He pulled out the mesh bag, crossed the sand to the water's edge and with great effort, tore his gaze away from Tessa long enough to wade into the water. He'd done a little research prior to his arrival. Night swimming wasn't the safest activity, thanks to the creatures of the deep, but Colton didn't plan to venture far from shore. How could he, with Tessa waiting for him, so lovely, so perfect, just a few paces away?

Her hair was longer than before, streaking well past her shoulders. A damp strand curled along her neck, flipping into a soft hook just above her breasts. Perfect breasts. Round and inviting and aroused. The moisture in Colton's mouth instantly evaporated and he marveled at her ability to remain still for so long. Though her breasts rose and fell with her soft breaths and her lashes occasionally fluttered, she remained motionless, just like Alina. Just as he'd asked.

And just like Reides, he'd soon coax her back to life.

Spurred with the thought, Colton splashed into deeper water, then dived, dousing his body completely. The cool currents twirled around him, momentarily tempering the strain on his cock. Good. He needed a healthy shot of cold to tone him down, dampen the intensity of his desire so he could see this seduction through as planned. Once thoroughly soaked, he emerged onto the sandy beach, shook the excess moisture from his hair and stalked toward his soon-to-be lover, the words from their novel dancing on his tongue.

"Alina?"

Water sluiced down his chest, his back, like a thousand slick fingertips. Salty drops coated his lips and tongue and stung his eyes, so he slicked his hair back, out of his way. Now was his moment of truth. No turning back. No time left to wonder what had possessed a sensible, logical, fact-loving man like him to embark on such a crazy mode of seduction.

Besides, he knew the answer. Tessa had possessed him. From the first moment he'd caught her eye in the West Palm Beach county courtroom, his die had been cast.

He slid to the ground beside her, grinning when the wool of a blanket soaked up the moisture on his calves and knees. She'd set the scene carefully, right down to a thick blanket beneath her and the gauzy sarong she'd wrapped around her body. She looked every inch the ancient Grecian maiden, tossed by the storm onto the shore.

When a droplet of water splashed from his hair to her belly, she flinched, but didn't utter a sound. Her control amazed him, nearly as much as the way the instinctive reaction drew his attention to her nipples. Centered high on her breasts, the dark tips announced her arousal when her voice could not. He expended every ounce of his self-control to keep from bending down now and taking her in his mouth. God, he wanted to taste her, all of her. Desperately, he wanted to prove his need. But first, as the scene dictated, he had to remove her clothes and draw her back into the water with him.

In the novel, Alina had already disrobed before she'd plunged into the water to rescue her injured lover. The innocent maiden hadn't realized that Reides half-mortal blood would heal him quickly or that because of his father's immortality, he could never die by drowning. Still, Colton couldn't fault Tessa for not stripping down before his arrival. Lying out in the open, naked on the beach wasn't the wisest thing to do for a woman who lived alone to do.

Still, they had agreed to reconstruct the scene as accurately as possible. When he reached to untie the knot on the sarong, his body tensed from the tendons in his shoulders to his swimsuit-bound sex.

She'd hardly tightened the knot. When he lifted her, he had no doubt that light material would flutter away like a spider's web in the wind. But just to be sure, he fumbled with the ends and in his haste, his fingers grazed her warm, pliant skin.

Her eyes flew open. She didn't speak, didn't move—didn't close her eyes again. And at that moment, Colton could think of nothing else but how green her eyes were. Sparkling with the reflection of firelight, they glistened like emeralds. No, he corrected. Lighter. More golden.

He swallowed deeply as he searched her irises for any hint that she'd changed her mind. If she wanted him to stop, she only had to say the word. For a split second, he thought he spied a flash of fear, but mixed with her natural surprise—he couldn't make a distinction between the two. Yet before he could search further, her lids dropped to half-mast and the curve of her smile was entirely sensual, entirely seductive. She closed her eyes, relaxed into his arms and with a soft sigh, beckoned him to continue.

A thrill shot through him. God, her fearlessness turned him on. Without delay, he lifted her, then kept his eyes trained on the surf as her dress fell aside beneath his feet. The scent of her perfume, light with musk and sweet citrus, fed his appetite to a ravenous hunger.

The torchlight faded behind him, but the glow of the ripe moon tempted him to take in the sight of her again. He resisted another look. He knew that one more glance at her would break his resolve to seduce her slowly and, literally, by the book.

He waded into the water, thankful for the cool, gentle waves breaking over his increasingly hot flesh. He held her close, then once the ocean splashed up to his hips, he lowered her so she floated on her back. He crossed her hands over her chest, and with one hand protectively buoying her beneath her back, he concentrated on his role.

"'This isn't your day to die, my love,'" he quoted, then with one strong, deep breath, pressed his lips to hers and plunged them both beneath the water.

DEPENDENT ON HIM for air, Tessa's mouth locked with Colton's. He tasted like mint and coffee, a heady combination as the sea swirled around them, lukewarm and lusciously inviting. He pressed her tight against him, possessive, protective. His chest crushed against hers, their legs tangled, all while the tide buoyed them in weightless delight.

No other woman in the world had ever experienced a first kiss quite like this. Safe beneath the waves, Tessa opened her eyes, but the dark currents masked his face. When they broke to the surface, Tessa forced herself back into her pliant role. In the scene, Alina was still unconscious. Alina would have to wait until after she experienced her first sexual pleasure before she saw her lover's face.

Of course, Tessa had already peeked. And what she'd seen had stolen her breath quicker than the ocean ever could.

Like no other man she'd ever met, Colton stunned her with the way his eyes revealed the depth of his desire. The first night they'd met, she'd noted how lust darkened and narrowed his irises, making her feel as if no other woman in the world had existed but her. On the shore, his silver-gray eyes had sliced through her, cutting her to the quick with white-hot need.

And though she'd read and reread the scene a thousand times in the past two days, each time experiencing a sensual thrill snaking through her body, she now battled a yearning unlike any she'd ever known. How would it feel to have a man make love to her while she pretended to be asleep? Would he follow the scene step-by-step, or would he deviate and experiment? She hadn't realized until this moment all the detail and nuance they'd left out of the scene itself, ripe fodder for her insatiable imagination.

Colton cradled her tightly, pushing through the tide toward the shore. Water rained down their bodies, spawning a sweet, intimate chill that primed her for what was to come.

Alina was now resurrected. Alive, but not yet drawn completely into the land of the living. Tessa pressed her lips together tightly, fighting the rush of anticipation.

The taut muscles of his thighs pressed against her hip as he lowered her onto the blanket. The ocean breeze lapped at the droplets on her skin, and when he moved away, a field of goose bumps prickled across her flesh, a response that intensified when he spoke the next line of dialogue from the book.

"'Damn you, Hades. Let her go! Alina, don't listen to the mad god of death. He craves you, wants your maiden flesh for his own.'" He rubbed his palms down her arms, up her legs, rubbing her briskly, but sensually, replacing the chill with pure fire. "'He'll tempt you with gilded promises, Alina, but only I can make your wishes true. Come back to me, sweet love.'"

Colton pressed his lips to hers again and Tessa needed all her self-control to fight the instinct to kiss him back. Instead, she relaxed her jaw and allowed his exploration. Forbidden sensations rushed through her as he ran his tongue beneath hers, then along her teeth, thrusting softly, learning her, pleasuring her. When his lips dipped lower, to her chin, her neck, she focused on keeping still.

You're Alina, she reminded herself. *You're unconscious. Unaware. You need your lover's caress to stir you, inject you with the will to live.*

Ah, hell. Tessa shifted on the blanket, ever-so-slightly moving so that her breasts were in the direct path of his descent, as if a sexy man like him would have any other destination. Still, while she wanted more than anything to experience lovemaking as Alina, she couldn't deny who she was or what she wanted. And she wanted Colton. Now.

His soft chuckle chastised her impatience.

"'I'll give you what Hades cannot, sweet love. A mortal's heat,'" he promised, his openmouthed kisses trailing down her breastbone with painful slowness. "'A god's desire.'"

On the breath of that pledge, Colton swiped a quick lick over her nipple, testing Tessa's ability to remain impassive long enough to experience the delights he promised. He lapped the seawater from her flesh with long, loving strokes. Creamy moisture pearled inside her and when he parted her thighs with his hot, muscular legs, she thought she might suffocate from holding her breath. His snug swimsuit restrained his sex, but the hard curve of his cock taunted her until the sensation of his mouth encircling her breast knocked everything else from her mind.

He suckled her with care, adoring every inch of sensitive flesh with his tongue, lips and teeth. When he'd laved one breast completely, he shifted and aroused the other, enhancing his exploration with his thumbs. Currents of blue light shot through her body and she couldn't contain a desperate whimper.

"My lady stirs," he said, and if the line was in the book, Tessa didn't remember it. Nor did she want to. She only wanted to experience all the pleasure Colton so skillfully offered.

When he lifted away from her body, she nearly protested, nearly surrendered and opened her eyes. Sounds teased her ears. The snap of wet spandex. The crackle of peeled foil.

Then she heard a twist, like a top removed from a jar. She opened one eye, but he'd turned his back to her. She could see nothing but water drizzling from his hands into a small bucket he'd jabbed into the sand. When he turned, she closed her eyes tightly, though his chuckle revealed she'd been caught.

"Alina, once you wake, our scene will be over," he chastised, giving her a clear choice. She either fought her instinct to discover what he had planned, or she lost her chance at sensual delight.

She chose quickly, relaxing into the blanket. She trusted him. She wanted him. And no matter what sheer force of will it took, she'd have him.

He seemed in no hurry, but finally returned to her side, his body heat taunting her, the hair on his thighs tickling her skin. He smoothed his palm over her belly, dipping his finger into the crevice of her navel just before he poured something fragrant, light, yet gritty onto her skin. The texture shocked her, and the minute he added a drizzle of water into the mix, the crystals foamed.

"Mmm, sea salts," he said, pressing the abrasive blend across the expanse of her stomach, then up her ribs, tantalizing her, awakening any nerve ending that dared remain dormant during his sensual assault. He rolled the softening granules beneath her breasts, tucking them beneath the sensitive curve of her flesh, then spread a moist swath downward until his fingers teased the edge of her mons, but went no farther.

A cloudy fog of sexual expectation restrained her in a pleasured cocoon. How would the rough crystals feel against her tender nipples, or smoothed over her pulsing outer lips? Would he dare coat her so intimately, or did he just seek to arouse every inch of her body except the ones that begged for his attention most? She listened to his deep-throated groans as he poured on more salts and coated her neck and shoulders until she thought his unhurried, unfocused pace might make her scream.

When he skipped to her legs, she couldn't restrain a frustrated sigh. Even when he poured more lukewarm water, then used both hands to rub the crystals over her, she could think of nothing except the parts of her that silently cried for his touch. He lovingly massaged her feet, her ankles, her calves. Her inner thighs shook from the gentle force of his rubdown, the tickling twirl of water, the bubbly mix of salt and soap. He touched her everywhere and nowhere, enthralling her so entirely that she didn't realize this wasn't part of the original scene until he twisted the cap off another bottle of fresh water and rinsed her skin clean.

"You glow with life, my love," he said, turning away from her again, this time returning quickly. He feathered something soft and absorbent against her skin. A natural sea sponge, she guessed. He dabbed her lightly, never in the same place twice, never allowing her to know where the downy sponge would press against her skin until she thought she'd go mad.

She didn't want a sponge, she wanted him. Squeezing her eyes shut tight, she feared if she attempted to look up at him she'd wrestle him to the ground and take what she wanted without any more waiting.

"You deserve such sweet attention." When he applied the moist sponge to her heated center, she instinctively opened her thighs. He pressed harder, releasing a trickle of cool moisture that ignited pure fire deep within her.

"My sweet Alina," he said. "I suspect you taste as sweet as the sea."

He answered his own supposition, tossing aside the sponge before he lifted her leg to his lips and scorched a path from the tip of her toes to her inner calf. He curved his body onto the blanket, following the trail over her thighs, stretching her leg over his shoulder. Tessa heard soft, pleasured moans and when he stopped his ascent, she realized the sounds came from her.

Her labia pulsed, hard and hot as her heartbeat. When his tongue parted her, she cried out in surprise, nearly overpowering the sound of his own insatiable groan. He pressed one hand across her smooth and scented belly, holding her still while he coaxed her to the brink of delirium.

Nips countered strokes—his lips chased the fire of his thirsty, lapping tongue. Her eyes flashed open, but she saw nothing but intense flashes of color, as if the torches rained embers around them to stoke the blaze coursing through her flesh. She reached for him at the same moment he lifted his body completely over hers. With one certain thrust, he turned the shower of sparks into a full-fledged conflagration.

His rhythm was hard, but steady. His sex filled her, stretched her, and with each surrender, her pleasure increased. He spoke. Somewhere in the distance, his voice urged her further toward the edge. What he said, she had no clue. Words didn't matter. Only the intensity of his sex sliding into hers, pumping her with the power of his body, her body, joined and hot. She wrapped her legs around his waist, clutched at his damp skin with hungry hands, her fingers digging into the tight muscle. She couldn't let him go.

Wouldn't. Not even after they tumbled into the madness, their pleasured cries echoing and drowning in the rush of sea and sand.

Tessa didn't know how much time passed before reality crept onto the beach like a frothy wave. A soft kiss brushed on her cheek, then tapped her on the tip of her nose. With a flutter of lashes, she opened her eyes and met the silver stare of her fantasy lover—a man who'd made this night so real, she knew she'd changed forever.

"Hello," he said.

His dark hair, just as long and rakish as she remembered, swung across his forehead.

"Hi, yourself."

Suddenly shy, Tessa glanced aside, but Colton tipped her chin back so that she had nowhere to look but at him. "Are you Alina now, or Tessa?"

She bit her lip. The man was incredible, but that she'd known for a long time. Still, in the glow of such overwhelming satisfaction, she couldn't form a phrase that was anything less than the truth.

"Tessa," she answered. "I've been Tessa since the moment you arrived. And I'll be Tessa after you leave, too."

Colton shifted onto his elbows, lifting his weight, but not breaking their connection. His grin was nothing short of incorrigible, as if he knew a naughty secret he was finally ready to share.

"Well, you see, that's the catch, isn't it? I've decided I'm not leaving for quite some time."

CHAPTER SEVEN

COLTON WAITED FOR Tessa to protest, but she didn't say a word. Maybe she hadn't heard him. Maybe she hadn't processed the full meaning of his declaration. Or maybe—just maybe—she liked the idea of spending more time together. For now, she seemed utterly fascinated with his face, raking her hands through his hair. And so she could see him clearly, she tilted his chin into the light. She traced his eyebrows with her thumbs, then spread her palms lightly over his cheeks, ensnaring him with her sensual touch.

"You live up to your promises, don't you?"

He grinned. "I try," he said, without a trace of false humility. He'd put a great deal of thought into tonight's seduction and her appreciation gleamed in her mysterious eyes, curved her bold mouth, emboldened her adventurous caress.

"Try? No, you succeed," she clarified, arching one thin eyebrow. "Wasn't easy for me to remain so still and docile. Not my nature, you know?"

He chuckled, dropping his chin so he could inhale her amazing scent. Tart and sweet and intoxicating. "I suspected. That's why I picked this particular scene, then did a few rewrites."

She licked her lips, still swollen from his kisses. "You didn't have to be so imaginative. I was a sure thing."

He nuzzled her neck, growing harder with each little coo

that spilled from her lips. "You talk a good game, Tessa, but a sure thing you're not."

With a hearty laugh, she pushed him to the side, rolling them over off the blanket and onto the sand, so powdery and fine, the velvet-smooth texture cradled his bare back when Tessa straddled him. She grabbed his hands and pinned him to the ground, as much as a woman her size could.

"As I recall," she said, swiping a challenge of a kiss across his mouth, "in the original scene, Alina wakes up satisfied, but a bit angry. Here she's been pining for her mysterious lover night after night for months. Experiencing pleasures she's never known. When her man finally shows up, she even gives her life for him. Then the bastard sends her over the edge into orgasmic delight while she's half-asleep. She hardly remembers all the good parts."

"She'll get her revenge," he reminded her.

"I could do the same," she challenged.

He nestled his backside into the sand, not so surprised when his sex stirred again, still nestled amid her damp, intimate curls. Not enough time had elapsed for him to initiate a repeat performance just yet. Still, the fact that she reignited his desire so quickly proved his suspicions about Tessa sinfully correct.

"You could try," he challenged.

She moistened her lips with her tongue, smoothing the wetness across her soft skin with what he was sure was deliberate slowness.

"I just might," she answered. "Sooner than you think."

Shifting quickly, Tessa slipped away, twirling on the beach, nude and beautiful, her skin pearlized by the moon and then warmed by the fire. He was tempted to grab her and tug her back, but he had to tread lightly. He had her just where he wanted her—focused on the two of them and the amazing experience they'd just shared. Only minutes had slipped by, but Colton couldn't help but note that she hadn't mentioned his original proposition about making love in order to get his answer about marketing the book. Nor had she broached the sore topic of him leaving the minute she requested his departure— a last-minute condition she'd attached.

Nevertheless, he wasn't leaving—deal or no deal. Not that he intended to piss her off. Instead, he planned to make the notion of him leaving impossible for her to bear. He didn't much care if she threw a first-class hissy fit or called out her dogs.

The thought of the hellhounds he so often heard snarling over the phone caused a shiver to race up his spine. Rottweilers were not his favorite breed. So far as he was concerned, the vicious hounds were best suited to bikers and security companies. He glanced around. Only after concentrating did he hear muffled yaps from somewhere beyond the brush. He caught the glimmer of a light from a window high off the ground. If he hadn't looked, he might not have seen the house at all, a good fifty yards away and tucked behind an impressive collection of tall coconut palms and a thick wall of fat, leafy sea grapes.

He was curious about what her home looked like inside, but for obvious reasons, had no strong desire to leave the beach.

Tessa retrieved her sarong, shook out the sand and wrapped the material around her. Splotches of moisture marred the dress, but Colton couldn't complain about the view. Nude or dressed, Tessa stole his breath. He wanted her. Again and again and again.

She picked up his swimsuit and held it toward him, but he made no move to retrieve it. "Am I being dismissed?"

With a deep-throated chuckle, she tossed the suit beside him on the blanket. "No."

"Good. I'm glad you didn't let me have my way with you and then throw me out."

She dropped to her knees beside him, tucking her feet beneath her. "I'm not a heartless bitch, Colton, no matter how much I like to act like one."

He pulled up onto his elbows. "It's a strong armor, that persona."

"Sometimes," she admitted. "But it can also be a prison, just like anything else." She fiddled with the material of her dress, layering the gauzy material primly over her bare thighs. She turned and watched the water, spilling gently onto the sand. "You were pretty incredible."

Again the topic drifted back to the lovemaking. Colton tried to bite back a surge of pride, but then decided, why? He had to play to his strengths if he wanted a woman like Tessa. "You ain't seen nothing yet."

She glanced at him sideways, her green eyes glimmering with something close to skepticism—but not quite. More like wary expectation. "Oh, really?"

"Absolutely. I'm a man of many talents, many interests."

"And let's not forget the unstoppable ego."

"How could we?"

The duet of his chuckle with her unbridled laugh sounded like music to Colton's ears. He could be himself around Tessa, or he could be someone else entirely, like Reides, their hero. Why or how Tessa had swept across the distance Colton had learned to establish between him and the women in his life, he didn't know. And at this point, he didn't care. He only hoped that the connection they'd fostered over the phone and through the writing of the book could stand the test of being together 24/7. He wished they had more time to move slowly—an evening together here, a morning there. But the tried-and-true path to romance wouldn't work this time. For either of them. Besides, he had only a week before he needed to return to Chicago. Whether or not Tessa would take a leap of faith along with him, he had no clue.

Tessa sauntered beyond the reach of the torchlight, her hips swaying as softly as the breeze, drawing his gaze. She shook out her hair as she walked, and Colton noticed that the strands were not only longer, but lighter, spilling across her back like hot caramel sauce. He didn't think she could have grown any more beautiful.

He'd been wrong.

She reentered the light soon after with a small Styrofoam cooler.

"Thirsty?" she asked.

"I could use something wet," he answered.

She settled the foam box in the sand, then pulled a bottle of wine from the cooler. The glass dripped from the melting ice that surrounded it. "Are you attempting a double entendre, because I've heard better. From you, actually."

He laughed. "Yeah, that was lame. Obviously, I need a glass of whatever you're offering."

"I thought about serving Mexican beer, for old time's sake. But your visit demands something infinitely more special."

She turned the wine bottle toward him. From a woman like Tessa, he expected a rare vintage, maybe something from before they were born. Instead, he got a cartoon drawing of limes hanging on a dark green branch and the words *Key West* printed in a font as bold and brazen as the island community itself.

"Key Lime wine?" he asked, surprised.

"Very fresh and fruity. Don't knock it until you've tried it."

"I'll take you at your word. First, I'm going for a short swim. Care to join me?"

She shook her head, but reached across the blanket to where she'd left a folded towel. He accepted the offering and by the time he'd returned to their oasis on the beach, washed clean and revitalized, she had two glasses poured and settled on the top of the cooler and was slicing a knife through a thick-skinned mango. She sat with her knees parted, carving the tropical delicacy over the gap between her thighs so that the juices trickled onto the sand. He had the insatiable desire to lie just beneath her and lap at the sweet, dripping liquid with his tongue.

He toweled off quickly and wound the cloth around him as if he'd just walked out of the shower.

"Hungry?"

He squatted beside her, then sat. "Around you, I'm always hungry."

She handed him a sliver of mango, still cradled in the reddish green rind. "You're just full of innuendoes tonight, aren't you?"

"Or I'm just full of it."

She chuckled, then laid the knife and half-cut fruit on the makeshift table. "You? Never. You don't say anything you don't mean, remember?"

He lifted the fruit to his nose, took a sniff and found the scent pleasantly subtle. Honeyed and exotic, but light. He bit into the bright orange flesh, surprised by the instant tanginess, smoothed immediately by a sugary finish. He hummed his approval.

"Never had mango before?"

"Not right off the rind."

She took a generous bite from her own wedge. "My dad and I could finish off a bushel of these in one week, sitting here, just like this."

Colton frowned, not sure he wanted their night together to remind her of her father. He snagged his glass and, as with the fruit, stole an exploratory sniff. Very limey.

"I'm sure you weren't drinking wine then," he said. Or having sex with virtual strangers.

Tessa laughed, then turned the rind so she could scrape the

last of the fibrous flesh off with her teeth. "When I was in the Keys with Rip, my childhood was not exactly traditional."

Colton drew a tentative sip of wine into his mouth. The first impression was strong citrus, but the crisp bite of a decent white wine made the vintage palatable. Fun, even. Unique. An appropriate drink choice for tonight.

"Was it traditional back in New York?" he asked.

She snorted, grabbed her wine and took a hearty sip. "In comparison to my time here, yeah. I guess. If nannies and co-tillions and picnics, where everyone dresses in their finest linen suits instead of halter tops and shorts, and where they serve vichyssoise and seared mahimahi instead of hot dogs and potato salad, are your idea of traditional."

Colton took another sip of wine. He'd been raised in wealth and privilege like Tessa, but he'd at least enjoyed an occa-sional hamburger-fest courtesy of his Methodist church or the local Scout troop. The Grangers of Lexington indulged in both old Southern sensibilities including coming-out parties and foxhuntings, and modern entertainment like baseball games and movie night. The diversity had permitted him to become a social chameleon, able to shift from situation to sit-uation without much discomfort. He wondered if the varia-tion between Tessa's divergent worlds of stiff, upstate New York society and loose-as-a-goose Key West living had done the same for her.

Just another of the many things that fascinated him about Tessa. Just another of the details he wanted to know.

"Did you see your father a lot?"

For an instant, Colton didn't think Tessa had heard him. Her head whipped toward the house, alerting him to the fact that the dog's barking had become louder, perhaps even more urgent. She turned toward the water and searched the horizon, then seeing nothing, shook her head and answered him.

"Not enough. But when I was here, he spent time with me every day, religiously, whether he was hung over or still entertaining some chick he'd picked up at Brew's. Between the hours of three o'clock in the afternoon, just after he woke up," she noted, "and sunset, when he'd shove off to go party until dawn, he was mine. He taught me how to torque a boat engine, fish for amberjack and hold my liquor. All in all, not a bad education."

The wistful lyricism of her voice made Colton wonder how different her life would have been if Rip had maintained sole custody of his daughter instead of her uptight mother. She likely would have had the street smarts to avoid a playboy like Daniel Reese. Then again, if not for Daniel, Colton and Tessa might have spanned their entire lifetimes without meeting.

He was about to admit as much when she jumped to her feet, again scanning the dark horizon. Setting down his wine, he joined her. "What do you see?"

"Nothing. But the dogs are going nuts."

"Maybe they don't appreciate my presence," he guessed, not entirely looking forward to his first introduction to her so-called pets.

"There's only one way to find out."

She looked up at him with big, innocent eyes. Before she even spoke a word, he gulped down his apprehension.

"Ready to meet the pups?" she asked.

He glanced back at the blanket, thought again about the treasure chest of condoms sitting on the dock. He had a lot more planned for this evening than doggie introductions. But with the distraction of continued howling, he couldn't expect her full attention.

"Do I have a choice?"

She wrapped her arms around his waist and pressed her nose to his bare chest. After inhaling deeply, she proceeded to rub her hands up and down his back, over his ass and down his thighs. His cock immediately rose to the occasion, bulging beneath the towel he was suddenly having trouble keeping attached to his waist.

"You should be safe," she said, pressing her cheek against his pecs.

"Oh, really? Why's that?"

She turned her face and kissed him in the center of his breastbone, precisely at the spot where his heart slammed against his chest. "You're carrying my scent," she told him, swiping a quick tongue across his nipple, which immediately and painfully clenched. "They'll either love you from the first moment they meet you, or they'll rip you to shreds."

He groaned when she turned her attention to his other nipple and tortured it in kind. "How reassuring."

Just then, a loud pop echoed across the water. A red flare streaked across the sky, sparks trailing in a sharp arc. The sound was followed by the roar of boat engines, growing louder and nearer.

He snatched up his swimsuit just as Tessa grabbed his hand and led them along the bushy trail she'd likely dashed through a thousand times. In seconds, they were climbing the steps to her second floor, onto a wraparound porch that allowed her a three-hundred-and-sixty-degree view of her island and the ocean that surrounded it. From the southwest, a yacht approached, motoring slightly above idle speed. Another flare shot into the sky with much hoopla and celebratory shouts, and even to the eye of a landlubber like Colton, the boat didn't look in trouble—not when he took into the account the half-dozen drunks dancing like tribesmen on the deck.

Tessa popped open a door and disappeared inside while Colton removed his towel and replaced it with his swimming trunks. When she reemerged, she tossed him a set of binoculars. "I don't know anyone around here," he insisted. "Shouldn't you use these?"

He heard the distinctive slide and lock as she loaded a shell from the magazine to the chamber of the twelve-gauge shotgun she'd told him a thousand times she could grab at a moment's notice. Good to know she hadn't been lying just to calm his overprotective instincts.

"Know how to handle this sucker?"

Colton chuckled. "While you were eating mangoes and learning about underage drinking, my father had me out hunting ducks."

She traded him the gun for the binoculars. He checked the safety and buoyed the ten-pound rifle in his hands, acclimating his hands to the shape of the weapon.

"Do you always come out armed when some drunken partiers venture too close to your island?" Colton asked, hoping the answer was an unequivocal yes.

In two strides, she leaned against the railing, training her eyes through the binoculars on the invaders coming eerily close to her dock. "Usually, I let the dogs out first. Then I back them up with firepower."

"Feel free to follow standard procedure," Colton volunteered, suddenly liking the idea of having two snarling, killing machines covering his back.

"Oh, I will." She tossed the binoculars onto a nearby lounge chair, grabbed his arm again and pulled him into the house, darting down the stairs to the utility area where she'd detained her dogs. "There's no way I'd deny Artemis and Apollo a chance to meet Daniel."

Colton stopped dead. His hand gripped the gun so tightly, his knuckles ached. "Daniel? As in Daniel Reese, your asshole of an ex-husband?"

Tessa pulled back a security bolt. Behind the door, the dogs raged, growling and barking and scratching as if possessed.

"One and the same." She shouted a throaty order to the dogs that immediately silenced them. When she opened the door, Colton saw two of the biggest, blackest dogs he'd ever laid eyes on, their barrel chests heaving and their tongues quivering with barely checked pants.

She leaned down and patted their heads, soothing them with nonsense words. A moment later, she motioned him closer. Grabbing his hand, she rubbed his palm over their ears. "Friend," she said to the pooches in a soft, childlike voice. To him, she whispered, "Let them sniff you."

The entire ritual took all of fifteen seconds. Soon the dogs were wagging their tails and circling them, then dashing to and from the door to the outside, more interested in the sound drawing closer and closer than the stranger their beloved owner had just introduced.

"Am I safe now?" Colton asked. He'd once doubted her stories about the ferociousness of her dogs. One look at their square jaws and demon eyes and he was a bona fide believer.

"You're safe," she answered, her green irises sparkling with their own devilish fire, making Colton wonder if he truly knew this woman as completely as he thought he did. The vulnerability he'd spied in her eyes over a year ago was nowhere to be seen. And the effect was wholly arousing.

"What about Daniel?" he asked, thinking the man was screwed and Colton was one lucky son of a bitch to get to bear witness.

She popped open the door and laughed when the dogs charged out ahead of them, growling and snarling as they shot toward the dock.

"He's in for the surprise of his life."

CHAPTER EIGHT

IN ALL THE YEARS she'd known him, Daniel Reese had been a lot of things. Selfish. Self-centered. Arrogant to the point of unintentional humor. But he'd never been out-and-out stupid...until tonight.

At least he—or whoever was captaining the fifty-five foot Bertram 510 fishing yacht—was smart enough to realize they would run aground if they didn't throw down anchor about thirty yards offshore. The hulking vessel might have been able to tie up at Tessa's dock, which her father had built over a deep trench on the island's southwestern side, but this novice captain had overshot it. For now, the man-infested yacht idled just off her private beach on the southernmost point of the island, its passengers likely attracted to the tiki torches like some sort of buzzing, annoying bugs.

"What are they doing?" Colton asked, his feet planted firmly as he scoped the yacht with her shotgun.

Tessa paced the shoreline as the dogs crashed into the water, snarling and barking, providing what she thought should be a strong enough warning to keep Daniel and his cronies off her private land.

She looked into the binoculars again. No more flares were shooting into the sky, yet Tessa could guess the yacht had already caught the attention of more than just her and Colton. Two men still danced—badly—on the sleek bow, though

Tessa could no longer hear any music beyond whoops and hollers from the clearly drunken revelers. She couldn't see Daniel anymore—or the man she'd thought was Daniel when she'd looked from the porch.

Maybe Heather's information this morning had just spooked her, injected her with images of her ex-husband so that she was seeing him now in the face of some frat boy toying around with his buddies on Daddy's big boat. She let the binoculars drop to her chest on the strap she wore around her neck and rubbed her arms. Her skin continued to prickle.

No, Daniel had to be among the carousers. Her jerk radar was on full alert.

"Can't tell. Only idiots would approach with the dogs going nuts like this," she said, shouting over Arty and Apollo's monstrous din.

"In other words, Daniel should be here momentarily."

Tessa snorted. "Feel free to shoot on sight. This is my island and my No Trespassing signs are numerous and well lit."

Colton lowered the gun and eyed her intently. "You're serious?"

She couldn't help but grin. Her father had installed the signs years ago and all she'd had to do was make sure the battery packs on the buoys were changed on a regular basis to ensure that she'd met the requirements necessary for protecting herself. Technically, trespassers actually had to be on her land before she could, in the eyes of the law, shoot first and ask questions later, but reports of her strict security measures usually kept the curious away. The sober curious, anyway. The intoxicated tended to forget their good sense.

Tessa guarded her privacy, but in all the time she'd lived here, the mere appearance of her dogs had been enough to run off any interlopers except reporters who'd camped out before she acquired her pets. Leave it to Daniel to push her limits.

"I'm fairly good friends with the sheriff and you already met Willa from the Coast Guard," Tessa said, "but if you'd rather fire a warning shot, to be polite, I won't think any less of you."

Colton cleared his throat. "So now my masculinity is in question?"

She walked close to him, brushing her body lightly against his. Who the hell was he kidding? Not even Arnold Schwarzenegger would question this man's machismo. "Never, Colton, never. But I'm counting on you practicing more restraint than I would. Besides, it's better to avoid spilling any blood in the water. I've got enough sharks around here, if you know what I mean."

As if on cue, an engine roared, not deep and rumbling like the yacht's twin inboards, but high-pitched and whiny like an outboard typically found on the end of the ten-foot tender. Seconds later, a small, semiinflatable vessel roared across the gentle waves, straight toward her shore.

The dogs nearly lost their minds. Fearful for their safety, Tessa ordered them to her side. Twice. Reluctantly, they complied, dripping wet and panting as they circled and whined until she commanded them to sit.

"You're letting him on Speed Key?"

Tessa removed the binoculars from around her neck and traded them with Colton for the gun. He hesitated before handing her the weapon, but with one intense glare, she reminded him whose name was on the rifle's permit.

"I won't have him thinking he can harass me at will. I'm going to put an end to whatever he's up to, right here and now."

As the tender drew closer to where they stood, the sounds of raucous laughter broke over the guttural growls simmering from the dogs. The bow of the inflatable boat skimmed over the sand and then jerked to a stop when the drunk in charge of the outboard engine failed to lift the propeller in time. Daniel and two friends literally spilled onto the beach. They laughed uproariously at their clumsiness, quieting only when they heard the distinct and sobering sound of Tessa cocking her rifle.

Daniel looked up with painful slowness, his ocean-blue eyes red around the irises, but still breathtaking for their color and clarity. Too bad for him, the hypnotic hue didn't have any effect on her anymore. Tessa grinned, both surprised and relieved that his gorgeous stare couldn't reduce her to a puddle of needy girliness anymore. In fact, his bright baby blues merely provided the perfect target between which to aim her best shot.

"What are you doing here, Daniel?"

Swiping fruitlessly at the sand and shell clinging to his damp and wrinkled chinos, Daniel did his best to stand up straight, an expensive bottle of scotch still dangling from his fingertips.

"Now, is that any way to greet your favorite ex-husband?"

The dogs bared their teeth. Tessa couldn't see them since she wasn't stupid enough to take her eyes off her ex, but she watched terror pale Daniel's sun-kissed tan. He took a stumbling step backward.

"What the hell are those?"

Tessa loosened her grip on the rifle, dropping her trigger hand to smooth her palm over Apollo's head. "Hellhounds. You'll no doubt be seeing them in the afterlife, so you might want to get acquainted now."

Daniel's friends must have suddenly realized that their sophomoric and clearly spontaneous trip to her private island might not have been the best idea for an exciting night in Key West. Apollo bared his teeth and both yahoos scrambled into the tender like crabs, as if the inflatable material could some-how protect them from sharp, saliva-coated canine teeth.

She eyed them both with a grin. "Should've gone to Duval Street, huh, boys? More fun to be had there than here."

Artemis lunged forward, her paws kicking up sand. One of the men screamed like a girl. Tessa ordered her dog back into place and bit the inside of her lip to keep from laughing. For once in her life, she had the upper hand with Daniel, thanks to two ferocious dogs, a shotgun and Colton. He stood so close, his body heat injected her with a renewed sense of confidence that flowed through and around her, as the ocean had when he'd taken them on their midnight swim.

Orgasms must make her especially sassy, because right now, she felt as if she could take on the whole free world and maybe even a few small dictatorships.

"Why are you here, Daniel?"

Her ex-husband's eyes darted from the dogs to Colton, who stood with his arms crossed over his impressive, naked chest. "Who the hell is he?"

Tessa glanced at Colton. The answer danced on her tongue, something along the lines of *the god of a man who just gave me the best sex I've had in years,* but sharp and biting as the crass comment would be, it would cheapen the experience she'd shared with Colton just to get another dig into her ex.

Anyway, Colton had to make his own decision about out-ing himself. Dropping his name to Daniel, even if he'd more than likely forget it by morning, could stir trouble neither one of them needed.

Living out more of their mutual fantasy wouldn't be so easy if Daniel decided to unleash his ire on Colton for some perceived slight. She knew Daniel well enough to know that's how he'd react, so she said a little prayer that Colton would keep his mouth shut.

"I'm a friend of Ms. Dalton," he answered, his tone deep and masculine. "That's all you need to know."

Amen.

Daniel snorted, eyeing Tessa with pure, unadulterated scorn. "At least you've graduated to real men instead of pool boys and housekeepers."

His remark died a quick death the instant the gibe left his lips, a zinger with no zing. She'd had enough of his lies and her outrage had faded a long time ago, right about the same time as the tan line on her ring finger. Daniel probably believed all the lies he'd told in court, convinced by two years of telling the stories over and over to every sympathetic woman he wanted to lure into his bed and to every tabloid still desperate enough to want to run a worn-out story.

She shifted her stance, but kept the gun aimed steadily. "Well, I started with you and then worked my way up through the sexual chain until I got to the top. Why don't you just go back to the ocean like the bottom-feeder you are and leave me the hell alone?"

He cleared his throat and attempted to stand up as straight as his drunken body would let him. "I want to talk to you."

"Call my attorney."

"Your goddamned attorney isn't going to get you out of this one. You've forgotten who you're dealing with."

At this, Tessa lowered the weapon and arched her brow. She couldn't have Daniel thinking that she had to rely on a shotgun to fight her battles. And she was done hiding out and avoiding him in hopes of burying that part of her past.

She handed the gun to Colton. "No, I know exactly who I'm dealing with—a bitter, small man who can't let go of the past. Move on, Daniel. We have nothing to say to each other. Ever."

"Tell your friends to back off."

"What?"

"I lost my table at Erina's."

Tessa swallowed a chuckle. "The restaurant?"

"The only decent restaurant in this tourist-ridden town!"

Okay, that was so not true. But Erina's, a relatively new addition to the Simonton Street offerings, would appeal to Daniel because it was probably the most expensive, European-style eatery in town. The wine list alone would make any connoisseur weep and coupled with a menu that changed with the owner's mood and a fawning Czechoslovakian proprietor, the place reeked of new money. If you were seated immediately at Erina's, you were somebody in the eyes of the nouveau riche.

Apparently, Daniel was now a nobody. Why? Erina had been trying to establish a relationship with Tessa for months. Tessa guessed the woman's motivation lay in the fact that Erina had once enjoyed a torrid love affair with Tessa's father, Rip, and that now that she'd returned to the Keys, she wanted back into Key West royalty, such that it was. Little did Erina know that Tessa was the last person who could get her where she wanted to be. She had no time for anyone's royalty anymore.

"I don't know what you're talking about, Daniel. I haven't been to Erina's in months."

"The maître d' said you were a regular. That she couldn't seat me because she was friends with you."

Erina's had no maître d'. Showed what Daniel knew. Erina sat her customers herself.

"I can't help it if Erina has discriminating taste."

He pointed his finger at her, sloshing whatever was left in his scotch bottle, probably a mixture of liquor and seawater. "I've been coming to the Keys for years. I won't have you ruining my vacation."

"Every day of your life is a vacation, Daniel. This is my home now. If people don't like you because of the hell you put me through, I say more power to them. You made your own bed of lies to sleep in. Take it like a man."

Rage boiled in Daniel's eyes and Tessa knew without a doubt that he wanted to rush her, lock his fingers around her throat and squeeze. He might have tried, if not for the little obstacles of her dogs, her gun and Colton.

Oh, and Willa, who marched in from behind her, off the path from the dock, flanked by two of her crew. A twenty-five-foot Port Security Boat skimmed the water toward the yacht, a bullhorn announcing the impending boarding of the vessel.

"She's giving you good advice, Mr. Reese. You should take it."

"Who the hell are you?"

Tessa relaxed. The dogs wagged their tails at Willa's approach, but stayed put as commanded even when she leaned down and gave them both generous scratches behind the ears. She took in Colton and his impressive naked chest, brief swimming trunks and bare legs, then proceeded to confront Daniel eye-to-eye.

"I'm Captain Willa Dawson. We saw your flares. They're for emergencies, you know. Not fireworks. We also received a complaint of someone driving a vessel while under the influence."

"I wasn't driving," he slurred.

"Really? I've got twelve witnesses down at Mallory Square who will testify that you were—and one of them is the sheriff. He called us in, since the waterways are our turf. And if that's not enough to stick to your ribs, I'm figuring I've got trespassing to add to your growing list of offenses, Mr. Reese. Am I right?"

Tessa pressed her lips together. God, would it be petty of her to press charges and watch Daniel get his ass hauled off to jail for a night in Key West's lockup?

Yes, it would be. Petty, petty, petty.

"You're one hundred percent right, Captain Dawson," Tessa replied, aware of the snicker from Colton, who still stood behind her. "I'll be more than happy to file charges… first thing in the morning."

Willa nodded to her cohorts, who menacingly stalked forward and grabbed Daniel by the arm.

"You can't do this to me!" he shouted.

Tessa rolled her eyes. "Daniel, you're so predictable. Why don't you do yourself a favor and *not* act like the outraged spoiled rich brat for once? Cooperate with the Coast Guard. Go quietly. Forgo calling your cache of attorneys for a few hours, sleep it off, pay the fine and get the hell out of Key West. No one wants you here."

Daniel was too busy sloppily struggling against his handcuffs. "I'm going to make you pay for this, Tessa."

At least his two friends had the good sense to keep their mouths shut. They surrendered willingly, even if one did throw up on the sand shortly after being hauled to his feet, apparently with a little too much speed.

Daniel seethed and raged and cursed and threatened and, true to his upbringing, acted exactly the way any privileged asshole with less sense than a croton bush would in the face of three arresting officers. At one point, the pain of watching Daniel behave like a drunk but pampered idiot forced her to turn away. Damn him. She wasn't even able to enjoy his moment of humiliation because she couldn't forget that only ten short years ago, she'd been stupid enough to marry the guy. And worse, she'd been completely in love with him at the time.

Enamored. Entranced. Head over heels.

Idiot.

"You okay?" Willa asked, laying her hand gently on Tessa's shoulder once her boys had Daniel and his more compliant friends hauled away to the dock.

Tessa forced a grin. "Couldn't be better. Did Rick really report Daniel and his friends for driving under the influence?"

Willa's smile could have lit up the whole beach. "I knew I liked that landlubber sheriff."

She wiggled her eyebrows lecherously, but Tessa only smirked. She knew her friend only had eyes for Leroy Brewster—though since their affair was publicly unacknowledged, it might mean they weren't exclusive, so she supposed if the aptly named Sheriff Rick Romeo showed interest in Willa, her friend might take a little bedroom detour.

"Thank him for me. He's got sharp eyes," Tessa said.

"And good ears," Willa added.

"What does that mean?"

Willa shrugged innocently, which made the hairs on Tessa's arms stand on end. Willa hadn't been innocent about anything since approximately the fifth grade. Or so Tessa had been told.

"It means you've got more friends than you think here on the Key, Tessa. Makes me a little embarrassed that so far, acquaintances of yours are doing more to annoy your ex-husband than your friends are. I'm going to meet with Heather and Brew. We're going to have to pick up the slack."

Tessa bit back a smile—right along with an insincere request that her friends leave Daniel alone. "You guys need to stay out of trouble. Rick just did us a favor, but he isn't one to toy with the law."

Willa waved her hands at Tessa dismissively. "Rick wouldn't dare arrest me."

Tessa leveled her with a look.

"Okay, he'd arrest me if I gave him a good reason. But," she said, wiggling her eyebrows again, "that's not really such a bad option, you know, that man and a pair of handcuffs."

Tessa laughed and Willa jogged off after clapping Colton

on the shoulder, mindful that she had an arrest to complete. For the next few minutes, Tessa and Colton watched in silence as the Coast Guard boarded and secured the yacht, leaving the tender bobbing on her beach.

Once the show was over, Tessa grabbed a towline, yanked the inflatable securely onto the shore, and then returned to the beach blanket and the last strip of sliced mango. The dogs romped around her, then settled at her feet whining for a morsel of fruit. She gave in almost instantly and the Rottweilers, who'd been vicious snarling beasts only a few minutes ago, now slobbered gently on her hand, evoking warm giggles and a bittersweet smile.

Colton watched her, now that the beach had grown quiet, stealing a few moments to realize the absolute weight and importance of the last hour of her life—and his.

"Boy, you weren't kidding when you said you were too busy living to write," he quipped.

She chuckled. "And here I thought I was exaggerating just to get under your skin."

He slid onto the blanket beside her, adjusting his legs so he didn't accidentally kick Artemis, who was happily chomping on the oversize mango pit. "You're under my skin, sweetheart. Have been for a hell of a long time."

With a deep sigh, Tessa wiped her hands on the blanket and eased to her feet. She spun toward him, but took a few steps back, creating a physical distance Colton knew wouldn't give her what she was looking for. They'd only been together for an hour or so, and yet, the chemistry between them was undeniable. He wouldn't go so far as to call their connection comfortable, but it was uncomfortable in all the right ways.

When she opened her mouth to speak, he stood and pressed a finger to her lips.

"Stop and think, Tessa. You're on emotional overload right

now, thanks to your drunk and clueless ex-husband. Don't let him ruin what we've started."

She reached out and cupped his cheek. "I'd never do that, Colton. I'm done letting Daniel influence my life. I've been done for a long time."

And yet, when Colton moved to rub her bare arm, she stepped out of his reach and started to collect the remnants of their beachside rendezvous.

"But he still affects you, Tessa. You can't deny that."

"Of course I can! I can deny it until the day I die, strongly and loudly and insistently."

"Doesn't make it true," he countered.

"Wanna bet?"

Colton chuckled. "Not when you have that stubborn look in your eyes. I get the feeling you'd do whatever it takes to prove me wrong. And I don't want to waste another moment of this night. Do you?"

After a few tense seconds, a smile dissolved the intense expression on her face. She licked her lips expectantly and eyed him through a naughty, narrow gaze.

"Did you bring any clothes with you?"

"Will I get extra points if I say no?"

She laughed, shaking her head. "Suddenly, I have a strong desire to go dancing. I'm not sure anyone will look twice if I took you to the island in only a bathing suit, but you might be a little more comfortable doing the Macarena in dry clothes."

The moment lasted with her expression dead serious until his smile faltered and she started to laugh. Colton couldn't imagine feeling any warmer outside on a sultry tropical night dressed only in a wet swimsuit, but he did. This woman was amazing. Exactly how was he going to convince her to leave this paradise to join him in Chicago, with its tall buildings, congestion and freezing cold winters?

Well, he'd already given it his best shot with his moves on the beach. Now, he had to top it off on the dance floor. He'd come here prepared to do whatever he had to—he certainly wasn't going to stop now.

CHAPTER NINE

Fluttering her fingers over the top of the aquarium, Aphrodite watched the creature she'd just acquired alight from the rainbow stones at the bottom of the tank, its iridescent scales reflecting a kaleidoscope of colors from pleasing deep blues to palest pinks. Its fluid, gelatinous movement turned the creature into a transparent butterfly of the sea with all the same breathtaking qualities as the gentle insects that flitted over the fields and valleys of the mortal's earth. Aphrodite had had to pay a great price for this treasure of the deep, and even the powerful Poseidon would never know that his bargain with her for a mere rare sea flower would cause his son's downfall.

"Aphrodite!"

She looked up, bored and cool, despite the rage echoing in the air. She scooped a handful of enchanted snails and tossed them into the water, watching with mild interest as the undulating creature violently devoured each and every one.

Morpheus materialized in front of her, his chest heaving and his nostrils flaring even before he attained complete form. His cloudlike hair billowed wildly around his face and his fists, tightly clenched, revealed the breadth of his rage.

"What have you done?"

She arched a brow at his desperate expression. She had no time for his pathetic histrionics.

"You forget to whom you speak, Morpheus. Check your tone. I am a goddess of Olympus, not some mortal handmaiden who has taken some potent draft to counteract your dreams."

His anger retreated seconds before he dropped to the floor. On his knees, he reached for her garment, raising the diaphanous hem to his lips. *"Forgive me, my love. I am your servant and slave."*

His claim made her laugh the light, tinkling trill that held the male gods of Olympus in thrall. He spoke the truth, of course, but she'd never expected he'd admit his servitude out loud. Her dalliance in his scheme must have affected him more deeply than she'd anticipated.

Not that she cared one way or another. Morpheus had outlived his usefulness.

Interference and manipulation of her fellow Olympians and the mortals they toyed with was Aphrodite's sport of choice. Morpheus should have known better than to challenge her at the game she'd practically invented. He could only hope but lose with a modicum of his pride intact. He had, after all, enjoyed the sensual attention of the goddess of love. For this, he could walk away boastful.

"Can you not see I am occupied?" she asked wearily. *"Be gone, Morpheus. I'm in no mood for you this eve."*

"Please, Aphrodite, indulge my outburst. Perhaps he lies, but Poseidon sent word that his son, Reides, disappeared from his home a fortnight ago. He claims you provided the boy with an enchanted map which led him to the woman in his dreams."

"Boy?" Aphrodite asked, amused. Reides was young, yes, by the standards of Olympians, but he was nothing less than a perfectly intriguing man. Mortal, but with the outward appearance of immortality and with half of his blood flowing from a siren, a creature mysterious even to the Titans who created them. Reides posed an irresistible puzzle to Aphrodite, not unlike her new pet in her aquarium. Born of the ocean and possessed of magical qualities not yet fully realized, Reides would provide more than a moment's amusement for her. Thwarting Poseidon and Morpheus was only an entertaining part of the game.

For now, Reides had his Alina, but all was not sweetness and love in their sanctuary beneath the sea. And still, Aphrodite could not content herself with watching the drama unfold in the magic mirror. No, she'd decided yet again to interfere—and this time, to lure Reides straight into her clutches.

"Reides intrigues me, Morpheus. This you know. My curiosity is all your doing."

"Poseidon's son is none of your concern," Morpheus said, his voice sufficiently tentative and small.

"You made him my concern when you tempted me with his beauty. You promised I could have him and so I have simply taken steps to have what is duly mine."

"I'm not done with him."

She grinned indulgently. The dream god bored her, but so long as mortals continued to exist and require sleep, Aphrodite realized she'd likely have use for him at another time. She could not risk turning him into an enemy.

At least, not tonight.

She wiped her hands on a cloth of woven gold, then smoothed her palms lovingly under his chin. He remained prostrate and likely would until she dismissed him. Oh, how the tides had turned.

"You've had your pleasure at his expense, Morpheus. Likely, you no longer remember the slight which caused you to seek revenge against Poseidon in the first place. Move along to someone else. Reides is mine now."

"But for how long?"

This voice, distinctly female even though the timbre reached the deepest tones and echoes, boomed across the cavernous chamber. In an instant, Artemis strode across the polished floor, her leather sandals tapping an ominous tattoo, her bow slung over her shoulder and her silver-tipped arrows creating a deadly halo behind her. Aphrodite could not keep her breath from catching. While not quite as intimidating as the warrior goddess, Athena, Artemis was the huntress and fiercely protective of the mortal maidens she guarded. Aphrodite was keenly aware of the lines she'd crossed in allowing Reides to find Alina, though technically, she hadn't broken any decree since Reides had not willfully set foot on the shore of the floating island—rather, Alina herself had brought him there.

"You are interfering where you have no right," Artemis claimed, her words wisely diplomatic. In terms of power, she and Apollo's twin were evenly matched and often at odds. But what Aphrodite lacked in brute strength and physical speed, she gained in sheer cunning.

Her day had just become more interesting.

"I have every right, Artemis. Reides and Alina are in love. It is my responsibility to see that they are together."

Artemis snorted, tossing back her thick mane of

earth-tone hair, reminding Aphrodite of the great mares in Zeus's stable. "Alina is under my protection. You and all on Olympus knew of my decree."

Aphrodite smiled indulgently. "With all due respect, Artemis," which was none in Aphrodite's estimation, "your protection was for Alina's sisters. You spirited them to your island sanctuary to lick their love-stricken wounds. Their sister was but a child at the time. Now she is a woman. She deserves a chance at true love."

"Reides cannot love her."

"Why? Because he's a man and you have long been convinced that no man can love a woman for more than a few hours?"

"Precisely," Artemis said with a sneer. "Besides, he's not a man. He's the son of a siren. Even he does not understand the legacy of his birth."

Aphrodite shrugged. She honestly had no convincing argument to this claim because she knew the prophecy. What would Reides become if he knew the whole truth? What would happen to Aphrodite's life of comfort and power and pleasure if the Oracle's prediction came to pass?

In most cases, Aphrodite cared not if the love matches she created lasted one hour or one day or one year. She simply paired the mortals together to amuse herself. Such doings were her lot, as ordered by Zeus. If she took pleasure in toying with the emotions of others, so be it. Love was, after all, the ultimate risk. Though the stakes were higher this time, she'd treat Alina and Reides no differently.

Aphrodite waved her hand at Artemis, dismissing her ire, then stepped away from Morpheus, who still clung to the hem of her dress. She tugged herself free and with a wave of her hand, dispersed him like the formless god he truly was.

"Return to the wood, Artemis, and forget your worries over this maiden, Alina. You may help her overcome her grief when the time is right. Reides's hour of loving her is nearly at an end. She will be yours soon enough."

Breathless and dizzy, Alina rolled away from the edge of the water. Despite the torches flaming on the damp stone walls, the cave was cold. She curled her naked body against the sand, desperate for the kind of warmth that came only from the sun. She hadn't seen daylight for so long. Days. Her eyes had adjusted to the dim light, but her skin seemed to shrivel tight against her muscle and bone from the dampness of the atmosphere. The man she'd sacrificed her life for, the man who'd haunted her dreams with the intense eroticisms he'd since shown her firsthand, now kept her his prisoner in a dark and wet ocean cave with no immediate plan for her release.

"Alina? Why do you desert me?"

His voice rippled through and over the water, deep and throaty and hypnotic, the timbre vibrating off the cones of stone dripping from the cave ceiling. Alina squeezed her eyes tightly shut, determined not to turn around, not to gaze on his beauty, which glistened with a magic she couldn't deny. If she so much as glanced at him, she'd be lost.

Her chest heaved, too heavy for steady breath. She concentrated on all she'd surrendered in the name of obsession—her sisters, her father, her life above the sea.

"I want to go home," she whimpered.

His chuckle echoed against the dank stone. "Face

me, Alina. Tell me with your gaze in mine that you truly wish to leave me."

She attempted to swallow, her lips raw from the sea-water and from the intensity of his endless, intoxicating kisses. She couldn't deny that when he touched her, her mind cleared of any thoughts of her home or family. When he slipped his hand between her thighs and plied his fingers through her sensitive pink flesh, she forgot everything but wanting him. The instant his tongue circled her nipples or his teeth tugged at the aroused nubs, her mind concentrated on nothing but wanting him inside her, pumping into her, fusing their bodies until delirium engulfed her completely.

But then he stopped and abandoned her for the sea, where he lived and rejuvenated. The sensations of pleasure ebbed and for those few clear moments, she ached to see the sun and feel the warm rays penetrating her skin.

She missed her sisters, her father. She ached to run free across the shore, to climb the sharp rocks of the lookout and feel the jab of the stone in her hands and feet. Her hunger for fruits and berries became ravenous—that which she'd taken for granted before now possessed her every clear thought.

What a foolish girl she was, captured by a dream, by a manlike creature she could not comprehend. For her selfish desires, she'd become a lost soul, no better than Persephone in Tartarus, trapped by desires she couldn't sate.

She'd broken Artemis's bond. The gods would forsake her. She'd never escape.

"I cannot look on you, Reides, and speak my mind, as well. You are Poseidon's son. I know little of men, but *the power of the gods is no secret. You keep me captive here against my will."*

She heard water sluice and drip down his body as he emerged from the dark, still cave lake where he lurked between seductions. Great Zeus, but she'd never anticipated this turn. Reides, the son of a siren and the progeny of the sea god, Poseidon, had battled the fierce Hydra and the trickeries of his powerful father to reach her on the lost island. Reides had crossed the will of Artemis and cheated Hades of her soul when she'd nearly died trying to save him and he'd infused her with life.

When she'd first awoken in his arms, the joy in his eyes had been palpable. He'd wept with utter and unmistakable gratitude for every breath she took, explaining who he was to her in a mad rush, pledging his devotion and promising an immortal love. He'd fed her from his own hand and while the textures of seaweed and uncooked fish disagreed with her palate, the sustenance rejuvenated her with incredible speed. He'd found this sanctuary for them and in the glassy solitude of polished stone and obsidian water, they'd finally made love passionately and without care.

She tried to shake the memories aside, but he'd invaded every inch of her. He'd revealed to her the mysteries of her body, of the pleasures trapped within her flesh. He'd gifted her with the mindless promises of physical surrender. Her heart had been overwhelmed at the idea that they'd remain together forever.

But now, as time slipped on with the tides, her heart ached with uncertainty. Like the door of a cramped closet, the darkness closed in on her. And, at this moment, as she waited for him to act, she heard nothing but her own lungs and heartbeat, for her lover excelled at stealth.

Only when the water dripped onto her shoulder did she know he'd neared. She shivered more intensely as he knelt beside her, even when the warmth of his skin reached out to her, just like any man who lived above the ocean depths.

"I use no magic on you, love," he claimed. "You are here because you willed it so. I keep you hidden because I suspect both Artemis and Poseidon will seek us out, to destroy us, to forbid our love."

She squeezed her eyes so tightly shut, her lids burst with vivid hues of gold and orange—colors she would never truly see again if she remained in this prison. She'd already defied the gods of Olympus. What punishment could be worse than banishment to a place that never warmed?

"You lie! You hold me captive with your kisses. When you touch me, I cannot think."

As if to torture her, he slid a finger across her arm. "I cannot help but touch you, Alina. We are destined to be together, can you not understand? Why else would my father scheme to keep us apart? Our union must portend some great shift in power. That's why Aphrodite gave me the map. She's the goddess of love. She wishes only for our union to triumph."

With gentle slowness, he traced a lazy path up Alina's arm, across her shoulder, then down to her breast, but when the glossy surface of his nail ignited her desire, shooting hot shards of lust into her, she fought his assault. She scrambled to her feet and despite the aches in her body, wildly kicked up the sand in her attempt to escape his powerful touch.

"What if our destiny is to exist in this cave forever, like Narcissus beside his pond? I cannot bear to stay *here, Reides. I need the air, the sun, the wind. I am a creature of the earth, not the sea. You cannot imprison me!"*

In the uncertain light, Alina wondered if the wounded look on his face was real or if her imagination willed her to see compassion where none existed. She could not leave without his help. The only entrance to the cave existed deep in the depths of the inky, mysterious pool. She could not hold her breath long enough, nor could she see in the dark to find her way to the surface.

If she tried to leave without him, she'd die. But if she stayed? Her spirit, slowly seeping from her body each time he enticed her into sensual ecstasy, would surely drift away into oblivion.

"I wish only to love you, Alina."

"Then show me, Reides. Not with lovemaking, but with sacrifice. Prove your love by releasing me."

CHAPTER TEN

COLTON FOLLOWED the smell of coffee from his guest bedroom toward the kitchen, his groggy brain waging a fierce battle between his daily desire for caffeine and his immediate and desperate need for some form of aspirin. Tessa hadn't been exaggerating when she'd claimed she and her friends partied hard. She held her liquor like no other woman he'd ever met. They'd danced until the bars had closed and the bartenders had kicked them out, and yet, upon their return to the island, she'd still had enough energy to reenact another scene from their book. In the wee hours of the morning, they'd played out the chapter that followed Alina's rebellion, in which Reides attempted one last time to keep his lover in his secret cave. The pleasures had been mind shattering and for the first time, sweet, shy Alina had shown prowess all her own.

Since Colton had written the scene originally, anticipation of having Tessa ply her talents on his body had nearly driven him insane. The first touch of her lips on his sex had sobered him completely, and then intoxicated him much more powerfully than rum ever had. And though he'd generously poured his own fantasies onto the page, he couldn't help but believe that Tessa had somehow invented new ways to arouse him, to pleasure him, to explore this fascination between them that only seemed to expand each time they came together. He'd caught himself more than once thinking he had indeed slipped into some perfect dreamworld he, like Alina, might never escape from. Only in Colton's case, he had no desire to leave.

On his way down the stairs, he stopped and adjusted his shorts. Maybe he needed a cold shower. As much as he had designed this week to be about using sex to convince Tessa that they were perfect for each other, he had to be smart. Too much of a good thing—natch, a great thing—could work against him.

Their every interaction couldn't be just about the physical. Even the most inventive acrobatics and incredible pleasure wouldn't keep them from requiring a change of scene. Like Alina, they needed to see the sun.

And he wouldn't lose Tessa now. She was an amazing woman, and not just because of her sexual fearlessness. She'd stood up to her ex with more moxy than he'd seen in a long time. Despite the temptation, she didn't dwell on hurts from the past, but grabbed hold of the future, even when staring down her abhorrent former husband. She seemed to use every moment to yank herself further toward her new and better life.

He'd been in Key West for less than twenty-four hours, and yet he'd never had so much fun. From Tessa's wild range of friends to her wicked sense of humor, Colton couldn't think of a single thing about her that didn't intrigue him—including his niggling suspicion that her bravado and strength were a shield, hiding something personal from him and, perhaps, from herself.

Once his bare feet hit the cool tile of the first floor, he heard a mechanical whirr coming from a room to his left, just off the kitchen, which was empty. He stopped long enough to pour himself a cup of coffee, but skipped his dusting of sugar. He followed the sound and found Tessa standing beside a long, tall bank of windows in her home office, manning a fax machine as it spit out page upon page of text.

He slid his coffee onto her desk and attempted to wrap his arms surreptitiously around her waist from behind, but she stopped him with a sharp elbow to the gut.

"Good morning to you, too," he said with a guttural grunt, stepping backward. She hadn't really hurt him, but only because he did crunches every morning, hangover or not.

She spun and her eyes blazed.

Uh-oh.

"Too much tequila last night?" he ventured.

She grabbed a handful of paper and slapped him across the arm with the pages. "No, apparently, I can hold my tequila, but I still have trouble with trust. How could you do this, Colton? I was clear on how this had to be done." She gestured to the fax machine. "I love my first publisher, but I'm ready to grow and try new things. This whole project has been about moving on. I don't understand why you couldn't trust me to handle this part of our deal."

Maybe he had more to drink himself last night than he remembered, because he had absolutely no idea what the hell she was talking about.

"Slow down, Tessa. My brain has apparently adjusted to the Key West way of living."

"Can't keep up? You sent our book to Greenwise!"

Okay, that was an easy enough phrase to interpret. Greenwise was the small press who had published Tessa's fairy-tale stories before her divorce.

"No, I didn't."

"What were you trying to do?" she continued, stalking around him, obviously not registering his clear and honest denial. "Surprise me? Show me how magnanimous you could be by arranging the whole deal as some sort of gift to impress me? The sentiment is sweet, I suppose, but this is business, not some sort of seduction game."

He arched a brow.

"Okay," she admitted with a jab of her finger, "I guess I've let you turn it into a seduction game, but I can't play around with the book deal, Colton. You'll ruin everything."

She waved the pages at him, so he took it upon himself to snatch them from her hand and try to figure out what exactly had bunched her panties so tightly around her oh-so-curvaceous ass.

The pages were straight from *Son of the Siren,* with no author name in the header, just as they'd created in the file. Even the page numbers contained the same odd formatting Tessa insisted on, with the asterisk by the number, which Tessa only deleted once she'd finished her final draft.

No mistaking—this was their manuscript, straight from one of their computers.

"Where did this come from?" he asked.

"From Greenwise, from Vivian, my editor." As she spoke, the volume of her words increased along with the speed. What Colton knew about the publishing business, he'd learned from her. Apparently, this breach had thrown her into a first-rate tizzy.

"How did she get it?"

"She called my agent at home late last night, giddy with excitement that I was giving her an exclusive on my first new manuscript since Daniel screwed me over. She spent twenty minutes promising to mortgage her house if she had to in order to pay my advance."

"I thought you and Audrey wanted to sell this book to the mass-market publishers?"

She huffed loudly. "We did! We do! And you knew that, so why did you send it to Viv?"

"Me? Slow down, Tessa. I didn't send our book to anyone. What makes you think I did?"

"Who else would have access?"

"Your agent?" he asked, straight-faced. He didn't know Audrey Burnham from Adam, but the woman had a reputation as a publishing shark. If she thought sending the book to Greenwise first would somehow up the value of the book to other publishers, he had no doubt she'd make such a ballsy move, even without Tessa's knowledge.

"She didn't! She wouldn't. Greenwise can't offer the money she knows I want and they don't have the clout to influence an auction. Trust me, nothing means more to Audrey than her commission. Besides, she called this morning furious that I'd made a move without her. Took me fifteen minutes to talk her down."

Colton scanned the pages again, looking for some clue as to who could have somehow gotten their hands on these pages. He found nothing. His days as an investigative reporter were long in the past, and even then, he hadn't been the best in the field, one of the reasons he'd moved on. He preferred following a story for the long haul, meeting with people, gauging the effects of public policy on the actual public.

Still, he had to give this a shot. "Calm down. Back up. Who has had access to the book?"

Tessa huffed impatiently. "Audrey, who didn't send it, me, who didn't send it and you…"

"…who didn't send it. Tessa, I may have established that I'm willing to manipulate you to get what I want, but I'd never do anything to hurt your chances of selling the book the way you want to. I know how much this means to you. I didn't send our manuscript to anyone."

She blinked a few times and Colton could see her struggle to make sense of what he'd said. He knew she'd eventually believe him—Tessa might possess a quick temper, but she wasn't unreasonable. If there was one thing they'd established between them since their first meeting, it was honesty. Even when he was attempting to trick her into something—like how he'd used the publication of the book as a means to orchestrate their affair—he did so pretty much out in the open.

She swallowed thickly. "Then who?"

Colton tossed the papers down on top of the fax machine, which was still spitting pages into the tray. Apparently, whoever had sent their manuscript to her former publisher had gotten their hands on every page, right down to the most recent ones they'd written just a week ago.

"I don't know. Does anyone here have access to your computer? Your housekeeper, maybe?"

Tessa's shoulders drooped. She'd built up quite a torrent of anger this morning and now she didn't have anyone to lash out at. Understanding how much she'd had riding on the successful marketing of this book, he took her gently by the hand and led her into the kitchen, leaving the fax machine humming as the last page slid onto the tray.

"Maggie? She couldn't have. I'm home when she cleans and besides, I don't let her in my office. I clean it myself. I usually pen Arty and Apollo in there while she works on the rest of the house. What about you? Is there anyone in your apartment when you're not home?"

Once they were in the kitchen, Colton found another mug, then hunted around for the creamer and sweetener he knew she took with her coffee. He must have looked clueless, so she took over while he went back to the office to retrieve his forgotten cup.

"My housekeeper comes and goes when I'm not home," he said when he returned, "but my computer is password protected. Besides, why would a cleaning lady poke around in my computer?"

Tessa took a perfunctory sip from her drink, her mind

clearly more interested in figuring out the mystery than injecting her system with caffeine. "To get at your financial information? Use your e-mail account?"

"Those are different passwords entirely. I set up the book on a separate hard drive with all kinds of protections and I don't even have a shortcut icon for it on my desktop. In order to get at the manuscript, she would have had to be specifically looking for it."

Silence ensued as both of them tried to find another angle to explain how their secret manuscript had landed on the desk of the wrong editor. They had sent the files back and forth using e-mail, Colton reiterated in his mind. Maybe somehow, the most recent version had been intercepted by someone who…what? Recognized her writing style and decided, for no good reason, to send the manuscript to the last publisher Tessa wanted to pitch to?

This didn't make sense. And despite Tessa's claims otherwise, his money was still on Audrey. But he had no proof—just motive and opportunity. When he got a chance, he was going to order a thorough check of this agent of hers—see if she had a past of shady dealings with her clients.

Tessa seemed to think Greenwise couldn't up her value in an auction, but Colton wasn't so sure. When publishers bid against each other, advance payments could get astronomical. Of course, if Greenwise didn't have the capital or the clout, he could see her point.

But for now, he had to talk Tessa down. "Does this ruin everything?" he asked. He couldn't help selfishly thinking that if the book deal went south, he'd have no other reason to remain here with Tessa and she'd have no other reason to continue their affair. Unless she wanted to. And while Colton suspected that she did, her pride in her wild and independent lifestyle could easily get in the way.

"No, thankfully. When I spoke to Audrey, she said she'd take the fall, tell Viv that she sent the manuscript to her by mistake."

How convenient. "Does this ruin your relationship with Viv?"

Tessa blew out a frustrated breath. "I don't think so. Maybe. I've been up-front with her. She knows I want something bigger for this book and that Greenwise doesn't have the money or the distribution venues to do the project justice. I'll call her later myself and smooth things over. I just don't understand how this could have happened."

The phone rang, interrupting their chance to discuss the matter further.

Tessa answered and after a few minutes of chitchat, her eyes lit up like twin stars. "You're shitting me," she said to whomever was on the other end of the line.

Shaking her head, she listened intently as the person on the phone continued whatever amazing tale they were spinning. With each word, her grin grew until she was practically giggling like a schoolgirl.

"Oh, this is delicious. I can't imagine what Rick was thinking."

Rick? The local law?

She glanced up at Colton, her face reflecting none of the confusion and desperation he'd witnessed only moments before. He didn't know what was going on, but whatever reversed Tessa's dour mood was okay by him.

"Not Rick? Rita! Oh, I'm going to have to buy our favorite prosecutor a drink next time I see her. Yeah, we'll be there around two. I wouldn't miss this for the world."

She disconnected the call and her grin was nothing short of wicked.

Colton was almost afraid to ask.

"Who was that?"

"Willa. She just got back from Daniel's arraignment."

"Quick justice in the Keys."

"For a small place, we have a lot of drunks to move through the system on a typical Friday night."

"Did the judge throw the book at him?"

Tessa practically skipped to the refrigerator, where she took out a dozen eggs, a half pound of bacon, bagels, cream cheese and orange juice. Whatever she'd just learned about her ex had clearly jump-started her appetite.

"Trespassing is a serious crime, not to mention driving a boat while under the influence. Did you know he actually ran over one of the Coast Guard's buoys? Seems like such a little thing, but around here, that's just not done."

"So the judge did throw the book at him," Colton concluded with a grin.

"Actually, Daniel's lawyer flew in from Miami, so book throwing was out. But the prosecutor made a deal they couldn't refuse."

Colton frowned. Plea bargaining was not his favorite judicial tool. "And you're happy about this?"

She downed the rest of her coffee in two quick gulps. "Just wait until you see what Daniel agreed to do. Why don't you whip us up some breakfast? I have to find my camera."

TESSA ASSIGNED HERSELF a generous fifteen seconds of guilt for taking glee in what she was about to witness. At the end of her allotted time, she flipped on her digital camera and wondered just which Palm Beach newspaper she'd send the picture to first. The one that had printed the account of the floral delivery guy who'd insisted Tessa had tipped him with a twenty-dollar bill and then an afternoon between the sheets or the rag that had printed a chronological list of every man, woman and sex toy who'd claimed to have shared her bed.

Hell, she'd send them each their own copy, along with a bill for her services in upping their circulation.

"You sure you want to do this?" Colton asked, his hand brushing her elbow gently just as she was about to sling open the door to Brew's Pub.

She stopped short. "Are you kidding? Call me shallow, but don't you think I deserve this?"

His gaze grew serious and no less devastatingly alluring than this morning when they'd taken time after breakfast to walk off his delicious omelets by strolling the full circumference of the island. When they'd reached the spot where they'd made love the first time, Tessa had caught herself turning quiet and pensive and too much like the woman who'd once been married to Daniel Reese. Though she'd tried to be open and honest with Colton, she couldn't help suspecting that the woman she showed him, with her carefree attitude and devilish lifestyle, wasn't a true reflection of who she was any more than the demure corporate wife she'd been with Daniel. Looking into Colt's eyes made her ask too many questions about who she really was, what she really wanted from her life—the answers to which she simply wasn't yet ready to confront.

"You deserve everything you want, Tessa. But one of the things you've been most proud of over the past year and a half is the way you haven't let your ex-husband ruin your future. You've created a new life, with new friends, and now a new passion, with the book. With me." He lowered his voice, but not his intensity. "But in twenty-four hours, he's intruded twice, stirred up past hurts and resentments. Do you really want to move backward?"

Tessa frowned, knowing Colton had a point. And yet, this was one opportunity she knew she'd never, ever, get again. "If I was a nobler woman with higher moral standards, I might agree with you. But right now, I'm going to milk this moment for all its worth. And after we leave, I promise I won't give Daniel Reese one more thought for the entire duration of your stay. And probably longer."

For good measure, she made a crisscross sign above her heart and then held up her right hand beside her cheek just like any good Girl Scout. It only took a split second for both of them to dissolve into laughter.

"You talk a good game, you know that, Dalton?"

She punched him playfully in the arm and shoved the camera back into her purse. "Yeah, but you've got my number. Look, maybe you're right. Maybe watching Daniel lose his dignity isn't the best thing for me."

Colton's gray eyes lit like polished pewter and he slipped his arms around her waist and pressed her close. The hard warmth of his body instantly transported her mind from thoughts of revenge to fantasies of incredible sex.

"You once said to me that your old life was one step forward, two steps back," he reminded her. "I'm thinking we should concentrate on a more forward momentum."

"Do you have a suggestion?"

His eyebrows narrowed and his mouth quirked into such an irrepressible grin, she suspected her heart skipped a beat. The man could look like such a brazen pirate when he wanted to. Give him a sword and a flowing white shirt, tight breeches and thigh-high boots and she'd be lost for sure.

Pirate's wench, here I come.

"I have a few ideas I'm kicking around. I think a brainstorming session is in order, don't you?"

If he only knew what her brain had already come up with.

CHAPTER ELEVEN

WILLA PICKED THROUGH the massive pile of chicken wings—greasy, crispy and delicious to the point of being illegal—chose the most plump specimen and took less than a minute to devour every sopping, hot-sauce sluiced morsel of meat. With finesse, she tossed the leftover bones toward the plate where she and Heather were stacking their remnants—and missed by a country mile.

Darn.

"Oh, busboy, think you could grab that for me?"

Daniel Reese did indeed have a sneer worth millions, even if those big bucks hadn't been able to sway the prosecutor, the judge or the district attorney overseeing the Monroe County courts. Daniel's high-priced attorney had quickly and effectively negotiated a deal so the prosecutor would drop all charges against his client once he paid a fine and agreed to community service. But Rita Martinez, who'd shared a drink or two with Tessa and the gang at Brewster's more than once, had insisted on instant compliance with the terms of the agreement. Mr. Reese was, of course, only a visitor to Key West. He could, with great ease, use his high-priced attorneys to delay his community service hours for years. Rita happened to know of a local restaurant owner who had loaned several members of his staff to the local Meals on Wheels while the regular volunteers attended a state-mandated workshop on nutrition. Mr. Roy Brewster, a long-standing Key West conch and pillar of the community, could use extra hands to keep his business afloat—a business that made more than its fair share of charitable contributions to the indigent and needful of their small island community.

The judge, who'd also been known to stop into Brew's for a drink during his fishing weekends, had instantly agreed.

Twenty hours bussing tables at Brew's and Daniel could be on his merry way, his record clean and his wallet just a little lighter from the five-hundred-dollar fine.

If only Tessa would show up, the crowning glory of the night would be in place.

Daniel swiped the stray chicken wing off the floor using a napkin, despite the double pair of surgical gloves he'd squeezed onto both hands. The hairnet was the pièce de résistance, though. She had to thank Brew for that one.

Willa waited until Sonia whistled Daniel over to clear the empty cups and plates off a booth in the corner before she turned to Heather, who somehow managed to devour a dozen chicken wings without smearing her lipstick.

"Do you think Tessa's going to miss this?" Willa asked.

Heather dropped her wing carefully onto her plate, grabbed a tiny napkin from the dispenser on the table and wiped her slim, graceful fingers clean.

"Wouldn't think so, but now that she's got that big, hunky, incredibly gorgeous man with her…" Heather said, raising her volume only for the words that described Colton Granger "…she might have better things to do than witness her ex-husband's indignities."

Willa nodded, snagged another wing and tore through it with relish. She couldn't remember the last time she'd had this much fun with something so simple. She reached for her beer and wasn't so surprised when the greasy cup slipped from her fingers and splashed to the floor.

That one got a full string of filthy epithets from Reese, followed by a stern rebuke from Brew.

"Watch your mouth, rich boy," Brew barked from behind the bar. "No one curses in my place but me."

The regulars applauded and Brew punctuated his warning by balling up a wet towel and tossing it at Daniel's head. He ducked, causing the sopping cloth to strike Reese's attorney—who he insisted stay with him for the duration of his "sentence"—square in the nose.

Heather nearly choked on a celery stalk.

"Check, please!" Willa joked, dissolving them both into irrepressible laughter that stopped only after Daniel cleaned the mess and then stared at them both with a sharpness Willa had only seen once before—in the eyes of a sociopath she'd once picked up for suspicion of piracy.

"What's your problem, Reese?" she challenged, slamming her palms on the table and standing to full height. She had at least an inch on him and, no doubt, his Pilates was no match for her military workouts. "A sense of humor too expensive for even you to afford?"

He glanced over his shoulder at his lawyer, who was busy trying to recover from being smacked in the face with more than a lawsuit. "You're just eating this up, aren't you? I had no idea you were such good friends with my slut of an ex. And yet, you arrested me. I guess conflict of interest doesn't mean much here?"

The crack about her unprofessional behavior earned him a choke hold on his collar. The slut comment forced Willa to squeeze until he made little croaking noises from the back of his throat. The crowd in Brew's barely noticed. Wasn't the first time Willa had put the squeeze on some jerk for talking out of turn and it wouldn't be the last—though it might be Reese's last coherent comment if he didn't get her message loud and clear.

Even Heather barely blinked, filling her time with tearing a little towelette out of a tiny paper packet and cleaning underneath her nails.

"My only conflict is deciding whether or not I can choke the life out of you in front of so many witnesses and get away with it. You already know where the prosecutor stands. And the judge. Your money and influence don't mean squat here, Reese. We take care of our own."

When his eyes made little motions toward rolling back in his head, Willa released him with a push. He flew back into an occupied table, sending nachos and pitchers of beer flying into the air. Now the screaming started, the loudest coming from Reese's attorney when a plateful of chili-cheese fries smashed into his tie and tailored shirt.

"You shouldn't have done that," Heather sang, not the least bit reprovingly.

Willa scrunched up her face, considering her next move. Much depended on Reese's response. If he remained on the floor, Willa could see her way to letting the whole incident slide, maybe even tipping Sonia extra for having to work with Reese for even one night, much less five. If he came back for more, she might be looking at a couple of hours in the brig.

Brew slammed a shot of tequila on the table beside her, which she immediately scooped up and gulped down. It'd be worth it.

Within seconds, Brew had the situation under control. He ordered pitchers of free beer and piña coladas for the crowd, lifted Reese off the floor and banished him to the kitchen, then sent his cutest waitress, Rebecca, over to appease the ire of the attorney, who'd already started sputtering about corruption and restitution. Becky had the sense to gift the man with a complimentary Brew's Pub T-shirt and a very tall, undoubtedly potent Long Island Iced Tea.

Heather finished the last chicken wing, this time sucking her fingers clean. "I can always count on a good time when you're around, Willa."

Willa chased her tequila with a long swig of Heather's beer. "You'd think Tessa would have remembered that."

"Actually, I think it's great she didn't show," Heather declared. "Daniel shouldn't mean anything to her anymore. And from what you've told me about this Colton Granger guy, she's most definitely moving forward in an interesting way."

Willa dipped a long thin carrot stick into the chunky "bleu" cheese dip and sucked away the piquant dressing. "He's a looker. And he certainly handled himself when Daniel trespassed on the island. No false bravado, just an impressive set of abs. He let Tessa handle things. A girl's gotta admire that."

"Unless Tessa wanted him to handle things and he was too chicken to tangle with the rich and powerful Daniel Reese?"

They snorted in unison.

Willa went on, "Maybe Tessa really has finished with her ex. But just doesn't seem right to have the guy right here, prime for the picking, and no one wants to take a chunk out of his hide for all the heartache he caused her in the first place."

Heather took back her purloined beer and finding it empty, waved to Brewster for another. "Well, just because Tessa really doesn't want to get involved doesn't mean her friends can't take over for her," she suggested. "I mean, that was our original plan, remember? Before he invaded her privacy?

How can we live with ourselves if we allow Daniel to run around Key West for the next week, likely trying to cause trouble for her? If he hurts Tessa again, it'll be our fault."

Willa grinned, loving the way this woman thought. In all fairness, they'd given Tessa the choice to be the mastermind behind the downfall and humiliation of her ex-husband and she'd declined. But just because she'd chosen to spend her time romancing a superhot journalist instead of joining their scheme didn't mean they had to miss out on all the fun.

"You know this is juvenile, right?" Willa pointed out.

Heather indicated a pause with a raised finger, then bent down to retrieve her bag from beneath the table. She tossed aside a stray soiled towelette and then dug inside to retrieve a stack of photocopied newspaper clippings. "I thought you might think that, being a respectable officer in the Coast Guard and all, so I made a little collection for you. A history lesson, so to speak."

Willa pawed through the papers, each headline more lurid and demeaning than the last. All about Tessa. All disgusting and seedy to the point that she couldn't believe anyone could survive this kind of public humiliation.

"Where did you get these?"

"Library. Internet."

Glancing through the articles reminded Willa of driving by a car wreck. She never *wanted* to look, but couldn't help herself. She made excuses that she only looked in order to assess the damage and offer help if she could, when really, she just wanted to catch a glimpse of gore.

But not this time. Tessa had told her about the attacks, but seeing them for herself was gruesome. Now, however, she had the perfect opportunity to offer the kind of help only she could render. Daniel Reese didn't come to Key West every day and after this week, she doubted he'd ever return again, lobster season or not. If the man was going to get his well-deserved comeuppance, it had to be here and now.

The more she read, the more she planned. Daniel Reese was going down, Key West style.

"So," Heather said, "when do we start?"

Willa slammed the papers down. "No time like the present. But first, I have to make a few calls."

TESSA GLANCED AROUND, unable to chase away the fear that she was about to reveal too much, too soon. Since Colton had come to stay with her on Speed Key, she'd kept him out of her bedroom, claiming that her private rooms had nothing to do with the scenes and fantasies they were recreating. She couldn't have told a bigger lie. Every splash of color on the wall, every framed print, every brocade pillow reeked of another time, another place, a fantasy first created with words on a page.

Her words. Her page. Her fantasy.

But now, the truth was about to come out, though under the circumstances, she doubted Colton would be distracted by it for more than a few moments.

A light rap on the door caught Tessa's breath and sent her heartbeat into double-time action. She adjusted the see-through material of her beaded wrap, which she'd fashioned into a toga draped across only one breast, leaving the other bare. Pressing her hand to her chest, she willed the beating to slow. Now Colton would know how obsessed she'd become with the story they'd created together, with the eroticism of the sensual interactions on the page—and he'd discover how she'd brought their fantasy to life long before Colton had made his bold suggestion.

She stepped to the open window, then after a deep and cleansing breath, invited him to enter the room.

She closed her eyes, concentrating on the sound of the surf rushing and receding off the shore below, on the chirp and whine of the crickets nestled in the tropical plants that surrounded the house, on the honeyed scent of blooming hibiscus. When she'd first visualized Reides' suite in his house on the coast of the island of Crete, she'd been completely aware of how she'd patterned his room after her own. But at the time, she'd anticipated that no one would ever be privy to the details. Then Colton entered—and his growl of approval sent a wicked thrill through her bloodstream.

"You've been busy," he said, straying immediately from the script of their book.

She really didn't care. In fact, she was glad. Reenacting the scenes point for point had been a fascinating way to start their affair, but little by little, their relationship had expanded. The more they got to know each other, the less they had to depend on prechosen words.

"No," she said firmly.

His arched brow told her he understood. She'd decorated the room this way long before she'd known he'd be visiting.

"The room suits you, suits us."

She swallowed, tasting the cool wash of mint she'd swirled in her mouth before he'd come. She'd taken so much time preparing for this rendezvous—as if this were a first date rather than a scheduled session of lovemaking. She'd braided beads into the hair that dangled alongside her cheeks, bathed in fragrant lavender oil and dabbed her skin with a complementary perfume, making sure to touch those hidden private areas Colton would soon explore. Why she wanted tonight—and every night they were together—to be so perfect, she wasn't sure. A dose of reality might do them both some good, might douse the fires that continued to rage between them with scalding intensity. But then again, what would it hurt if the fantasy lasted a little longer?

"Did you enjoy the sun today?" he asked, returning to the dialogue, but with a stilted cadence that testified to what she suspected—being anyone but themselves was growing more and more difficult.

But she had to stick to the plan. Yes, she admired Colton. Yes, she respected everything about him from his strong belief system to his inherent self-confidence. But he wouldn't say the same about her once he understood the demons she dealt with on a daily basis. Her fears. Her weaknesses. Her confusion over what she truly wanted from her life, beyond the publication of the book. He thought her to be strong, healed and whole when she was honestly nothing of the sort.

She smiled shyly, slipping on the expression she'd written on Alina's face so many times. "The sun suits both of us. How long can we remain in this paradise?"

He crossed the room, eyeing the bed as his leg brushed against the burnished red satin coverlet.

In the scene, Reides had used that moment to think about the many trysts played out on his bed, with mortal women like his maid or with any number of the Nereids and water nymphs who'd left their watery homes long enough to enjoy the pleasures of land-bound lovemaking. Every affair had been fleeting and intense—pleasurable but forgettable. Tonight would be different. Reides had vowed to prove his devotion to Alina by spiriting her away from the dark, hidden cave she'd considered a prison and hiding her in the last place he figured his father would look—in Reides castle beside the sea from where he'd first escaped. He needed to abolish the last of her fears and prove that his devotion would not burn out as her sisters had assured her. His rooms in the palace were a temporary haven from all the jealousy, angst and spitefulness that plagued them—just like Tessa's house in the Keys.

How long would Tessa and Colton last? Longer than their

fictional lovers? The current outline said that the star-crossed characters would have a happily-ever-after. But outlines could change as easily as the direction of the wind.

"We will stay for one night," he replied, answering her query with words they'd written only a few weeks ago. Little by little, they crept nearer to the last scenes they'd crafted of the novel. Soon, Colton would have to make a choice— agree to Tessa's marketing plan for the book and keep writing—or abandon the project, and her, altogether.

The idea made Tessa's stomach ache.

Even after spending a few days together, she had no better idea of which way his decision might go. He'd forbidden any discussion of the topic and frankly, there was nothing left to say. He knew how badly she wanted to sell the book. In her pursuit, she'd opened every aspect of her life to him—her body, her home—everything but her heart. She knew that's what he was after, but even her overwhelming desire to see their novel on bookstore shelves couldn't push her that far. How could she open her heart when she didn't know what he'd find there? How could she allow him to try and figure out what she wanted from her future when even she hadn't been up to the task?

Colton broke into her personal space, tentatively touching her arm with a single finger on the point of her elbow. "Tomorrow, if you still wish, I will return you to your island sanctuary. To your father and your sisters. By my word, I shall never again return to you if that is your demand. Not in the flesh. Not in your dreams."

Colton claimed no acting ability, but Tessa begged to differ. The finality in his voice stabbed her. God, had they been aware of how their book mirrored their own affair? Just like Alina, she had the power to dismiss her lover from her life forever and pay an exacting price for his fulfilling her desire.

But would she? Would Alina dismiss Reides? Would Tessa deny Colton a place in her life? They hadn't written that far. Hadn't explored that far.

So while they both knew the mechanics of the love scene, and they both accepted how the power of this interaction would forever change the relationship of their two main characters, neither knew the outcome.

Tessa tore herself away from the window.

"I can't do this, Colton."

She pushed past him, but he grabbed her hand and tugged her against his chest, bare and tanned and ever so slightly oiled. The coconut scent sizzling off his skin nearly drove her mad. Her mouth watered. Her nostrils flared. Nothing could quite stir her juices like the tropical scent of suntan oil on the chest of a man like Colton.

"I don't remember that line of dialogue," he said, testing her.

She met his gaze, her suddenly overwhelming fear lessened by the sweet smile crinkling his amazing gray eyes. She hated to disappoint him—hated to break her word. But what she'd agreed to was clearly beyond her capability. She was nothing like Alina. She wasn't innocent or naive or entranced by the promise of true love. How she'd managed to write the character with such clarity was a true testament to her talent for fiction.

Writing Alina was one thing. Being her was entirely another.

"I can't be Alina for you anymore. I'm not an actress."

"You've done amazingly so far."

She shook her head so that the beads of her braids slapped lightly across her cheeks. "I guess I've used up all my acting ability on myself, not that I had much to start with."

"Then maybe it's time we start being ourselves?"

She bit her lip. "No."

"What are you afraid of?"

"What am I *not* afraid of? Colton, I've never let a man into my psyche the way I've let you. You know things about me. I've revealed more through the character of Alina than I ever have in any of my previous stories. She's the girl I wanted to be. Full of romantic expectations. Not afraid of her sexuality or of taking risks for true love."

"Wanted to be, or was?"

Every muscle in her body cramped from her desperate attempt to hold herself together. Could she remember those pre-Daniel days without castigating herself for her naiveté and stupidity? And what did regrets help now anyway? The damage was done.

"I don't think I was ever as innocent as Alina," she said.

"I think you're wrong," he said, running his hands up and down her arms, creating a gentle warmth and a slow-building friction. "You told me yourself you were sheltered growing up in New York. You had tutors and carefully orchestrated play dates, with several nannies overseeing all the fun. You never went to school until junior high, and then, it was an all-girl's academy with strict rules for socializing."

She glanced around, suddenly unable to bear the weight of his compassionate stare. "In the summers, I had Rip."

"How many times? How many days did you really spend with your father overall, in your entire life? Fifty? Sixty? I can see it in your eyes, Tessa. You idolize him because you never really knew him, because every moment you spent with him was rare and precious. You lived in two extremes—your mother's closed and isolated existence and your father's world of hedonistic excess."

A thick lump formed in her throat. "What are you, a part-time psychologist?"

He chuckled. "No, just someone who's spent a lot of time thinking about you, trying to figure out the best way to get to you so you won't shut me out. I want you, Tessa, and for more than just sex. I care about you. But you've got issues and while I want to help you work them through, I refuse to let them ruin what we have together."

"What we have together? What we have is a good working relationship and great sex. What more can you possibly want?"

A quick glance into his eyes told Tessa she'd made a huge mistake in posing that particular question. The dark ring surrounding his pewter irises seemed to thicken as his pupils enlarged. Still pressed close to him, she could feel the quickening of his heartbeat, the jump in his body temperature. To an untrained eye, Colton appeared to be simply sexually aroused. But Tessa knew better. She'd challenged him deep in his core, far inside the reaches of what made him such an honorable and honest man.

"I want all of you, every inch, starting with the very thing that frightens you the most."

CHAPTER TWELVE

DESPITE THE SUBTLE struggle Tessa launched against his embrace, Colton knew that ultimately, she wouldn't run. Yes, he'd presented a frightening challenge to a woman who'd made an art out of escaping rather than facing her deepest fears, but he had just as much confidence in her latent courage as he did in his resolve to make Tessa see what was undeniably true—they were meant for each other.

With amazing ease, their souls had become intertwined during the writing of their little book of sex, betrayal and divine soap-opera drama. Here on her island, they'd connected more deeply, as if they'd been just as destined to be together as their fictional lovers. Yet in a way, their lovemaking had led them to a fork in the road—an ultimate test. If Tessa couldn't deal with her past or with the woman she'd become because of Daniel, then Colton couldn't invest his heart completely by falling in love.

He wasn't afraid of a woman with neuroses. What woman didn't have them? Hell, what man didn't? The whole scenario he'd cooked up to entice Tessa into an affair proved he had his own issues with obsession and control to deal with. But he hadn't forgotten his core inspiration for their deal. A weeklong fling was fine, but he wasn't willing to invest any more of his time and emotions in a relationship destined for doom. He didn't *want* to call it quits. His affection for her ran too deep. Yet he needed some hint, some clue that she might at some point be able to peel away the layers of her inability to commit to reveal the real, vulnerable, headstrong woman he knew existed. He accepted that her past had shaped her, but he wouldn't buy that old hurts defined her. She'd been burned, but not charred. Not ruined. Not incapable of trying again.

She sighed, settled into his unflinching embrace and laid her cheek gently on his chest. The scent of her hair tantalized him and the soft sensation of her skin on his made him wonder why he'd had to bring this all up before they'd made love. Sometimes, he could be so dumb.

"You have no idea what frightens me, Colton."

"No, I don't know. Not for sure. But something more than your ex has you running scared, Tessa. In fact, you handled him without flinching. Whatever is keeping you from opening up to me will remain a mystery until you let me in."

She tensed, her back rigid and tight. "If I let you in, if I show you what frightens me, I have to acknowledge my fears myself. I'm tired of being scared, Colton. I just want to live life and enjoy and forget about everything else."

He held her tighter, brushing a soft kiss on the crown of her head. "You mean live life on the surface, never digging too deep so that you don't open up a dangerous hole you can't get yourself out of?"

She snickered humorlessly. "That about sums it up."

"That's normal, after all you've been through, Tessa. But you've never been one to shy away from the good, the bad or the ugly. You faced down your ex-husband, both in the courtroom and the day before yesterday on the beach—and he's about as bad and ugly as they get."

This time when she pulled away, he let her go. Absently, she untied her transparent toga and retied it so that both breasts were covered, though still visible beneath the see-through material. The enticing shape of her areola provided a dark outline for her oh-so-sensitive nipples. Though they were lax now, he anticipated the moment when the night would turn back to seduction and he would suckle them to tight pinpoints.

His mouth watered. "What's stopping you now?" he asked brusquely, suddenly impatient.

"I'm stopping me," she answered finally. "I'm not happy about it, but it's the truth. I like my life. I don't want to change."

"I don't want you to change. I just want you to see what we could have together if you just push a little further, if you just take a risk."

She shook her head violently. "What if I liked my life exactly the way it was before you came down here and decided to blackmail me?"

"Blackmail? That's an ugly word."

She smirked. "Not when *you* say it, or when *you* do it. You're clever and irresistible, Colton. I don't regret one minute of what we've had together. But you can't force me to give more. There's a damn good chance that I simply don't have it in me."

She sounded so final, so certain of her convictions, that he would have had to be an arrogant fool to think he could change her mind simply by staying in her life, and sharing her bed, a little longer.

But he'd been called worse than arrogant or foolish. Colton trusted his gut instinct, which told him undeniably that he and Tessa belonged together, if he could only convince her to work beyond the apprehension that still colored her life, no matter how much of a tough, bad girl she pretended to be.

"You have wonderful, untapped things in you, Tessa."

"How can you be so sure? Seems to me I'm all tapped out."

"You don't look at you the way I look at you."

The corner of her mouth quirked into a grin. "You mean with unbridled lust?"

He matched her saucy smile with a purposefully lecherous laugh. "Any man with eyes would look at you that way."

"Daniel never did."

"I don't believe you."

"You should, I was there. Yeah, I guess when we were in college, he was all hands and tongue and dick, but once he put that ring on my finger… I guess I should have known, but I was too stupid in love with the first guy who looked my way to see the truth. I was such an easy mark to him. A rich, well-dowried virgin ripe for the picking."

"Daniel is the scum of the earth. Everyone knows that. You can't take his opinion of you into consideration. What about your other boyfriends?"

That made her laugh, out loud and from the belly. "Other boyfriends? Who are you kidding? Rip may have let his friends fornicate on the couch next to my bedroom during one of his parties, but I was strictly off-limits to anyone and everyone of the male persuasion, particularly boys my age. I met Daniel my first semester at Cornell. To say that I went to college naive and unprepared is the greatest understatement of the year. He might have treated me like crap after we were married, but he made college a magical adventure. He took me places, introduced me to his friends, brought me out of my shell, even if it was only to mold me into the woman he wanted by his side at frat parties on Friday night and the country club on Saturday. I had no business marrying the first man I ever slept with, but I did."

"What about the second?"

She crossed her arms. "Who says you're the second guy I ever slept with?"

He stepped back, somewhat staggered by what she'd just inadvertently admitted. "Who says I was talking about me?"

"You're going to deny it?"

Despite his best efforts, Colton's ego surged. For over a year since her move to Key West, she'd been taunting him with her sexual exploits. He'd always hoped her claims were exaggerated, but now he knew for sure. Tessa clearly knew how to party, but she also knew where to draw the line.

"No. I'm done denying anything when it comes to you." He bridged the distance in two bold steps, but fought the instinct to drag her into his arms and onto the bed so they could erase this conversation with long, hot, wet kisses and pleasures of the flesh.

"You know I want you, Tessa."

"You've had me."

"Part of you, yes. I want more. I've never made a secret of that."

"And I haven't made a secret of the fact that I don't think I have any more to give. Why do you keep doing this to us? Why can't we just have our fun and then go back to our respective corners of the world, better and infinitely less horny than before we came in?"

"Because I don't settle for less than everything I want. Not anymore."

"Why? Maybe it's time to delve into your psyche, Dr. Phil. Maybe it's time we start exploring why you instantly felt so connected to me, why you are so irrationally convinced that I'm the woman you could love for the rest of your life."

She was right. Maybe it was his turn to spill, his turn to dive into the depths of his heart and soul and pull out the answers to the questions she asked.

Then again, maybe he'd just kiss her silly.

"Enough words. I'll *show* you why."

He gave her no time to protest, but grabbed her roughly by the arms and yanked her flush and hot against his skin. Instantly, he felt her nipples prickle at his bare chest, spawning a wash of sensations that ignited the oil he'd smeared over his chest before coming to her room. Slipping back into character, Colton took Tessa by the hands and led her toward the bed. Once the backs of his knees hit the edge of the mattress he stopped and, imploring her silence with his gaze, untied the knot at her neck, then slowly, sensually, unwound the material from her body. He allowed the last strip of gauzy material to slide across her skin and then pool to the floor, then without a word, without breaking their stare, stripped down to nothing himself.

At this point in the story, Reides had coaxed Alina to make love with sweet but sincere words. Reides, son of an immortal, refused to be denied by anyone at any time, much less by the woman who'd occupied his dreams until he'd nearly gone mad.

All Reides' manipulations made for great drama, but wouldn't do much to advance Colton's personal quest to win Tessa's heart, so the man who created Reides remained silent. Instead, Colt climbed onto the bed, lay down with his hands hooked behind his head and beckoned his lover with a tentative smile.

Tessa hesitated, then took a deep breath and climbed beside him. She must have understood his desire to strip the scene of the dialogue, because she pressed her lips together and didn't speak, even after she reached across to the headboard and grabbed a small bottle of oil she'd hidden there.

He quirked a brow at her. Hadn't he prepared for the scene in that way well enough? Reides used the emollient to keep his sea-starved skin moist, not realizing the advantages the slickness would provide in the bedroom. Colton had slathered on some suntan oil he'd found in the guest bath cabinet, just to give the scene another layer of authenticity.

But when she tilted the label of her bottle toward him, Colton quickly squelched his objections. The Greek gods had their fair share of magic toys, but he'd guess none of them ever bought mint-flavored lotion that heated when rubbed on the skin.

With a wicked grin, Tessa straddled his waist. Colton used every ounce of his concentration and self-control to keep his hands planted on her hips, his thumbs digging lightly into her flesh. Though they'd dropped the pretense of spouting the dialogue shared by Alina and Reides, the essence of the scene remained the same.

In the chapter as written, Reides instructed Alina in the ways a woman pleasured her lover. Without experience, Alina had needed the coaching. Tessa, on the other hand, could call her own plays. She didn't need signals from him or a script to ignite her imagination. Just by planning ahead with the oil, she'd already evened the score.

She unscrewed the bottle top and squeezed, releasing a stream of golden oil that immediately scorched his skin. The sensation made him wince until she slid her fingers into the lotion and spread long trails of oozing fire across his chest, his shoulders and down his arms and belly. She scooted backward and before he could protest, smeared the slick emollient over his sex.

The sensation nearly sent him bucking off the bed. As his skin flamed, she tightened her grip, stroking with unyielding firmness in a relentless rhythm. He squeezed his eyes shut, uncertain which physical wonder demanded his attention more—the incredible heat sizzling across his flesh or the delicious, insistent motion she created with her hands.

The heat built and burgeoned. Just when he thought he might lose his mind, Tessa took him into her mouth. With sweet, luscious licks, she cooled the fire and built another con-flagration even more consuming.

Inspired, Colton slicked his hands down his chest, collect-ing remnants of the oil, which he spread over her breasts as she lovingly sucked him to near madness. He flicked his slip-pery thumbs over her nipples, but an eternity of pleasure seemed to pass before he heard her coo as the lotion worked its magic. Intensity built along with the raging blood in his ears and the exquisitely painful tightening and throbbing of his sex. He wanted her so badly and at the same time, he wanted nothing more than to go over the edge with her lips wrapped around his cock.

Through a haze of sexual stimulation, he watched her sit up, grinning like the Cheshire cat. He groaned, both thankful and pissed that she'd stopped when she had. But the gleam in her eyes told him she wasn't done with him. Not by a long shot.

She crawled over him to reach for the oil again and when she did, he captured one breast in his mouth.

Tessa hesitated then tossed her head back and allowed the sensations to assault her. With just teeth and tongue, Colton soon had her tottering on the edge of orgasm. She could feel the liquid heat seeping from her sex, prepping her, taunting her, making her body thrum for his touch. She shook her head, desperate to deny what she knew so intimately—she and Colton connected in ways she'd never experienced before.

With a strangled cry, she attempted to move out of his range, but he grabbed her hips and held her fast while he pushed her further toward orgasm. He alternated his attention between each breast, using his fingers to pluck and pinch her moist skin until she couldn't think straight. She shifted and when his cock touched just the folds of her sex, the shudder-ing began. She couldn't stop the orgasm now, even if she wanted to. And she most certainly didn't want to.

Colton eased her onto her back and before she could protest, had his mouth locked on her, torturing her clit with his tongue. A million tiny explosions racked her body. She grabbed Colton's hair. The action spurred him so that he folded Tessa's legs around his shoulders and lifted her high so that he left no part of her untasted.

When the frenzy abated, he curled her beside him and grabbed the edge of the comforter to wrap around her.

Spooning his body with hers, Tessa could feel the rock hardness of his sex against her buttocks, but she couldn't immediately speak. Yes, she wanted to finish what he'd so deliciously started, but couldn't until the sensations still thrumming through her body abated.

After a few minutes, she attempted to turn around and return the sensual favor, but he stopped her with an insistent shush.

"It's been a long day, Tessa. Get some sleep."

She twisted her neck so she could see his eyes, which were dark and liquid with what she instantly recognized as barely checked need. "We're not finished with the fantasy," she said, once again attempting to turn and finish what they'd started.

He offset her move by snuggling closer. "No one is more painfully aware of that fact than I am."

"Then why are you holding me captive?"

"Can't you guess?"

He tightened his arm around her waist.

She huffed. "I'm not in the mood for games."

With a sweet kiss on her shoulder, Colton chuckled. "Well, you're not in the mood for sex, either. Admit it, Tessa. You've had your thrill. Now, you're sleepy. Can you imagine anything more delicious than burrowing into the comforter, laying your head on that soft pillow with me hard against your back and drifting off to sleep knowing that the first thing I'll want to do in the morning is make love to you?"

Despite her best efforts, Tessa couldn't help but let her eyes drift closed as she mulled over his suggestion. Honestly, she couldn't think of anything more wonderful than his little scenario. Yes, she wanted to make sure he was just as sexually satisfied as she was, but there was something incredibly seductive about a man making you come and then asking for nothing in return. In terms of sexual firsts, this one just topped her list.

Since she'd stopped struggling, Colton released his tight hold and lightly stroked her hair, just beside the temples. Little by little, her eyelids dropped and her body practically molded into the warmth created by Colton's body heat. In moments, she was seconds away from sleep. In the morning she'd figure out what he really wanted from her besides a shot at her heart, but for the moment, she decided simply to close her eyes and dream about the dawn.

IN THE UTTER STILLNESS of the night, Colton heard his cell phone trilling from the other room. He cursed, glanced at the clock and realized that for starters, no one would call him in the middle of the night if there wasn't an emergency. Not to mention that there was no way he could fall asleep with his cock still as hard as a bone. Gingerly, he eased out of bed, then quietly padded to the guest room.

The night was sultry, so strolling around naked didn't so much as inspire a chill. Still, he wrapped a towel around his waist before retrieving the phone, checking the missed call number and then hitting Redial.

His sister, Grace, answered on the first ring.

"Sorry, were you busy?"

Colton cleared his throat. "Is something wrong with Mom or Dad?"

"Those two? They apparently spent the day horseback riding, complete with a picnic under those willows by the lake. Then they invited me over for dinner and spent the entire night making goo-goo eyes at each other. They both got lucky tonight, of that I'm certain."

"Good thing someone did," Colton muttered.

Grace made that little sound with her tongue and teeth that meant she was shaking her head and looking into the phone with exaggerated pity. "Poor guy. Your Key West fantasy isn't working out?"

Instinctively, Colton turned his shoulder away from the door. Tessa seemed dead to the world, but he didn't want her thinking he'd discussed his love life with his sister—which he hadn't. And wouldn't. He and Grace got along fine, when they weren't sniping at each other in the way that only brothers and sisters could.

"I don't know what you're talking about," he said.

"I'm talking about Tessa Dalton Reese? You remember her— the erotica author you mentioned when you asked me to check out her agent. The one whose house you're staying at right now."

Grace Elizabeth Granger, his younger sister by six years, had followed her big brother into a journalism career. But while he'd suffered through investigative assignments, Gracie thrived off them. Nothing thrilled her more than poking around and discovering tidbits of information someone somewhere had wished would remain buried.

"How'd you know I was in Key West?" he asked.

"I don't reveal my sources."

Colton frowned. "Did your sources give you any information about what I asked about or did they focus only on my personal travel plans?"

Though Grace was now back in Richmond as one of the top reporters for the local crime and political beat, she'd gone to college at Columbia University in New York and had interned at a publishing house. She still had a few contacts and had, at Colton's request, checked into the business practices of Tessa's agent, Audrey Burnham. He half wished that Grace had waited until morning to call, but he appreciated his sister's night-owl tendencies. And what the hell, he couldn't sleep anyway, not with Tessa nestled so close and him trying to prove some ridiculous point about putting her needs first.

Luckily, a tête-à-tête with his sister was just what he needed to cool his jets.

"I hear her house in the Keys is amazing," Grace baited.

"Forget about Tessa," he ordered, not that a commanding tone would make a hill of difference with his headstrong sister. "What did you find out about her agent?"

Grace sighed dreamily. She always did have more than a healthy interest in sexual matters, probably because his parents, despite their continual horniness, tended to ignore the fact that their daughter was a red-blooded American female, attractive in an above-average way. And despite the Grangers' demonstrative relationship, they expected their daughter to be pure as the driven snow.

Which, of course, drove Grace insane.

"Burnham's got a pretty good reputation," Grace finally answered. "Not a top dog, but she trained with the best when she worked for William Morris back in the eighties. She's been on her own for over twenty years and has made some impressive deals."

"Any questionable ones?"

"Lots of them, but that's par for the course. Publishing is a tough business."

"Any lawsuits by clients?"

"None. In fact, I couldn't find a single former client who'd ever written or said anything publicly against her. Most of her clients have been with her ten years or more."

"Then she always works in her client's best interest."

"Seems that way."

"Do you think she had any reason to send Tessa's manuscript," Colt said carefully, since he hadn't confessed his personal involvement in the book to his sister, "to her former publisher without her permission or knowledge?"

On the other end of the phone, Colt could hear his sister's fingers flying over a computer keyboard. He doubted whatever she was typing had anything to do with his questions about Audrey. Grace was a world-class multitasker. Until recently when she'd developed some health problems that had forced her to undergo a full regimen of physicals, he'd suspected she used pharmaceutical means to keep up her insane pace. He'd learned she was just highly energetic. What she probably needed was a great big dose of Key West. He'd hardly thought about his own job for days.

Until his phone had trilled, he'd forgotten about the freelance assignment he'd offered his sister to check into Audrey's business practices. Hell, he'd forgotten about Audrey, and the screwup with Greenwise Publishing.

"Audrey Burnham isn't one to make mistakes, but they happen to the best of us," Grace said. "And from what you've told me, she's the only person who had access to the manuscript, right? Maybe her assistant was pissed off about something. Maybe it was just a crazy mix-up."

"That's what Tessa thinks," he verified.

"Well, if you don't have any other theories you'd like me to check out, I should be letting you get back to your lover."

Colton frowned into the phone. "Who says she's my lover?"

"Mom."

"What?" Colton stood and his towel fell. Not surprisingly, his rigidity problem was now a thing of the past.

"I told her about your trip to Key West."

"You told her about Tessa?"

"Sort of hard to rat you out without that little detail."

He groaned, flopped back on the bed and raked his hand through his hair, calculating and scheming exactly how he was going to pay his creepy little sister back for such betrayal.

"And you did this, why?" he asked.

"To amuse myself," she replied, though Colton could see through his anger long enough to realize she probably had an ulterior motive. She was probably dating some ex-convict biker dude she met at the courthouse and wanted to soften the blow of her inappropriate bedmate choice by shifting their mother's attention in his direction. "Mom nearly went through the roof. The scandal! The infamy! Really, Colton, you should be ashamed of yourself, involving yourself with a woman of such a notorious reputation."

Great. Now she was quoting a lecture he hadn't even heard yet. Well, at least not recently.

"You are so screwed, Grace. You forget all I know about you. Next trip to Kentucky, you're busted," he promised.

"Yes, I suppose I am," she said with a bored sigh that told him she couldn't care less. "And then I'll get you back and the circle will continue. Call me if you need anything else, okay?"

He jabbed the end button on the phone and spent the next ten minutes plotting revenge against his sister. Then he climbed back into Tessa's bed, focused on the sweet hum of her breathing and anticipated the dawn.

CHAPTER THIRTEEN

WILLA SIDLED UP to the bar, keeping tabs on Daniel through the corner of her eye. Brew's Pub overflowed with both regulars and tourists—the full range of people desperate for a safe haven from the festivities on Duval. While not quite as wild as Fantasy Fest, Key West's raucous answer to Halloween, the action one block over had escalated to blush-worthy proportions—and Willa rarely, if ever, blushed. But the police had started dispersing the crowds and consequently, the entire staff at Brew's, including Daniel the busboy, hadn't had a break in over two hours.

The last of the busboy's good humor deflated when a party of eight stormed in and immediately ordered one of everything off the appetizer menu, three pitchers of beer and then proceeded to move chairs and tables to accommodate their oversize group.

Sit tight, Danny-boy. Your old pal Willa is about to arrange the kind of shore leave that will make all your dreams come true.

Okay, maybe not *his* dreams—though she couldn't be sure. Never knew about those rich boys. But she was quite certain this plan would cap Daniel's week in Key West in a way he'd never forget.

The possibilities tumbled in her mind as Brew sidled over and poured Willa a well-deserved shot. She glanced at her watch. Heather was due back from her assignment any minute.

"Our boy isn't looking like much," Brew said, tossing a careless glance in Daniel's direction.

Brew wasn't lying. Perspiration coated Daniel's face and his professionally cut-and-styled hair spiked with sweat. The apron Brew had issued him wore an abstract masterpiece in orange chicken-wing grease, piss-colored beer and if she wasn't mistaken, a female handprint rendered in ketchup.

"We can clean him up. Underneath all that shit, he's still the same handsome, soulless bastard with more money than sense."

As if on cue, one of the women sitting at a booth with her friends, drinking umbrella-topped daiquiris turned up her smile's wattage and batted her lashes as Daniel retrieved a stack of plates off the table. Even working as a busboy, Daniel was a chick magnet. Neither Willa nor Heather could understand the allure, but then, neither one of them had ever pursued a man who regularly spent the entire sum of an average yearly income during one trip to Neiman Marcus.

Though he'd worked like a dog during his court-mandated community service, he'd never resisted an opportunity to flirt with the women in the bar. Thanks to Daniel's lawyer, who was still in the corner despite his recent vocal declaration that his sizable retainer wasn't worth the billable hours he was missing by remaining in Key West, she also knew that Daniel's honey of the moment had left the island, apparently bored with waiting for him poolside while he paid his debt to Monroe County. Poor guy was probably already lonely.

And wasn't Willa magnanimous as all get-out in helping him find a new squeeze? Poor guy deserved a sure thing, right?

Willa threw back the shot and slammed the glass down on the bar so Brew could immediately refill. "What else you got for me, Brew?"

"I got a room upstairs," Brew said, wagging his thick, salt-and-pepper eyebrows.

No subtlety from this big lug, and yet, Willa still experienced an electric thrill that sizzled through her bloodstream whenever he looked at her with such unbridled lust.

"Not my turn to get laid tonight," she answered.

Brew licked his lips and on his well-weathered face, the gesture wasn't so much crude as it was sexy as hell. With no Scottish brogue, she couldn't quite compare her sometimes lover to Sean Connery…but he was damned close in every way that counted, right down to the twinkling blue eyes. The only difference was, Connery twinkled for just about every red-blooded woman in the free world. Brew sparkled just for her.

"Who says it's not your turn?" he asked.

"I say. I don't want to miss any of the fun."

"Ah, come on, babe. There's always time for a quickie. That's why they call them that, you know."

"Ya think?"

Brew's eyes crinkled with humor while he filled a beer order for Sonia and rang up two tabs from the patio. After admonishing his waitress to push the onion rings, he leaned his elbows on the bar and moved in close, so close that the scent of tobacco, beer and Chaz, which Willa guessed he'd gotten off eBay, kicked her resolve in the gut.

"It's going to take a while to get Daniel properly loaded," he pointed out.

Through the window behind Brew that gave her a bird's-eye view into the kitchen, Willa watched Danny-boy sipping from his foam cup through a straw. At Willa's request, Brew had laced the guy's cola with rum. If Daniel had noticed the booze, he hadn't said a word, probably thankful for a little hooch to get him through the indignity of bussing tables in a Key West dive for the second night in a row.

"Not too loaded," she insisted. "I want him at least partially conscious when he realizes what we've done to him."

"Wouldn't be half as good as what I'd do to you if you snuck upstairs with me for fifteen minutes."

"A whole quarter hour? Don't tempt me," she warned with a wink, knowing she'd easily waylay the entire plan if Brew sweetened the pot in the way only he could. "Give me a break, Brew. I've got to keep on task. Tonight's operation requires expert planning and execution. If we push too hard, too fast, old Daniel might bugout of Key West before he's properly taught about what happens when he messes with one of our friends."

Brew chuckled. "He's got a court order that's gonna keep him here at least two more days, whether he likes it or not."

A sultry shiver not unlike the ones she experienced when Brew whispered to her in that gravelly, smoke-filled voice of his skittered through her bloodstream. Nothing turned her on more than revenge. Well, except for Brew. She hoped his libido lasted because by the end of the night, she was going to be hot to trot.

"God, don't you love the American justice system?" she asked.

Brew slid a second tequila her way just as Heather slipped in through the swinging doors. She glanced around and spying Daniel disappearing into the kitchen with an overloaded tray of empty plates and cups, scurried over to them, graceful on her four-inch heels.

"We're all set. Randa's the headliner tonight!"

"Hot damn!" Willa shouted, quieting herself when Daniel slinked close by the bar with a damp rag clutched in his hands and a scowl on his face. The three of them leaned forward conspiratorially, but Daniel had long given up on looking in their direction. The only one he trusted in the least was Brew, and that's only because the man had gone out of his way to treat him fairly—even if he did work him hard. But everyone who worked for Brew worked hard—including Brew. Still it hadn't been easy to get Brew to take such an even hand with the guy, but Willa had been very convincing. They'd need that trust later. Of this, she was certain.

"Okay, then," Brew said, yanking up the apron that had dropped somewhat below his ample belt. "Let's get this party started."

Willa took her cue, leading Heather out of the bar after quickly tossing a few bills down to cover the tab. Brew had long ago insisted she didn't have to pay, but Willa wasn't the type for freebies. At one point or another, her fling with Brew would be *finito* and when the break came, she wanted it clean.

She and Heather lingered outside the door.

"Is Randa still at the Paradise Club?" Willa asked.

Heather nodded. "Of course. She's still the hottest ticket there."

"Heard the Garden was trying to poach her."

"She's considering her options, but for now, she's all ours."

"And you showed her Daniel's picture?"

Heather bounced up and down, nearly unable to contain herself. "Yup. And I did a quick rundown of his history with Tessa, though she cut me short. She'd read the whole story in the *Star*. And Tessa made quite the impression when she brought her agent in to see Randa's show last week. Weird how Tessa has that effect on people. Randa can't wait to get her hands on the man who messed with her new buddy."

"Well, then," Willa said, hooking her arm through Heather's. "Let's not keep randy Randa waiting."

TESSA DIDN'T THINK she could feel any freer than she did at the moment she and Colton burst through the doors of Brew's Pub, panting from battling the crowd on Duval Street. Hand in hand, they'd survived the jostling of what seemed like a thousand revelers, each more outrageous than the next, who had somehow managed to organize a party and parade on very short notice. Usually, in the Keys, festivals from the stoic to the outrageous were planned and executed with tons of advance notice so that merchants and tourism officials could take full advantage of the increased population of people willing to part with their money. But every so often, a party just broke out in the streets and the locals either joined in or escaped to neutral ground. Like Brew's. In this case, she and Colton had ventured into Old Town to find Willa, who'd left a cryptic message on Tessa's answering machine.

She hadn't heard it until well after three o'clock. As promised, she and Colton had made love almost instantly after waking up. Then, she'd taken him fishing. He was an expert wrangler and by noon, they'd filled the cooler with red drum and returned to the island to clean and cook their catch. They'd blackened the redfish on a pan over an open fire, drunk wine on the beach and then made love on the chaise lounge on the patio under the hot afternoon sun, with only a sweet breeze to blanket them. Sometime before checking her messages, Tessa had realized that Colton fit like a conch inside a shell here and yet he spoke about cold, windy Chicago as if it were the Promised Land. Even if they were to overcome her difficulties in committing to anything beyond a romp on the beach, they'd still be geographically opposed.

But for this evening, Tessa decided not to worry. She knew Colton had to go back to his job in Illinois sooner rather than later. He'd have no choice but to leave her behind and though she knew with each passing moment that she'd suffer for his absence, she would push aside her regrets for now.

Tessa pulled Colton toward the bar where Brew looked very surprised to see them.

Incredibly surprised.

As in, so surprised, something was up.

"Tessa? What the hell are you doing here?"

Tessa leaned back, bumping her head against Colton's shoulder as a well-soused group of guys all wearing Barenaked Ladies T-shirts pushed past them to get to the patio out back. "I'm looking for Willa," she shouted. Between Jimmy Buffet crooning about changes in latitude and the bark of laughter and animated conversation from the bar patrons, she could hardly hear herself think.

Brew frowned. "She ain't here."

He grabbed a bottle of rum and turned his back on them while he mixed up a batch of piña coladas.

With a glance over her shoulder, Tessa caught Colton's raised eyebrows. Despite the crowd in the bar, a definite chill snaked through the room—emanating directly from Brew.

When a seat opened up, Tessa slid on and after a quick chat with the guy next to her, convinced him to move down one so Colton could join her. The guy tipped his NASCAR cap to Colton, then passed them the pretzels.

Colton eyed Brew warily. "Maybe he just doesn't like me."

Tessa shook her head. "Nah, that's not it. Brew doesn't like anyone. It's never been a reason for him to be rude to *me*." She glanced at her watch. The pub was busy, but because she'd known Brew since childhood, she'd never had to wait more than a minute for service. Most times, she'd barely settled into a seat before he had some concoction delivered directly into her hands. At the moment, however, he seemed particularly interested in skewering the right combination of orange, cherry and lime to garnish his drinks with. Something was definitely up.

Tessa looked around and noticed that while Daniel's attorney was poring over some chicken-wing-stained papers in the corner, her ex-husband was nowhere to be seen.

"Notice who's missing?" she asked, palming a half-dozen pretzels.

Colton looked around. "Maybe he has the night off."

Tessa shrugged. "Not if he wants to earn his hours and get back to West Palm. I didn't want to run into him, but I have no choice if I want to find Willa. He has to be here every night in order to fulfill his community service."

Colton caught Brew's attention with a wave. Brew returned the gesture reluctantly.

"That's the craziest community service I've ever heard of, you know that, right?" Colton said to Tessa. "If this was Chicago, I'd probably launch an investigation of the criminal justice system."

Rolling her eyes, Tessa wondered how things might have turned out differently had her divorce case been tried in radical Key West rather than stuffy West Palm Beach. Every day's testimony would have been celebrated with drinks at sunset and all tales of her supposed sexual acrobatics would have been greeted with cheers instead of shock and derision.

God, she should have moved here years ago.

"You can't hold Key West to the standards of the regular world," she reminded him. "We just don't work that way."

"You've really settled in here, haven't you?"

Though she noticed a tinge of sadness in his voice, Tessa decided to ignore it. The facts were the facts. He lived in Chicago. She lived in Key West. Though other parts of their relationship had undergone radical change in the past few days, some truths could not be altered.

"Key West is my home now, Colton. It's more than just an address. It's a state of mind."

He glanced away and when his gaze returned to hers, his grey irises twinkled with that all-too-familiar charm that made her insides melt like ice cream on the pier.

"I understand the appeal now. But you know, since I've arrived, things have gone downhill. Used to be you could at least get a drink pretty quickly."

Tessa caught Brew's eye and this time, with an exasperated look, lured him over.

"What can I get you?" he asked, greeting them with a wooden smile.

"Willa," Tessa answered, though at the same time, Colton said, "Beer."

Brew reached for the tap at the same time that he answered Tessa. "I told you, she's not here."

"Her cell phone is turned off," she informed him.

Brew shrugged. "Maybe she forgot to charge up. She won't be back tonight. Place is crowded. Maybe you and your lover boy ought to go back to Speed Key."

That did it.

Tessa leaned forward and snagged Brew by the shirt. "What's going on, Brew? Where's Daniel?"

Brew glanced down at her hand, annoyed. "I gave the bastard the rest of the night off."

"Then why is his mouthpiece still here?"

"The barrister likes the wings. I think he's got a thing for Becky. How the hell do I know? You leaving or what?"

Tessa released him and he backed away like a dog that had just been caught piddling on the carpet.

"You always so rough on your men?" Brew groused.

Tessa cracked a saucy grin. "When I have to be."

Colton leaned in close. "What do *I* have to do to make you so forceful?"

She caught the teasing gleam in his eye and countered his playfulness with a kiss on the nose. "You can start by getting me out of here."

The relief on Brew's face nearly made her laugh. She contained herself, not wanting to give herself away. Brew was a damned good liar when he wanted to be, but lies of omission were not his forte.

Colton took a sip of his beer. "I thought you wanted one of Brew's special mai tais."

"I've got a new craving now."

She grabbed his hand and yanked him out of his chair. He spared one minute to gulp down a good portion of his drink and throw down a few bills, before he allowed her to maneuver him toward the door with her arms wrapped around his waist.

Colton's eyes darkened to stormy slate. "I like the way you think."

Tessa glanced at Brew, who made great drama out of ignoring her.

Guilt, pure and simple.

"Don't be so sure," she said.

When Sonia slid past, Tessa tapped her on the shoulder. She didn't break from her embrace with Colton, but instead leaned her cheek on his chest. Not only did she love the feel of his taut muscles beneath her skin, but her face was blocked from Brew so that he couldn't see what she was saying.

"Sonia, where's Willa?"

The waitress stopped, distracted by her quest to find a pen in her big 1980s hair, then jotted something down on her pad, likely a leftover detail from her last order. She chewed the corner of the pen while she looked over her notes.

"Paradise Club," she answered absently.

Tessa thanked the waitress and then tugged Colton the rest of the way out of the bar.

"Let me guess. We're going to the Paradise Club."

"Yup."

"Why?"

"I have a feeling we're going to avert a huge disaster."

THE PARADISE CLUB sat smack-dab in the center of Duval
Street, not far from Sloppy Joe's, the infamous bar beloved
by Ernest Hemingway, one of Key West's many claims to
fame. No doubt the novelist who valued grace under pressure
above all else would have been perplexed by the scene inside
the PC. It took a few minutes for Tessa to connect all the
pieces of the puzzle, but luckily, she was alcohol-free and
therefore able to perform some basic feats of logic.

First, she noted Heather and Willa sitting rather unobtrusively
in the back, their froufrou drinks nearly untouched. Then, she
took into consideration Randa Divine on stage—wearing her favorite slinky black dress with the slit up her thigh, a rhinestone
choker and five-inch heels on an already five-foot-ten body—
singing about the material girl in her best Madonna voice. But
the most perplexing clue of all—and most telling—was Daniel,
seated front and center on stage while Randa circled, flirted,
touched, groped and kissed. And the man didn't object.

"Looks like your ex found a girlfriend," Colton said.

Tessa skewered him with a wide-eyed stare. Girlfriend?
When's the last time he had his eyes checked? Granted, Randa
was a first-class drag queen, but even the most undeveloped
gaydar could scope this one out, right?

"Looks that way," she said with a snicker.

He arched a brow. "Am I missing something?"

"That's a distinct possibility," Tessa said wryly. "Let's
catch up with Willa and Heather. I don't doubt they've been
the ones playing matchmaker tonight."

Though Colton's perplexed look remained plastered on
his face, Tessa didn't want to give away the secret just yet.
The longer she let it ride, the greater the potential for a fun
reveal. God, men could be so dense in the presence of statuesque women with double D breasts.

Tessa slipped through the crowd carefully, not wanting Randa to catch sight of her in case it would ruin whatever craziness Willa and Heather had clearly cooked up. By the time they reached the back of the bar, Randa had segued into "La Isla Bonita" and had added a bright red boa and a lace mantilla to her costume. Daniel was leaning forward so far that when Randa cast her boa around his shoulders and started reeling him toward her, Tessa suspected he might fall out of his chair onto the runway stage.

"Here they are," Tessa said, breaking through the audience right in front of Willa and Heather's table. "Lucy and Ethel in the Tropics."

Willa stretched forward and pushed Tessa out of the way. "You're blocking my view. I want to see his face when he finally catches on."

Heather giggled and sipped her drink. Giggled? Heather, despite her breezy persona, never giggled. Just how long had they been here and how many rounds had they had?

"Catches on to what?" Colton asked.

Tessa scanned through the crowd and caught sight of Daniel again. He was standing. He was dancing.

"What did you do to him?" Tessa said, swallowing a laugh.

Willa shrugged. "Just added a little flavor to his soda over at Brew's and tipped the bartender here to make sure his drinks never needed a refill. I didn't think you'd want to see this."

Tessa shook her head, her chest aching with restrained laughter. "I don't want to see this. What are you paying Randa with, Chanel?"

"Nah, it's a freebie," Willa assured her. "She likes you."

"Everyone likes you," Heather said, in a strangely vapid agreement.

Tessa hooked her thumb over at Heather. "What is she drinking?"

Willa rolled her eyes. "Anything she can get her hands on. You know, I never realized that she can't hold her hooch. We're going to have to work with her."

The Madonna set finally finished and the crowd was universally on their feet, applauding, whistling and whooping their approval of the drag queen's fabulous voice and even more fabulous body.

The reaction of the crowd suddenly surged into full-blown cheering. No amount of standing on her tiptoes revealed the cause of the excitement, so Tessa joined Heather and Willa, who'd climbed onto their chairs.

When her gaze finally lighted on the stage where Daniel and Randa were making out as if they were in a private hotel room, Tessa toppled over into Colton's arms.

"What's going on?" he asked, hesitating before lowering her to the ground.

Tessa could hardly breathe. God, she shouldn't be enjoying this. She was fairly certain she was destroying her entire store of good karma by taking such delight in Daniel's impending calamity, but she couldn't help herself. "Daniel's getting lucky," she said with a snort.

"On stage?"

"Welcome to Key West."

Sooner than she expected, Tessa heard a screech coming from the direction of the stage, a yelp so high-pitched, it managed to pierce through the whoops and cheers of the crowd. Heather and Willa gave each other high fives, then jumped down to the ground.

"Our work here is done," Willa declared.

The screams had not stopped, though the crowd had started to quiet.

Colton stretched, but apparently couldn't see a thing. "What the—that sounds like…"

Tessa bit her bottom lip. "Daniel. I think he just figured out who he's been kissing all night. And I believe that scream's our cue to get the hell out of Dodge."

CHAPTER FOURTEEN

HEATHER AND WILLA tossed a few twenties on the table and started toward the door. Colton grabbed Tessa by the arm. "What do you know that you're not sharing?"

She wrapped her arm around his waist and propelled him forward, even though every instinct in his body screamed for him to stay. Something was going on here and he was in the dark—maybe missing out on some punch line only women could get? He didn't know, but he meant to find out.

"I can't believe you're so blinded by big boobs and long legs," Tessa cracked.

"Whose big boobs?" he asked, somewhat offended. Well, Randa did have one hell of a rack, but he wasn't one to ogle another man's date.

"Randa's! For Pete's sake, Colton, she's a man! And judging by that scream, Daniel just made the bulging discovery."

The audience was now laughing hysterically and over the din, Colton could hear Randa chewing Daniel out. Words like "rich-boy pig" and various epithets about the size of Daniel's johnson—or lack thereof—rang through the room.

Then, they heard a thump, then a smack, another scream and then the breaking of glass. Oh, great. A riot was going to break out and they weren't anywhere near the door.

For Pete's sake, Colton, she's a man!

He froze. The words played over in his head. Good God.

Had he really stared with appreciation at some drag queen's fake tits?

Colton pushed away from Tessa and made his way through the crowd to get a closer look. Well, not too damned close. From the way two of the bouncers were shoving their way toward the stage, Colton was lucky to grab one glimpse of Randa, who'd somehow lost her sassy, blond wig.

Holy shit.

By the time he caught up with Tessa near the exit, her eyes were filled with tears of laughter.

"You really didn't know?"

Colton hadn't known a lot of drag queens in his lifetime, but he was pretty sure that Randa was one of the best. Despite her statuesque build, her facial features were delicate, her hands finely boned and her breasts—well, real or not, they were the stuff men dreamed of.

He shivered. "I'm going to get you for this," he said, laughing despite his best efforts.

"Don't blame me! I had nothing to do with this."

"The hell you didn't!"

This was from Daniel, who'd been shanghaied by the bouncers, each of whom had him by one arm. His left eye was red and swollen. Apparently, Randa had gotten in one good lick before Reese had been dragged offstage.

Colton took Tessa by the hand. "You don't have to do this again. Let's just get out of here."

"Sure, run when you've been caught, you ungrateful, crazy bitch. Couldn't be satisfied with ruining my reputation, could you? You had to—"

"Ruining *your* reputation?" Tessa repeated, incensed. She shook her hand free of Colton's, dug her fists onto her hips and stalked toward Reese with fire in her eyes. Luckily, the bouncers held the jerk steady. "What the fuck are you talking about, you worm? You're the one who made me the brunt of jokes on the late-night talk shows. You're the one who made me look like a nymphomaniac whore!"

In his attempts to free himself from the bouncers, Daniel kicked out, nearly catching Tessa in the chin. Colton yanked her back and when Daniel lost his footing, the bouncers let him fall.

He rose up on shaky balance, spittle flying, and the bouncers stepped back. "You were a whore. And from what I can see—" Daniel said, skewering Colton with hate-filled eyes "—you still are."

Colton hadn't really formulated the idea to punch Daniel dead on the nose, but the action seemed to precede the intent. By the time the red haze cleared from Colton's eyes, Daniel was lying flat on the floor, a trickle of blood oozing from one nostril. His eyes were closed.

He was out cold.

Colton started to lean forward to see if he'd killed him when Tessa snatched his hand and pulled him toward the door.

"Tessa, what if he's dead?"

Tessa huffed. "He'll be fine, but I don't want to see you arrested for assault. Come on!"

One of the bouncers clapped him on the shoulder. "He ain't worth going to jail for, man. I'll tell Randa you kicked his ass. She'll dedicate her next show to both of you."

Between Tessa's tugging and the bouncer's push, Colton didn't have much choice but to leave. Heather and Willa were waiting for them at the corner of the street and they took off together toward Brew's. By the time, they reached the patio out back, which had a much thinner crowd from earlier, Tessa had recounted the entire story to the two women, ending with Colton's knocking Daniel flat on his back.

"My hero," Tessa said, leaning her head on his shoulder.

Willa accepted a pitcher of beer from Sonia and proceeded to pour. "First round is on me! I never would have pegged you as the physical type, Granger. Not with your fists anyway."

Colton frowned and rubbed his knuckles. "I'm usually better at holding my anger in check, but he went too far."

Heather, who at Willa's orders was drinking a Sprite, toyed with the cherry Brew had thrown in to soften the blow of being cut off. "I wonder if Randa's okay."

"Randa used to box back in college," Willa informed them. "I'm certain the shiner Daniel develops on his eye will have been thanks to her. But I am feeling a little guilty about what Randa had to deal with. I didn't expect Daniel to get violent when he found out he was sucking face with a guy."

"I don't understand," Tessa said wearily. "Sucking face with a guy is usually the highlight of my night."

Tessa winked at Colton, then returned her head to his shoulder, her hair a soft pillow against his skin. Combined with the beer and the warm, ocean-scented air, tension immediately began seeping out of his body. He could get used to this. Not the fighting or the drag queens or the crowds, but all those could be avoided in favor of midnight swims, delicious food, abundant drink and Tessa.

After determining that they would send a bouquet of roses worthy of a Derby winner to Randa first thing, they closed Brew's pub at three o'clock in the morning. By this time, Heather had sobered up and could get home with minimal help from Willa. Tessa and Colt decided to bunk out in Brew's spare room rather than risk motoring back to the island so late at night. And for the first time since Colton had arrived from Chicago, they fell asleep instantly in each other's arms.

Despite the fatigue of running on very little sleep, they rolled out of Brew's foldout couch just after dawn, returned to Speed Key, fed the dogs and then napped on the hammocks until nine o'clock.

When Colton finally opened his eyes, Tessa was awake and quietly stirring the sand beneath the hammock with her toe. He stretched. She smiled. Colt realized his whole world had turned upside down in the short spread of a few days. But sooner or later, he was going to have to leave paradise. In the real world, he had a job he loved, responsibilities he tolerated and family and friends he missed.

And then there was the city. Chicago wasn't exactly the polar opposite of Key West the way Manhattan was, but the dissimilarities between the Windy City and the home of easy living were clearly as wide as the distance between the Midwestern metropolis and the U.S.'s southernmost point. For all he and Tessa had in common, they had just as many differences, right down to the way they lived.

And yet, the thought of leaving her, knowing their relationship was doomed to long-distance impotency, churned his stomach—though he had to admit that the response could have been from the beer and wings at 2:00 a.m.

"Morning," he said.

She glanced up at the sky, then at him, with those hypnotic eyes of hers. "Just barely. Hungry?"

He squeezed her closer and breathed in the scent of her hair. "Always."

"For food," she said, pulling just enough out of his arms to send up the no-sex signal.

He decided not to complain. They couldn't have sex all the time. Could they?

"Yeah, but I'm not sure what I'm in the mood for. You're not going to believe this, but I'm thinking a big, juicy steak."

She smiled lazily and stretched, not unlike one of those six-toed Hemingway cats they'd caught sight of yesterday. He started rethinking the whole steak thing in favor of the delicious morsel in front of him.

"We'll go to Pepe's. Maybe afterward we can go to a few galleries. You've yet to shop with me, you know. You never really know a woman until you've shopped with her."

Colton chuckled, but the humor died quickly. "I know enough to know that shopping with you isn't going to give me any more insight than I have right now."

The twinkle in her eye faded. "Colton, you're not going to get all serious on me again, are you? It's a real drag."

With as much balance as he could muster after their wild night and early morning, Colton swung out of his hammock and dug his feet into the sand. Then, he took a deep breath, reminding himself that he couldn't let his natural impatience ruin whatever headway he'd gained with Tessa. Despite her reluctance to really open up to him, to really let him in, they'd connected this week. He didn't have a doubt that he'd gotten under her skin just as much as she had his.

"Point taken. I'm going to take a swim, then a shower, and then we can hit this Pepe's place. Care to join me?"

She crinkled her nose. She wanted to join him——he could see it in her eyes. But he'd irked her with his offhand comment and she wasn't quite ready to let go of her ire.

Stubborn to the last.

"You go ahead. I have some phone calls to make and I should take a few minutes to toss the ball with the dogs. They've sort of been ignored over the past few days."

He nodded and though she popped a kiss on his nose before sauntering back through the foliage to the house, Colton felt the tension crackling between them. They hadn't made love in almost twenty-four hours and like it or not, he had to face the possibility that the connection they'd formed had already begun to loosen. Though he'd never suspected as much until he'd hooked up with Tessa, Colton now realized that he was a romantic at heart. But he'd always known he was a realist—and the realist in him had already started hinting that without the physical side, he and Tessa were simply two different people thrown together in a situation that had nearly run its course.

Nearly. But not quite.

TESSA HAD SHOWERED and changed and was tossing a bright red ball to the dogs when Willa maneuvered up on Brew's powerboat and eased into the slip at the end of the dock. Giving the ball one last throw that sent Artemis and Apollo bounding into the brush, Tessa met Willa as she was tying off the line.

"How's Randa?"

"Loved the flowers," Willa said with a grin. "Claims she has another chapter for her memoirs. I think she wants you to ghostwrite them, but she's too shy to ask."

"She should write them herself." Tessa laughed. "I can only imagine how interesting her life has been."

"Yours has gotten pretty interesting with Colton around, hasn't it?"

Tessa blew out a frustrated breath and gestured Willa toward the other side of the dock where they could sit and let their feet dangle in the water. "I don't know how much longer he's going to be around."

"Are you screwing things up already?"

"Of course. It's not like I have a lot of experience in the whole relationship business. Besides, I like my life, Willa. I still don't know if I want more than a weeklong fling. But he does. He's made that clear."

Willa unzipped her fanny pack, extracted some lip balm and smoothed it over her lips. "Well, you've at least made some progress. Before he came, you didn't want more than one night."

Tessa tried to tamp down the chill that chased up her spine, despite the bright sun and eighty-degree temperature. "I know. It terrifies me."

"It shouldn't. What about the book?" Willa said, quickly changing the topic.

Suddenly, breathing became easier. "He still hasn't made a decision and to be honest, I haven't asked. I told you about the mix-up with my agent, right?"

"Yeah. Ever figure out how that happened?"

She shook her head. "Colton thinks Audrey did it on purpose, to drum up interest in the book, but I don't think so. She said she had nothing to do with it and I believe her."

"So is this causing problems between you two?"

"We haven't talked about it since it happened. Actually, we haven't talked about the book since…"

She wasn't about to tell Willa that they'd continued recreating scenes from the book and that the last time they'd tried, they'd strayed entirely from the text. She and Colton had come to an odd crossroads in their weird relationship. The truth was, the time had come for them to step out of the fantasy and into the realities of an interpersonal relationship. But with her nearly unwilling to dig deep into her heart to see what she found there, their chances of success were slim to none.

"How are things going with Brewster?" Tessa asked, suddenly hungry for information on someone's romance other than hers.

"We're chugging along." Willa leaned back on her elbows and glanced up at the sky. In the bright sun, the highlights in her light brown hair gleamed and her skin, only slightly weathered from exposure to the elements, took on a pinkish glow. God, her friend was so in love. And like her, she refused to see the truth.

"Does it bother you that he's so much older?"

"Brew? Nah. He'd be crusty and mean if he was still twenty-five. I just think a man that's gone this long without getting married even once must have a natural aversion to the whole institution, you know?"

"You want to get married?"

"Someday. Of course," Willa said, snapping a disbelieving look in her direction. "Don't you?"

"No."

"You hesitated."

"No, I didn't."

"Yes, you did," Willa said, her smile widening. "We've talked about this before and usually, you've got that *no* out of your mouth before I've even finished the question. You better face it, Tessa. Your life has changed since Colton stepped onto this island. You aren't the same person you were before. And I think that's a good thing."

Tessa scoffed, preferring to be insulted rather than face the inherent truth of what her friend was claiming. "I'm sorry I was so lacking before. I'm surprised you wanted to hang out with me."

Jumping to her feet, Tessa swiped the sand and shell off her ass, knowing she was being petulant, and not caring. As a child, she was rarely allowed to be snappish. Her mother had expected her to be quiet and her father had insisted she be clever. She was feeling a good, old-fashioned temper tantrum coming on that was over thirty-two years in the making.

In her typical unruffled style, Willa stood and scratched an itch on her nose. "Surprises the hell out of me, too. Spoiled little rich girls aren't usually my taste."

"I'm not spoiled."

"Aren't you? Come on, Tessa. Let's face facts. Sure, your ex handed you a raw deal. I think he's been sufficiently paid back, at least for the moment. And honest to God, I think you've come to terms with all that mess. Or, you're close. But now you've settled into your life on the Key and you don't want anything or anyone to disrupt it. You want to write your book your way, market it your way, live your way. You compromised so much in the past you don't want to bend at all anymore."

"And what's wrong with that? Haven't I earned the right to do things my way and my way only?"

"Yeah," Willa conceded. "If you want to be lonely. If you want to lose a guy who clearly thinks you could hang the moon."

God, Tessa didn't want to hear any of this. She shuffled off the dock and found a modicum of comfort in kicking the sand. "Why are you telling me all this today? Is it some sort of honesty holiday that I haven't heard of?"

Willa shook her head and then joined her, wrapping her arm around her shoulder. "I'm telling you because no one else has the balls to."

"Colton does."

"You should know," Willa quipped with an eyebrow waggle.

Tessa socked her in the arm.

"My point is," Willa continued, "you aren't listening to him, are you? Or to me. Or to yourself. You're desperately trying to hold on to the status quo because it's the safest place to be."

Tessa mock-whimpered, her shoulders shaking as her gaze turned helplessly to the sky. "How can living on my own private island, partying whenever the hell I feel like it and finally taking charge of my career be considered safe? Every day of my life is one big risk."

"To your physical safety? Probably. Your sanity? Most definitely. Your heart? Not by a long shot, babe, and you know it."

Thankfully, Colton took that moment to push through the

palms, with Artemis and Apollo jogging faithfully at his side. Good Lord, even the dogs had accepted him as part of her life. They didn't dance around him anymore trying to impress him or finagle treats—they just marched by his side as if he lived there. How come she couldn't manage to accept him in the same way?

"Hey, Willa," Colton greeted. "I don't suppose the sheriff sent you here to arrest me for assaulting Daniel Reese?"

Willa shook her head. "Out of my jurisdiction. Now if you try to drown him, which I'm neither suggesting nor discouraging, then I'll be back."

"Whatever did happen to Daniel last night?" Tessa asked.

Willa shrugged as if she didn't know, but Tessa knew better than to buy that for an instant. Willa Dawson was plugged into every avenue of communication on the island. But if there was something Tessa needed to know, she'd tell her. She hoped.

"Hopefully, he learned his lesson and won't mess with you again," Willa said, returning to the dock and unwinding the rope from the cleat beside her boat. "Want a ride back to Old Town?"

Tessa considered the option. If they hung out with Willa for a few hours, she could at least temporarily avoid any in-depth and personal discussions with Colton. She knew he planned to return to Chicago soon. Then she'd have her life back. Then she could redevote herself to mindless pursuits like shopping and dancing and fishing.

Just her. Alone. Well, not entirely. She had her friends. Good friends. Friends willing to turn Key West upside down to exact revenge on her behalf.

And yet, they weren't Colton, were they?

"I think we'll take a rain check," Tessa said.

Willa leaped into the boat, shoved off, started the engine, and then eased the power craft out of the slip. "I'm on duty for the next five days. If Daniel gets out of hand, you call Brew, you hear? It was nice to meet you, Granger."

Colton waved and for reasons Tessa couldn't fathom, she felt her body slump. Something about Willa's no-muss good-bye struck her as wrong and yet somehow familiar. Like reverse déjà vu.

Colton must have noticed her posture, because he wrapped his arms around her from behind and placed a soft kiss on the crown of her head.

"So, you ready to go?"

She turned and eyed him narrowly. "When are you leaving?"

He stepped back and cocked an eyebrow. "Is that a request for my departure?"

Frowning, she surrendered to her impulse and curled herself into his arms. "I'm not usually so subtle. No, I don't want you to go. I just know that you plan to."

He hesitated before he answered and when he spoke, his voice was low and deep. "My plane ticket is for three days from now, Tessa. We have three days to decide if what we've started is worth seeing through or if we should just count this all as a great diversion and cut our losses."

Tessa pressed closer to him, her cheek flush against his chest. She inhaled his scent, wanting nothing more at that moment than to imprint his unique blend of musk and cologne in her mind.

He could have been talking about the book. He could have been talking about them. She highly suspected he was talking about both—and all she knew was that she didn't want to talk about either. Not today. Talking would mean making a choice and for some deep-seated reason, Tessa suspected that no matter what she chose, she'd make the most serious mistake of her life.

CHAPTER FIFTEEN

The smoke from the fire was enchanted, Reides realized too late. He widened his stance and dug his toes into the sand and rock that surrounded the crystal-clear spring where he'd been swimming, but his body still wavered from the effect of the acrid aroma surrounding him. In moments, he had no choice but to throw himself down onto the plush, silk chaise that suddenly appeared beside him and glowed with a luminescence that meant only one thing.

An Olympian had come down from the heavens.

Reides tried to regulate his breathing so as not to breathe in more of the drugged smoke, but his firsthand knowledge of the rage of the gods thwarted him, and he panted with fear. Had his father, Poseidon, finally found him? Would he punish Alina for daring to love the son of a god? Perhaps Artemis had tracked them and he would pay for breaking the bonds of the goddess's protection of Alina and her family. He had, after all, stolen a maiden's innocence.

So tight. So moist and sweet to the taste.

Concentrating on his nubile lover, he stilled the wild beating of his heart. He wouldn't regret his choices, but he didn't wish to die for them, either.

And yet, even as his eyesight clouded and he fought

for the skill to speak, he realized the scene around him did not conjure images of either Poseidon, who preferred to appear in a fury of thunderous waves, or Artemis, who would likely charge in with her stag at her side, her deadly bow and arrow drawn and aimed. Instead, the night reeked of exotic and spiced aromas floating off the sparks in the fire. The warmth of the flames reached out to him and stroked his skin like the hands of a thousand concubines. In seconds, the spring-water had evaporated off his skin, but he didn't experience the tight dryness that normally began to choke him when the air stole the moisture from his flesh. He was caught in a soothing fog and he had no desire to leave.

Especially not when the spring burbled furiously at the center and golden streams of light spiked from deep within the pool. White foam soon frothed on the surface and the distinct scent of ambergris, sweet and aromatic beyond reason, assailed his nostrils. Reides attempted to swallow and shake his head to clear the disorientation, but his mouth remained dry and his vision tunneled. He could see nothing but the undeniable beauty of the woman who emerged from the spring.

No, not a woman.

A goddess.

Draped in a gilded fabric that dripped with glittering gems, she rose to the top of the water in full, luxuriant splendor. He knew instantly she could be no other than Aphrodite, goddess of love.

He must have murmured her name because she smiled and glided over to him, her arms outstretched.

"Yes, Reides. I am Aphrodite, born of the sea foam, creature of the ocean, devoted to fulfilling the most secret, most intimate desires of those who worship me.

Have you paid your homage, Reides? Do you deserve my approval?"

The smoke thickened. His nostrils flared as the burning scent of the fire nearly suffocated him, and yet he couldn't help but inhale deeply. With a wave of her hand, the wind blew the dark tendrils in another direction and for an instant, his vision cleared.

"Why are you here?" he asked. "Has my father sent you? Has Artemis?"

She forced a smile, but he could see in her eyes, which glittered like faceted sapphires, that she was not pleased by his question. "I take orders from no one, Reides. That you must understand."

He sputtered. "But Zeus—"

"We'll not speak of him." Her voice remained soft, the whisper of a gull's wing, yet her tone brooked no disobedience. She stepped off the rolling wave that had magically brought her to the shore. "I'm here for you and no other."

Slowly, Reides regained his ability to think. He managed to swallow and fill his mouth with moisture so he could speak unhampered. "For Alina, too? To bless our union? Will you offer your protection to lovers in peril?"

Aphrodite's eyes darkened into pinpoints of pure cobalt fire. "Alina has no need for you, Reides. The dreams Morpheus gave her ignited her obsession with sexual satisfaction. Soon, she'll find other means to experience pleasures of the flesh."

Reides shook his head. There were no other men on the island. He'd sent away all but a few female servants to tend to Alina's every whim and need. And they were together nearly every moment. He'd only come out

*alone tonight to the spring because Alina had tired of
the water, whereas he could not live without it.*

*"I don't believe you," he said, attempting to keep his
tone reverent, and yet insistent. "She's an innocent. She
does not have the heart to betray me."*

*Aphrodite rolled her shoulders, a light undulating
motion of her arms and hands that epitomized grace,
liquid movement and complete indifference to his claim.
Why did he notice every nuance of her gestures, every
inflection of her voice, which seemed to echo in his ears
and vibrate against his skin? Aphrodite's beauty was almost painful to behold and he suddenly understood why
men sacrificed their free will to earn mere moments in
her presence.*

*"Perhaps, in the beginning, her soul was as innocent
as you claim," Aphrodite said, her tone enchanting,
haunting. "But since you snatched her before she could
descend into the underworld, you've tainted her, Reides.
She's no longer the child she was while under the care
of Artemis. She's a woman. With desires. With needs you
cannot fulfill forever."*

*A chill rammed up Reides' spine, causing him to
shiver with both fear and grief. Lies from an Olympian
would not surprise him—fabrications and fictions
flowed from his father's lips with keen regularity. But
Aphrodite's claim tasted of truth. He'd shown Alina the
beauty of love—but also the ugliness. In his initial zeal-
ousness to keep her safe, he'd held her captive, against
her will. He'd given her no respite from erotic games,
no pause between feeding his hunger. She'd witnessed
the darkness in his soul and he knew without doubt that
she no longer trusted him the way she had that first mo-*

*ment when her eyelids had fluttered open and he'd
taught her the first lesson in fulfillment.*

*And as the son of a god, he also knew that Aphrodite
was a dedicated enchantress. She fed on the manipulation of mortals, just as his father, Poseidon, and his un-
cles, Zeus and Hades, and the rest of the residents of
Mount Olympus. Spawned by the jealous, powerful and
arrogant blood of the gods, Reides could easily guess
what this goddess of beauty and love meant to accomplish by coming to Crete, to his hideaway.*

*He anticipated nothing but destruction. And he had
no way to counter her machinations, no way to stop
whatever plan she'd put in motion.*

"Where is Alina?" he demanded.

"Looking for you," Aphrodite answered coolly.

*"She'll come here," he said confidently, knowing
Alina understood that this spring was his favorite place.*

*"She might have," Aphrodite countered, her light,
tinkling voice entirely confident. "But thanks to me…
and Morpheus…she dreamed you went to the fountain
in the garden outside your rooms at the palace. The deep
fountain. The one that flows with water pumped from
this very spring. The dream stirred her need for you,
Reides. She's mad with wanting—a last gift from Morpheus—one I paid dearly for."*

*From beneath the languid folds of her golden dress,
Aphrodite revealed a gilt mirror. For a long, torturous
moment, she admired her reflection. The haze from the
fire had increased again and when Reides rolled off
the chaise and tried to scramble away from the flames,
the smoke from the enchanted blaze pursued him like the
talons of an eagle, latching on with ferocious intensity.
Heat smothered him. His vision blurred to near darkness.*

He couldn't move, so when Aphrodite approached, she nearly blinded him with her radiance. He couldn't even close his eyes against the brightness.

"Look into this mirror, Reides. Watch your darling Alina discover the wonders of the sea."

She held the reflective oval inches from his face. The smoke rushed to the reflective glass like moths to flame. He blinked when the gray, choking mist seeped into the mirror and then swirled until an image came into view.

Alina.

Calling to him.

At the fountain.

With all the strength he could gather, he forced his eyes away. Aphrodite, the great seductress, was like any of the gods of Olympus. She would show him lies if she fancied the amusement.

But he couldn't resist for long. When he looked again, the smoke thickened. Incense flickered and flamed in the fire. An acrid odor now mingled with the scents of the rare spices. Anise. Cinnamon. Cloves. The same spices mortals burned in sacrifice to the gods. In the heat, his muscles nearly melted against his bones, and he still couldn't move.

"What do you want from me?" he asked, his voice choked.

"Only for you to see the truth," she answered sweetly, shrewdly. "Once you do, your mind will open to more glorious possibilities than can be bestowed by a mortal woman."

"I do not worship you, Aphrodite," he said, his lips barely able to move. "I am the son of a god. I need not pay tribute to anyone but Poseidon."

She eased closer, the mirror never wavering, as if it

hung suspended in the air. She grazed her fingers over his chest and the fire seemed to leap out and scorch his skin.

"You are also the son of a siren. A rare combination of enchanted blood. Exotic blood. Do you not know how that affects you?"

"I never knew my mother. She cast me into the sea shortly after my birth."

Aphrodite nodded, a tiny frown reflecting her pity. "And your father rescued you, but then locked you away on this island in Crete, with only your servants, the water nymphs and Nereids to amuse you. Do you know why?"

He didn't. Reides had posed the question to Poseidon on many occasions, but his father refused to offer an answer that made any sense.

In the mirror, Alina had circled the fountain several times, calling Reides' name louder and louder, sounding more concerned and worried with each pass. When she turned into the light spilling from the lanterns inside his rooms, he saw terror in her eyes. Did she think he'd abandoned her?

"Reides?"

Aphrodite's voice permeated his mind. The dulcet tone rolled over him, through him, sizzling into the stream of his blood. Her image swam in his eyes, her beauty so powerful, he could hardly see Alina any longer. But she was there, sitting at the edge of the burbling fountain, her gaze suddenly captured by something in the water and he had to strain to see when she dipped her hand in the darkened pool.

"Oh, look. She's finally found my little gift," Aphrodite announced. "What a fortunate maiden she is. To

*my knowledge, no mortal woman has ever experienced
the delights of a siren's psyche. Well at least they've not
survived to tell the tale. In your ventures into the sea,
have you ever met a psyche? They are creatures beautiful beyond words, full of color and whimsical shapes.
They are irresistible. They feed off the juices a woman
secretes when she experiences sexual arousal. And after
submitting to the pleasures of this unique creature, Alina
will lust only for the sea until she drowns within its
depths. But you would know that, since the psyche was
created by sirens, as vengeance against the women they
wish they could be."*

Her eyes darkened and her tone turned mocking and
cruel. *"You should have heeded your father's warn-
ings, Reides. You should have taken stock of the danger
you brought to Alina by teaching her the ways of love.
The psyche has no power over virgins."*

The fire that Aphrodite stoked with a long, golden
staff popped and crackled with each sweep of breeze.
Though Reides still could not move, his vision cleared
enough so that he could see Alina as if she were standing just a few feet away, her attention enthralled by the
fluttering creature in the water.

He could not stop her. Even if he'd had the strength
to scream out her name, she'd never hear his voice from
this distance. Once the psyche touched her, she'd be lost
forever. He'd snatched her away from death once. Was
this his punishment? To watch her die again, this time
because of the sexual awareness he'd awakened?

"Stop this," he begged.

In the mirror, Alina waded into the fountain.

"It's too late," Aphrodite claimed. *"I cannot. See
how fickle your lover is? She prefers the attentions of a
watery flower over you."*

"You've tricked her."

Aphrodite's eyes seemed to glow. "True. Watch her now, Reides. Read the ecstasy in her eyes. Imagine you are the one skimming your hand up her leg, extending your reach until you reach her breasts. Look, she's fully submerged herself. She understands what she must do. She's torn away her gown. The creature can take all manner of forms, can expand, harden, kiss with the lightest flicker of sensation or suckle to the point of madness."

With nimble hands, Aphrodite touched Reides from his arms to his shoulders to his chest. She removed his tunic and licked her lips as she ran a sharp-tipped fingernail over the length of his shaft, as her tongue swiped across his nipples.

"There. See?" she encouraged, all the while arousing him with her hand on his cock. "She's closed her eyes. Watch how she pants. Imagine the liquid heat pouring through her body even now, moistening her passage, readying her for the lover that will never come. But she'll come, Reides. Watch as the passion builds."

He wanted to turn away, but could not. He wanted Aphrodite to stop touching him, but even if he hadn't been frozen in place, he couldn't have denied her. Her beauty overwhelmed him. Even with Alina moaning in the mirror, her eyes glazed with that unforgettable expression she had just before she fell over the peak of sensual delight, Reides couldn't concentrate entirely on anything beyond the goddess's touch.

"What do you want from me?" he managed to ask, hanging tight to the knowledge that Aphrodite's machinations were not random. Was he some means of revenge against his father? Could he bargain for Alina's life? For his own?

Her tongue moistened her perfect, red lips. "I want you as my lover. As my slave."

"Take me, then. Spare Alina."

"But look at her," she crooned with a voluptuous pout. "This is sweet torture for her, Reides. I imagine the creature has expanded by now, has enveloped her completely below the surface of the water. The tentacles have thousands of tiny fingertips, each one able to induce the ultimate sensation. She'll die happy."

"Spare her," he begged.

She arched a brow and dropped the top of her gown. "Swear your devotion to me."

Reides' hands instantly came free. He reached out, cupped her breasts, pleasured her nipples with the pads of his thumbs as he breathed as deeply as his stone-hard lungs would allow. "I swear."

Her eyes blazed with power. With one gesture toward the ground, he fell to his knees. He did not stop arousing her, his palms growing addicted to the feel of her gossamer flesh against his.

"Swear that the pleasure you'll give me will surpass any your mortal lover has experienced," she demanded.

As if his arms had a will of their own, he reached forward and stripped Aphrodite's gown from her body. Roughly, he grabbed her by the hips, tugged her forward and spoke his pledge into the curls at the juncture of her thighs just before plunging his tongue into her. The honey-eyed flavor exploded on his palate. He gasped, but could not stop. Never had he tasted anything so delicious. He licked longer and deeper, parting her flesh with his fingers, needing the taste with the same urgency he needed to be one with the sea.

She lifted her leg over his shoulder and laughed

while he lapped into her like a parched beast. Sensations burst onto his tongue like wild colors. He bit her flesh, suckled and slurped. With her hands entwined in his hair, she held his face steady, encouraging his thirst with cries of triumph.

He snaked his hands up the inside of her thighs, parted her labia and bathed every inch of her with his mouth. His cock strained to the point of pain and the burning that had emanated from the fire now scorched him from the inside out.

With boldness born of lust, Reides grabbed Aphrodite's wrists and forced her to release her hold. He kissed a path up her body until the tip of his shaft teased the folds he'd saturated with his tongue. In one swift motion, he lifted her and impaled her on his sex. The sensations caused him to stagger until the smoke gathered around them in a hot, ashy thickness that buoyed his body as he pumped into her with unhampered ferocity.

The mirror dropped. Somewhere outside his consciousness, Reides heard the glass shatter into a thousand pieces. And he cared not. He cared for nothing but pleasuring the goddess. For now. For always.

TESSA PRINTED OUT the pages on the fastest setting possible. She didn't reread or edit, but grabbed the pages as they spilled off the printer and stuffed them into a manila envelope she'd rescued from the recycle bin. After a fortifying glass of scotch, she padded quietly to the dark bedroom where Colton slept and laid the envelope on the pillow beside his head.

He didn't stir. No big surprise. They'd packed a lot of punch into the day's activities—boating, shopping, eating, more boating, a little fishing, cooking, dinner, cleanup and then a soft, quiet session of lovemaking that had apparently tuckered him out. She fought the urge to reach out and touch the long lock of his hair that had fallen across his cheek. She couldn't wake him. She needed more sleep before he read what she'd so brazenly written.

After grabbing her pillow and an extra blanket, she left him snoring softly in her bedroom. She'd woken up only an hour after they'd finally fallen asleep and the scene had burst into her mind with such clarity, she'd had no choice but to sneak into the office and work until the fire of inspiration burned itself out. With a glance at the clock, she realized she'd worked for nearly four hours straight to produce a new scene that she'd had no business writing in the first place.

The scenario with Aphrodite, Reides and Alina had not been in the outline. Well, not in the same way. In the early version, Aphrodite had tempted both Reides and Alina with the magical psyche, coaxing them to use the dangerous creature as a way to enhance their sexual connection. The goddess had attempted a grand manipulation, but the lovers' loyalty, while tested, had prevailed.

In the scene that had woken her from sleep, Reides betrayed his true love with a goddess he couldn't resist. He cared for Alina, but circumstances only partly beyond his control pushed him to make love to the goddess he knew would ultimately destroy the woman he claimed to love. Tessa had written the pages from Reides' point of view—something that until now, she'd left to Colton. What would he think? Would he be angry that she'd invaded his turf? Would he see something in the scenario that she hadn't intended to reveal?

Unwilling to sequester herself in one of the guest rooms, Tessa whistled the dogs to her side. With them shuffling lazily beside her, still half-asleep, she unlocked the sliding-glass doors to the moonlit porch and settled into a hammock.

Artemis and Apollo circled a few times beneath her, then settled into a mass of dog fur, muscle and bone and instantly fell asleep.

Unfortunately for Tessa, sleep didn't come quite so easily.

COLTON HEARD the phone ring, but didn't look up from the pages he'd scattered across the bed. In the background, the sliding-glass door screeched open, followed by the patter of two adult feet and two sets of paws. Then a "hello" as she picked up the phone and a slam of a door. The office door, no doubt. Tessa had apparently gone back into work mode, whether he liked it or not.

Judging from the scene she'd just left for him on his pillow, she'd spent the night writing, proving one telling fact— she didn't need him anymore. Was this her way of dismissing him, showing him that his cooperation with the novel was no longer necessary since she could clearly write from Reides' point of view just fine without him? Or was there something more indicative embedded in the text, a message he'd have to analyze to understand?

He read the scene again, trying to ignore the steamy sexuality. By the time he flipped the last page over and Tessa appeared in the doorway, the only thing he decided for sure was that he hated every word.

"Good morning," she said softly, her brow furrowed.

Colton watched how her mouth pursed and for a moment, forgot about the scene she'd given him.

"What's wrong?"

Tessa swallowed, took a deep breath, then huffed out what he could best describe as a stunned sigh. "That was Audrey on the phone. There's a problem with the book. A big problem. One that very well could ruin everything I've worked for. Everything we've worked for." Her eyes grew glossier, but she valiantly fought back the tears. "And it's all my fault."

CHAPTER SIXTEEN

COLTON BOUNDED off the bed. The pages of the scene crackled beneath him, but he figured first things first.

"What happened?"

Tessa shook her head as if she either couldn't believe what she was about to say—or didn't want to. "I've been accused of plagiarism."

"What?"

With an expression of complete surrender to irony, Tessa strode across the room and sat on the bed, smack-dab in the middle of the scene she'd pounded out in the dead of night. "Audrey's been on the phone all morning. Apparently, I submitted some sample chapters to every major publisher in New York. Trouble is, I didn't write the story. I lifted it nearly word for word from an obscure piece of erotica written by a French author about fifteen years ago. Just my luck that one of the editors I supposedly submitted to read the piece recently and recognized it."

"You didn't submit anything. You don't do that, do you? That's Audrey's job."

"Apparently, the cover letter had her name on it. And mine."

Colton sat on the bed beside her. Even after his conversation the other night with his sister about Audrey's clean record, Colton had had a strong gut feeling that the agent had orchestrated the situation in order to build buzz for the book.

This situation, however, was entirely different. In the publishing world, plagiarism charges were dead serious. The act of stealing another author's words and passing them off as original was likely the lowest action a writer could take.

"Was it Audrey's stationery? Her postmark?"

Tessa shook her head. "I don't know all the details. Audrey said the editor who called was livid. Infuriated. Insulted. He promised to call *Publishers Weekly*, the *New York Times*—anyone who would love to jump on a story like this." She laughed, but the chuckle held nothing but bitterness. "I thought Daniel had trashed my reputation until there was nothing left. I guess I thought wrong."

Not knowing what else to do, Colton gingerly put his arm around her shoulder. "This is serious."

Tessa blew out a frustrated breath. "No one is going to touch me now, Colton, not without proof that whatever I'm submitting is mine and mine alone. I mean, it's not going to ruin my career, I won't let it. But, damn it, this isn't the type of notoriety I wanted!"

A heavy, burning pit formed in Colton's stomach. He knew the consequences of this situation would invariably touch both of them. He wasn't sure how, but he knew he had more than just a vested interest in Tessa to make him want to help. Not that he needed more motivation, but he had it. In spades.

"What do you want to do?"

"What can I do? Either roll over and accept my fate as a washed-up has-been or fight."

He cocked an eyebrow. "I wonder which one you'll choose."

This time, her laugh was more genuine. "What did you think of the scene?"

"I'd rather talk about who is trying to ruin you and why you think it's your fault."

She frowned, but nodded. "Well, after what Willa and Heather pulled the night before last, I'd say Daniel is our first suspect. This is so up his alley, going after my reputation. He trashed my personal life, but with no clout or knowledge about publishing, he couldn't touch me professionally."

Colton couldn't deny that Daniel had the most motivation to hurt Tessa, but such clever subtlety didn't seem like his style. "You're sure it was him?"

"No," she admitted. "But who else? You suspected Audrey for the mishandled proposal and I can see that. But why would she do this? It's career suicide."

"You think the screwup with Greenwise and this plagiarism thing are connected?"

She sat forward, elbows on knees. "Don't you?"

He concentrated. He didn't know. Chances were, the events were orchestrated by the same person, but at this point, they had too little information to go on. "Could have been anyone. The first time, the person who was trying to screw with you at least needed access to your computer, or mine, or Audrey's. For this little practical joke, they needed nothing more than the name of your agent and an old piece of erotica that nobody's ever read except for some jerk-off editor in New York."

She snagged her bottom lip in her teeth. "It reeks of Daniel. I can't help thinking he's somehow involved. Who else would want to ruin me?"

"His father?"

"From what you've told me, Martin has enough of his own problems to waste time messing around with a daughter-in-law he doesn't have to cut alimony checks to on his son's behalf. He wouldn't care."

"A rival writer?"

She snickered. "I'm not exactly Nora Roberts, Colton. Or Anne Rice or anyone else that the mass market has heard of and has reason to envy. No one even knows I'm writing again. The only person who would try to ruin me is Daniel."

Her point made sense. He had no idea how Daniel had discovered she'd started writing again, but the man did have the clout and the money to have any number of publishing people on his payroll.

"What do you want to do?"

Tessa shook her head and speared her fingers through her hair, which he just realized she obviously hadn't combed since she'd woken up. She was still in the silky tank top and pants she'd worn to bed the night before, though he'd noticed immediately upon waking that her side of the bed had been cold for many hours. Had she stayed up all night to write?

"I have no clue what to do," she admitted. "I guess I might as well take the direct approach and confront Daniel. We'll head over to Brew's before the lunch crowd and see what we can find out. But the most important thing I have to worry about is saving our book, our project. Now that my integrity has come into question, I don't know what's going to happen. We might have to wait to market the book until the furor dies down—if we can get it to die down at all."

Colton stood, watching as Tessa mindlessly gathered the pages of the scene she'd written and tapped them into a neat pile. He knew she was dying to know what he thought, but he wasn't sure he was ready to tell her.

"Why don't you go grab a shower? We'll go over to the island, have breakfast and plot our strategy with Daniel."

She contemplated his suggestion for a long moment, all the while staring at the scene she'd written, the one he'd yet to comment on. After a few more seconds, she left the pages on the bed and walked toward the door. "Sounds like a plan. In the meantime, I think I'll book a flight to New York. No matter who is responsible, I've got damage control to do."

At the forlorn weariness in her voice, he indulged the urge to cross the room and cup her cheek. "We have damage control to do. This is our book together, Tessa."

Glossiness quickly coated her eyes and she pressed her lips together tightly before speaking.

"You need to stay anonymous, Colton. Look at what's happened! Plagiarism, Colton. As a writer, I think I'd rather be accused of murder. My reputation was already in the crapper before this. Now all someone has to do is flush and I'm done as a writer. You don't need to put your good name at risk, too."

She was right. God, as much as he wanted to deny the truth, any association of his name with the blatant theft of someone else's words would not bode well for the journalism career he'd worked so hard to build. After all these years, he had finally earned the respect of his colleagues, the trust of politicians and community leaders and the confidence of his readership. The fact that she was innocent wouldn't matter. The accusations would make front-page copy, at least for the industry papers and magazines. No one would resist talking about such a sordid story, especially in light of Tessa's past, which would be heated up and served like a gossip's gourmet leftovers.

In a split second, he calculated how long he'd been in the newspaper business and the sum wasn't a small number. Could he really risk everything he'd worked so hard to build when Tessa could more than likely handle this all on her own?

Even though all his reasons for staying out of the situation stacked high and solid, Colton knew he had no real choice to make.

"We'll do this together, Tessa. That's just the way it has to be."

TESSA FLIPPED her cell phone closed after talking to Karen. Her attorney had been adamant. She could be in Key West in a couple of hours. If Tessa could just wait it out, Karen would confront Daniel and his attorney for her, carefully, without any allegations that might be misconstrued as slanderous. For the most part, Tessa didn't give a damn if Daniel sued her. She simply wanted to know the truth.

Colton came out of Brew's bar, his scowl verifying that her ex-husband was indeed inside, despite the early hour, just before ten o'clock.

"He's on the patio, helping with the setup."

"And his attorney?" she asked.

"Sowers is sitting at his regular table, pouring over some papers. A FedEx guy is in there having a coffee, waiting for Sowers to finish something that apparently needs to go out right away."

"So the lawyer's pressed for time?" she asked, figuring she could use the time crunch to her advantage. He wouldn't have as much leisure to argue small points.

"Looks that way. Tessa, what did Karen say?"

She rolled her eyes. As if he couldn't guess. "She said to wait for her."

He rubbed his nose, then looked at her from beneath those dreamy dark eyelashes of his. "Any way you're going to follow that advice?"

Lordy, it was already hot today. And dry. She needed a cool drink and no matter how much of a favorite she was around Brew's, she wasn't going to get served standing outside the door. "I told Karen to meet us in New York. She'll be more useful to us there. In fact, why don't you use your cell phone to check on our reservations?"

Colton shoved his hands into his pockets. "Nice try."

"You punched his lights out two nights ago. Do you really think he's going to want to talk with you around? Colton, this is my last shot. He finishes his community service today and then he's going to blow this Popsicle stand like there's no to-morrow. Once he's back on his home turf, the damage can only increase. If he's behind this mess, I need to stop him now."

With a frown that barely reflected his carefully checked rage, Colton clipped his cell phone off his belt and marched toward the corner at the end of the block where he'd get the best cell phone reception. She hated sending him away and if he thought she was doing so out of some need to confront her ex-husband on her own, he was sorely mistaken. She would have paid big money to have him by her side for this as he had been the past two times she and Daniel had tussled. She'd become strangely accustomed to having him near and for some reason, his presence didn't restrain her so much as make her bolder, more brazen.

But under the circumstances, she had to do this one on her own.

She walked inside and Sonia, who was filling saltshakers, gave her a shout-out.

"You're early today. What can I get you?"

"Just a bottled water," Tessa answered. She eyed the attorney, who was, as Colton described, sitting alone at his table, a cup of coffee balanced on top of a tottering stack of papers, folders and if she wasn't mistaken, court briefs. "Make that two, will you?"

Sonia waved and smiled while she screwed the last of the silver tops back onto the shakers. Tessa took a deep breath and strolled over to the attorney, trying not to look the least bit confrontational. With Daniel likely buzzing with the wild anger of a certain stinging insect, she decided she'd catch more bees with honey, just this once.

"Mr. Sowers?"

Startled, he looked up. His glasses slipped and he nearly upended his coffee, but Tessa caught the cup and put it safely on a nearby table.

"I'm sorry. Didn't mean to startle you."

"Mrs. Reese."

"Dalton, really, thanks. I hope you don't mind the interruption."

"I'm actually incredibly busy, trying to meet a deadline. Daniel is out on the patio. You should be pleased to know that we're taking the last flight out tonight, as soon as the sheriff verifies that my client has fulfilled his community service hours."

Tessa grinned, but not too much. As eager as she was for Daniel to leave, she couldn't seem overly anxious or she'd put the man on the defensive. Well, even more so than he clearly already was.

"I'm sure Daniel will be happy to put this incident behind him. Look," she said, then hesitated. She didn't like standing over him, giving the impression that she considered herself above him. With a gesture, she indicated her desire to sit and with nervous graciousness, he nodded his consent. "Thank you. Look, I want to make a few things very clear to you, things that might help you advise your client more effectively. Before Daniel showed up on my private island, I had no idea he intended to have anything to do with me during his vacation here. I did not ask my friends to make him feel unwelcome. He brought their rancor on himself when he treated me so badly during the divorce."

The attorney sniffed, but neither agreed nor objected.

"What I mean to say is, I don't want to fight with Daniel anymore. I don't want to talk to him or send messages to him through my attorney. I want our divorce to be a thing of the past and I intend to make sure my friends leave him alone from now on."

"That would be appreciated."

She smiled and nodded. Sonia bustled over with the bottled waters, which she deposited on the table next to theirs since Sowers had papers on every flat surface. Tessa grabbed a bottle and offered it to the attorney, who took it with a nod of thanks.

"Someone has put a plan in motion, Mr. Sowers, that will likely disrupt the forward momentum of my return to publishing." She'd rehearsed that line twice before leaving Speed Key, knowing she had to confront the lawyer in language he'd not only understand, but appreciate. His eyebrows narrowed, indicating that she indeed had his attention.

"And you suspect my client?"

"He has strong motives to want to hurt me."

"He didn't press charges against your lover. Wasn't that enough to make you believe he's dropped his vendetta against you?"

"It would have been his word against fifty witnesses who would have all claimed Daniel slipped, fell and smacked his face against a table," she replied, her voice steady and firm, but not defensive. She was stating a fact, not gloating—definitely not threatening. "I'm not here to play games, Mr. Sowers. I just want Daniel to leave me alone."

She heard Daniel chuckle behind her. *Damn.* She shouldn't have sat with her back to the patio entrance. She'd wanted to explain the situation to the lawyer, bring him on board, before she spoke with her ex.

"Leave you alone after all you've put me through this week?" he asked, his hand moving to his bruised and battered eye. "That's a fairly tall order."

Containing her anger as best as she could, Tessa turned to face him.

"I don't think it should be, Daniel," she replied. "You had plenty of practice ignoring me when we were married. Once you had a ring on my finger, a social secretary and a paid escort could have fulfilled your needs just as well as I did—and would have saved us both a ton of grief."

"Paid escorts usually don't come with pedigrees."

"Pedigrees don't mean shit, Daniel, and you know it."

He had a pedigree that would have made the members of the Kennel Club drool, and he was nothing more than a mongrel who knew only how to attack and to hurt. She kept that opinion to herself. She hadn't come here to pick a fight.

He wiped his hands on a white towel dangling from his apron. "What do you want, Tessa?"

How he managed to still sound superior and pretentious was beyond her.

She stood, crossing her arms blithely over her chest.

"I want to know if you're the one who's trying to keep me from publishing my new novel."

Daniel's face twisted into an expression that was a combination of disgust and disbelief. Daniel was a good liar—but only when he'd had time to prepare and practice. "Why would I give a damn if you ever publish those trashy books of yours again?"

No matter his initial surprise, she had to push further and make sure she was barking up the wrong tree. "Because you know it hurt me to lose my career before."

His laugh was hollow. "The money you made from your 'career' barely covered the cost of the electricity bill to keep your computer running, much less your clothes and jewelry."

"That may be, but you know I loved writing. If you didn't know that, you wouldn't have used it to attack me in court."

"How soon you forget," he said with a snicker. "I would have used anything to attack you in court. Reeses don't like to lose."

"Then maybe it's your father. Maybe he's the—"

Daniel cut her off with a flat palm in the air. "Save your suspicions, Tessa. After this week in Key West, one thing has been made perfectly clear to me. You're not worth my time anymore. In fact, you're nothing but trouble. You always have been."

For some odd reason, Daniel's assessment made Tessa smile, even warmed her a little right in the general area of her heart.

"It's not so easy to attack me now that I have my own friends, is it?"

Had he less manners, he probably would have spit on the floor, judging by the disgusted look on his face. "Your so-called friends are yokels and freaks and prime candidates for the mental ward."

Tessa stood, her grin now reaching from ear to ear. "God help me for saying this, but for once in your pathetic life, Daniel, you're right about something. My friends are all those things, but they are also loyal and clever and determined. You keep that in mind if you ever decide to try and come after me again, you hear?"

Daniel jerked forward, but Tessa stood her ground even when the attorney jumped to his feet and grabbed Daniel tightly around the arm. "Four hours, Mr. Reese. That's all you have left here. Let's not do anything to jeopardize your legal situation, please?"

With a nod and a quick goodbye to Sonia, Tessa left the bar, suddenly and for the first time, truly feeling released from the albatross that was her past. Daniel didn't matter anymore. She'd been telling herself that for over a year, but now, she'd stared down the truth of it and triumphed. By the time she caught up to Colton leaning against a palm tree on the corner of Simonton and Eaton, she was practically skipping.

He flipped his cell phone closed and eyeing her obvious glee, smiled at her with wary eyes. "So I take it you caught Daniel red-handed?"

She bounced on the balls of her feet. "Nope. He's clean.

He's too self-absorbed with his own petty dramas to dig deep enough into my life to pull off such an attack. Besides, he's not making a move without his mouthpiece and Sowers is working overtime to keep Daniel out of my face."

"What about your former father-in-law?"

She'd meant to fish around with Daniel for more information on Martin Reese, but the conversation hadn't gone in that direction, at least, not for long.

"You told me yourself that Martin was wrapped up in some serious problems in Chicago," Tessa reasoned. "Why would he bother to spend any of his time or resources on me a year after I kicked his son to the curb? Doesn't make sense."

Despite that she had absolutely no clue who might be trying to ruin her reputation as a professional author, Tessa couldn't keep herself still. To a tune she heard only in her own mind, she danced around, spinning in clumsy pirouettes and delighting in the way her breezy skirt fluttered in the wind.

Colton crossed his arms tightly over his chest. "Just what did you drink when you were in Brew's? Did Daniel slip you something?"

Tessa stopped humming long enough to answer. "He slipped me my freedom."

"You've had that for over a year."

"Yeah, that's what I thought, too. Boy, was I ever wrong."

With nothing to stop her, nothing to hamper her overwhelming enthusiasm for the very simple practice of breathing, Tessa launched herself into Colton's arms. She wrapped her legs around his waist, nearly throwing him off balance, until she pressed her lips against his and they tapped into that certain equilibrium only they seemed to share. Kissing him out in the sunshine, in the middle of a street bustling with tourists and locals alike, her skirt flying high and probably revealing her panties, Tessa experienced a keenness of sensation she'd never felt before. Her lips and tongue and teeth seemed to vibrate as the flavors of Colton's mouth merged with hers— tangy orange juice and cool breath mint. His cologne tempted her with spicy heat and seductive promises. Even the muscles in his chest, arms and legs supported her with undeniable strength and power.

When they stumbled back against the sturdy trunk of the palm tree, they both laughed, but didn't break the magnetic connection of their lips.

"We're making fools of ourselves," he murmured.

"Yes," she agreed, then tugged her arms around him more tightly.

With a weary groan, Colton pushed her back. Not too much, just enough so he could look into her eyes. "Our flight leaves in three hours. We need to pack."

Tessa liked the idea of returning to the island, but she couldn't care less if she had a change of clothes and clean underwear for the next couple of days. She just wanted Colton to satisfy other, more pressing needs. "Back to the island sounds perfect."

With Colton buoying her bottom with his hands, she hopped down, and then gave a little wave to the gaggle of red-hatted women in purple shorts who'd stopped just outside of the Simonton Court Inn to watch their display. At Tessa's unabashed acknowledgment, the women applauded and Colton turned the color of a British tourist who'd forgotten to apply sunscreen.

Invigorated, Tessa grabbed Colton's hand and started back toward the pier. His stride didn't quite match the skip in her step, but he kept up all the way to the boat and without instruction this time, released all the appropriate lines while Tessa powered up the engines and eased out of the slip.

Once they were clear of the no-wake zone, Tessa pushed

the speedboat to full throttle, sending Colton stumbling a few steps where he landed in one of the padded chairs.

"Whoa, Tessa. What's the rush?"

She laughed, throwing back her hair and allowing the wind to stream through it until she knew she must look like a madwoman.

As if he didn't know.

CHAPTER SEVENTEEN

EVEN OVER THE HUM of the engines and the slashing of the waves against the hull, Colton heard Tessa's sigh as soon as they neared Speed Key. An unfamiliar boat sat on the narrow beachfront near the dock and not too far from that, Leroy Brewster tossed a spongy football to Artemis and Apollo. The dogs hardly noticed their owner's return to the island, but Colton knew that wasn't why Tessa looked so incredibly disappointed.

After easing the throttle into neutral, she let the waves propel the boat into the slip. Before he even had a chance to catch his balance, she leaped onto the bow and tied off the line. She was accustomed to managing on her own, and for the first time since he'd come to Key West, that little detail bothered the heck out him.

"Brew is going to watch the dogs while we're gone," Tessa informed him, her voice low, as if a whisper could hide her frustration.

Colton smiled and tried to offset her distress with a peck of a kiss on her nose.

It didn't work.

"He's early," he said with a growl. Tessa hadn't been the only one looking forward to a little alone time. Since he'd met her on the sidewalk, giddy and amorous, he'd been torn. Of course, he wanted to make love to her—he was starting to suspect that he'd never tire of that particular activity, even after, oh, say, fifty years or so—but an anvil of tension was hanging over their heads. Well, over his head. The contents of the scene she'd written in the middle of the night still haunted him, not because she'd written from Reides' point of view without him—he really couldn't care less about that.

But Reides had cheated. He'd surrendered to his lust for Aphrodite and left his one true love, Alina, to suffer the tortuous and degrading fate of a woman enthralled by some weird sexual sea creature. What was going on in Tessa's mind that would push her imagination in that direction?

Clearly, his question would have to wait until they reached New York. Tessa grabbed her bag and Colton gathered the water bottles they'd used and tossed them in the cooler.

"I need to show Brew a few things, where things are and such. I forgot I'd asked him to meet us here," she said, her voice lilting with apology.

"Hey, that's cool," Colton said. "This is probably the first time you've left the dogs since you moved here, right?" The turn in conversation lessened the thick, heavy feeling in Colton's gut.

"Brew doesn't take many days off, but he was fishing this morning when I called and asked him to puppy-sit. Willa is on duty and Heather hates to travel by boat, so I'm lucky he was willing to help out."

He laughed. "Heather doesn't like boats and she lives in Key West?"

Tessa smiled and shook her head as if she couldn't understand her friend's aversion, either. "You can live here for years and never go on a boat, you know. I have a sneaking suspicion that they didn't even have water where Heather grew up."

"Which is?"

Tessa shrugged. "She won't say. Says she left her past behind her the minute she set foot on Duval Street. I'm the last person on earth who would question that philosophy."

And Colton was the last person on earth to want to broach that topic now that Tessa had clearly made some serious headway. He'd always suspected that the hurts Tessa had experienced in her marriage and high-profile divorce had been too overwhelming for her to release in just a year's time, but this trip had convinced him. Clearly, she'd been tethered by the betrayals of her past and as much as she'd tried to act otherwise, her ex-husband's appearance in Key West had thrown her into a turmoil of emotions—a turmoil that had suddenly calmed. He had no idea exactly what had transpired between Tessa and Daniel at Brew's a little while ago, but some sort of revelation had clearly injected her with that free-spirited love of life he hadn't really seen in her since the first night he'd stepped off Willa's boat.

Brew tossed the ball beyond the wall of foliage and the dogs disappeared in a barking, snarling rush.

"This a good time?" Brew asked.

Colton chuckled to himself while Tessa pulled her father's old friend into a hug. "Well, I was about to get lucky, but them's the breaks."

Brew scowled and Tessa had to sock him in the arm to jump-start his sense of humor. "You check out the house?"

"I still remember where everything is, if that's what you're asking. I threw my gear into the old guest room by the pool table. That cool?"

"*Mi casa es su casa,*" she replied. "I'm going in to pack. You sure you don't mind staying with my pups for a few days?"

With a tilted half smile, Brew shooed Tessa toward the house. "Seems like old times, crashing here, waking up with that amazing view, tapping into Rip's old wine cellar, which I've noticed you're keeping up. Yeah, I think I can suffer through."

She pointed a wagging finger at him. "No parties, young man."

At Brew's chuckle, Colton figured it was time for him to head toward the house, as well, and toss his things in his duffel. He might have caught up with Tessa on the walkway up to the house if not for Brew's viselike grip around his arm.

"Hang on there, Chicago. I'd like a word."

The dogs had retrieved their toy, but after Tessa took a second to wiggle her eyebrows in Colton's direction, she whistled to her pets and they followed her in. By the time Colton had turned, Brew had pulled a cigar out of his shirt pocket. Dressed in a braided captain's hat, an oversized and overwashed button-down with four pockets, a pair of loose khaki shorts with tattered hems and sandals that had likely lost both their flip and their flop over the past decade, Brew epitomized the look of a Key West Conch. From his frazzled hair and beard to his weathered skin, Colton figured he could be the poster-boy for living life at a leisurely pace. He wondered how long Brew had had the pub, how he'd known Rip Dalton and why a man his age was fooling around with a woman as young as Willa. But he stashed his reporter's instincts. For one, Colton doubted Ben would answer any of his questions. And two, Colton knew he'd been kept behind to be on the receiving end of a stern talking-to. His father had had the same look in his eyes many, many times.

"You smoke?" Brew asked, gesturing with the cigar, still in the protective plastic tube.

Colton shrugged and nodded toward the boathouse. They sat on a newly painted bench, their backs to the island and nothing but a glorious blue sea and sky in front. "A good cigar is impossible to pass up on a day like today."

"Well, these suck, but they do the trick."

Colton accepted the tube and in silence, they bit, spat and

lit their stogies until pungent, slightly cherry-scented smoke coiled into the air.

"You and Tessa getting serious?" he asked.

"Define serious," Colton countered, puffing lightly. One man's serious could be another man's fancy-free fling.

"You're sleeping with her."

"Is that your business?"

"No, but I know you are, so let's skip over the bullshit."

Colton cleared his throat. "I don't mean to be rude, but Tessa's over thirty, which makes her old enough to make her own choices."

"To be honest, I really don't give a shit what Tessa does with her private life, except for one thing."

Colton took a drag off the cigar, let the tobacco flavor roll around his mouth before blowing out the smoke. "Her father?"

Brew stretched his arms out from shoulders to fingers. "Rip was my best friend. We grew up together on the island, fished the same waters, dated the same chicks. He fronted me the money to start the pub so he'd have somewhere to hang out. If he were still alive, he probably wouldn't care who his daughter screwed around with."

"Are you giving me a talk on Willa's behalf, then?"

Brew sat back, his expression skewed in confusion. "Willa? She likes you. She wouldn't see any reason to sic me on you."

"Then what is this man-to-man discussion all about?"

"This is about me, my boy. Tessa don't know shit about this, but when she came back to Key West and opened up the house again, I remembered stuff I hadn't thought about in years. What it felt like to be young, living large and not giving a crap what people thought about you. Rip's death hit me hard, too hard. But now my life is back to normal and I thank Tessa for that."

"What did she do?"

Brew chuckled. "Nothing much. She just needed me. Sometimes that's all it takes."

Colton wasn't sure how to respond, so he concentrated on smoking his cigar down a few inches, enjoying the breeze on his neck and the steady beat of the waves against the dock. He'd done a lot of self-exploration over the past year since meeting Tessa, but he'd never looked at their relationship in such a simple way. The women he'd dated before, the women who'd left him so cold despite their beauty, impeccable manners and perfect suitability had all needed him in some way, but more as a steady escort to fund-raising dinners or for political clout—or for sex.

Tessa's needs were more elemental, more personal. She'd needed the kick in the pants he'd given her when her self-confidence had been shot and her ability to write had fallen by the wayside. More recently, she'd needed him to challenge her status quo, to coax out the sexually free and un-hampered woman she toyed with becoming. She'd needed him simply to be who he was. Her other half, perhaps?

Or was he imagining and oversimplifying in order to justify the fact that leaving her would be equal to cutting out his heart and throwing it into the surf? Because no matter how he formed his words, he doubted he'd ever get Tessa to admit how entwined their lives had become. In fact, if she fully realized how she'd come to rely on him—and he on her—she'd likely jump into the closest speedboat and zoom away without out a backward glance.

"You'd better get on up to the house," Brew said. "You go fix this thing with her in New York, but you make sure she comes back."

"I couldn't take her away from her home."

Instead of nodding as Colton expected, Brew's bushy eyebrows lifted over uncertain eyes. "You do what you have to, boy, to keep her happy."

Colton stood and without another word, marched back to the house. More than anything, he wanted to follow Brew's orders. He just wasn't entirely certain he knew how.

BY THE TIME THEY STEPPED into the lobby of Audrey's building in the Soho section of New York City, Tessa had the unexplainable urge to grab the nearest post or column or archway and hold on for dear life. Everything from the mad dash to pack, to the overbooked flight, to the delayed landing at LaGuardia, to the traffic in Manhattan had created a tornado of tension and activity Tessa couldn't wait to escape from.

She should have made Audrey come to Key West where they could have discussed this disturbing turn of events over margaritas and a sunset, but she had to face reality. Though she could write anywhere, publishing happened in NYC. She had to give Audrey the home-field advantage if they were going to settle this quickly and, with any luck, discreetly.

"Ms. Dalton?"

Tessa caught sight of a pretty brunette in an efficient black suit and adorable, spiked shoes. "I'm Cynthia Beck, Audrey's assistant."

Though still aching to grab something sturdier than a woman's hand, Tessa accepted Cynthia's gesture with firm politeness. "Nice to meet you in person, Cynthia. This is Colton Granger, my…friend."

She hesitated, but only because she wasn't sure what Cynthia knew, if anything, about Colton's partnership on the book. And saying "lover" just seemed too, well…obvious. But mainly, she still hoped they could keep his collaboration with her on the book out of the spotlight. It was bad enough that Tessa might lose her reputation as an artist and businesswoman. She couldn't imagine the fallout in Colton's career if his relationship with her and the book hit the news under the dark cloud of plagiarism accusations. Every word he'd ever committed to print would be called into question, every clever idea or award he'd won would become shadowed in suspicion. She couldn't do that to someone she cared about. Someone she probably even loved, if she'd take a few minutes to face reality.

"Is Audrey waiting for us?" Colton asked, shaking Cynthia's hand and then moving toward the bank of elevators, his shoulders and arms laden with their luggage, which they hadn't had time to deposit at the hotel since they still didn't know how long they would stay in New York.

"Yes. Your attorney," she said to Tessa, "has been here for the past hour shooting off all sorts of faxes and tying up phone lines. She's scary."

Tessa laughed, tempering her chuckle only after the guys getting off the elevator looked at her funny. What? No one in New York City had a sense of humor?

"Karen is not one to be crossed, that's for sure," she admitted. "I'm hoping she and Audrey will have the situation under control and we'll all be able to get on with our lives."

Cynthia nodded and pressed the button to the tenth floor. "Is there anything I can get you?"

Tessa watched the panel as the numbers rose. "I'm guessing a Rum Runner is out of the question."

For an instant, Cynthia's brown eyes narrowed with concern, but then she grinned, either catching on to the joke or managing to hide her initial reaction.

"Nothing is ever out of the question," she told them. "But Rum Runners would be hard to come by in a Manhattan office building. I can see what I can do, though," she said, eyeing Tessa uncertainly.

Colton shuffled closer to the wall when two women entered on the eighth floor. "Coffee will suffice, Cynthia, thanks. We'll reserve our celebrations until after this mess is handled, okay?"

"City slicker," Tessa groused, rolling her eyes.

"Lush," he shot back with a chuckle.

And despite their hushed voices vibrating with contained laughter, Cynthia looked effectively scandalized while the two other passengers tried their best to ignore them.

"So, Cynthia," Tessa asked, her volume vibrating in the tight space. "How long have you been with Audrey?"

"Six months a week from Tuesday," she answered quickly.

Right around the time Tessa started writing again. "Who did you work for before?"

They stopped on the ninth floor and the two women got out. Had they not heard of stairs?

"I was an intern at a publishing house."

"Really? Which one?"

Cynthia said the name and while Tessa was familiar with the company, she knew very little about what they published or who wrote for them. She wasn't sure if they published erotica or erotic fiction—information that would be useful.

Though Tessa had vehemently denied any possibility of Audrey's connection to the premature submission of their novel to Greenwise, a screwup by the assistant had always been a possibility in the back of her mind. Meeting Cynthia made her doubt that scenario. She was young, yes. But also professional in that crisp sort of way that likely made her a valuable asset to Audrey. She couldn't see Cynthia making such a boneheaded mistake. On the other hand, she was new and clearly eager. Maybe she'd thought she was being proactive when she'd sent in the submission.

They arrived on the tenth floor and Cynthia took a bag from Colton and directed him where to place the other two. Once they were unencumbered, Cynthia ushered them into Audrey's office, which overlooked Bryant Park. Audrey had leased the space before Mayor Giuliani had transformed Times Square, just a block away, into a tourist Mecca. Tessa knew her agent was sitting on prime New York real estate and would likely do just about anything to stay there.

Anything but betray Tessa.

The moment she and Colton crossed the threshold, Audrey jumped out of her chair. Karen, sitting on a corner of the desk, speaking forcefully toward the speakerphone, gave them a little wave. Audrey, on the other hand, greeted them with full-fledged hugs—even Colton, whom she'd never met.

"How was your flight?"

Tessa stuck out her tongue. "Long and cramped and devoid of warmth and blue sky and ocean."

"You're spoiled," Audrey said softly.

"Yes, I am," Tessa responded, equally quiet while Karen barked about libel lawsuits to whomever was on the other end of the phone. "But I'll deal. Any headway on figuring out who sent the submission?"

Audrey combed her fingers through her stylishly cropped gray hair. "We haven't really had that much time to deal with that side. Karen and I have been focusing on keeping the plagiarism accusation out of the media and convincing all the publishers who received the submission that you didn't send it."

Colton ran his fingers through his mussed hair, leaving a couple of strands standing up at an angle that made her giggle.

"What?"

Purposefully forgetting why she was here and who she was with, Tessa walked her fingers up his chest and then smoothed his hair into place. She didn't care that she'd just struck Audrey and Karen dumb with her actions. They needed to know that things had…progressed between her and Colton. They weren't just business partners anymore.

Not that they ever had been.

Karen disconnected her phone call and like Audrey, greeted both of them with a hug.

"You ready to talk turkey?" Karen said, gesturing toward the chairs in front of Audrey's desk.

"No," Tessa admitted, "but we have no choice, so let's get this over with."

As they sat, Cynthia popped in with a fresh carafe of coffee, bagels and mugs and promptly disappeared while Audrey took care of the hospitality.

Tessa accepted a mug with graciousness and wrapped her freezing-cold hands around the heated cup. She was all for air-conditioning, but something about the artificial air in the office building made her twice as cold as she would have been at home.

"Where are we so far?" she asked.

Karen added cream to her coffee as she spoke. "As far as we can tell, the bogus submissions were sent to eight major publishers, all addressed to editors who'd done interviews in a November issue of *Publishers Weekly* saying they were actively looking for erotica."

Audrey toyed with her empty mug. "Cynthia pulled the article and no other editors were mentioned. I checked around with a few other editors who were not interviewed in the article and no one received the submission. I think we've got them all."

"What did you do about the submissions?" Colton asked.

"Karen wrote a letter that I sent on my letterhead informing these publishers that the submission was bogus and sent specifically to damage Tessa's reputation. I asked them to hold on to the complete submissions, letters, envelopes, everything, until I sent a messenger to pick them up so that we could pursue criminal or civil action."

Tessa glanced at Karen. "Is this a criminal offense?"

Karen adjusted her glasses. "I'm a general practice attorney. I don't know that much about criminal law, especially in New York City. But I'm thinking that if we can prove who sent the submission in, we can at least sue for defamation. I have a call in to an old friend who is with the prosecutor's office here in New York. If this is a criminal offense somehow, she'll let me know."

"What about damage control?"

Audrey blew out a frustrated breath. "I think I got everyone to stay hush-hush about this for at least a few more days."

"Do they believe I didn't send it? That someone was setting me up?"

Biting her bottom lip, Audrey hesitated before answering. "Most of them are too busy to give a damn. Two had the class and foresight to be outraged on your behalf. A couple thought maybe that high-profile divorce of yours had sent you into some sort of psychotic tizzy and implied you should see a shrink."

Tessa took a big swig of the hot coffee to keep from cursing at someone who didn't deserve to hear her reaction.

Colton picked up the slack. "That's insulting. I hope you wrote those editors' names down because when we do send out *Son of the Siren*, we won't even give them a chance to bid."

Audrey's brown eyes brightened. "You're ready to send it out?"

Tessa couldn't breathe. After giving Colton the scene she'd written this morning, she could have sworn she'd screwed up any possibility of marketing the book with him. And the plagiarism scam had only made her more certain that his association with her was a horrible idea. Sure, they made great friends and even better lovers, but as a business associate, she was poison.

She stood up and stalked from the chair to the window behind Audrey's desk.

"I still have to work out a few details with Tessa," he replied cautiously, "but if we can clear this all up, I'm willing to sign over whatever rights you need me to so that Tessa can sell her story."

She spun around. *Her* story? It was their story!

Karen and Audrey both shifted uncomfortably, glancing over their shoulders at Tessa. Audrey's frown practically cut her face into two distinct halves, neither of them happy.

"What's wrong?" Tessa asked, returning to her chair.

Audrey stared at Karen, who held up her hands in surrender. Whatever news they had, Karen wasn't going to be the one to tell them.

After glancing around and realizing no one was coming to her rescue, Audrey took a deep breath and spit it out. "We can't sell this book."

"What?" Tessa asked.

"Not the way we originally planned," Audrey clarified. "Your integrity has been called into question, Tessa. You know how publishers are with plagiarism accusations. Lawsuits and countersuits—they cost too much money to pursue and defend. Even though this whole thing was a bogus attempt to hurt you and we've done our best to control the impact, some of the damage is already done."

Tessa sat back in the chair, her stomach aching and her lungs tight. "They won't trust that anything I send them is mine anymore, will they?"

Audrey reluctantly shook her head.

"Not at the moment. You can wait a year or so, let this all die down," Karen suggested. "But in all reality, Tessa, when you couple the accusations hurled during the divorce and now the shadow of plagiarism, you're a legal risk to any publisher who picks up your contract. You're an invitation to every crackpot wanna-be author to say you stole their stuff."

Colton leaned forward. "But Tessa wrote this—the idea was entirely hers. I'm a witness and my credentials are impeccable."

Audrey and Karen exchanged glances.

"You're willing to put your name on this project?" Audrey said, her eyes wide.

Colton frowned. He looked at Tessa and the longer their stares locked, the more pronounced his frown became. Deep lines furrowed his forehead and his eyes darkened with such sadness, Tessa forgot to breathe.

"No," he replied. "I'm sorry, Tessa, but I can't put my name on the book with you. Not now. Not in a year. Not ever."

CHAPTER EIGHTEEN

TESSA RAISED HER CHIN. "Wow. Well, that decision is made. Clearly, there's no point in discussing any of this. Sorry, ladies," she said to Audrey and Karen in her most flippant tone, "wasted trip."

She stalked back to the window, her arms crossed tightly. Tension crackled through the room like static electricity.

Colton took a deep breath. He'd pissed her off, as he suspected he would, even if making her angry and putting her on the defensive hadn't been his intention. His reasons weren't selfish for once in his life. He had to show Tessa that she didn't need him to win back her credibility. She could do this on her own. She deserved to.

With a glance, Colton convinced Karen and Audrey to leave the room. On her way out the door, Karen took a second to pat him on the arm in support, and then shut the door behind her.

"That's not what I meant, Tessa," he said, not rising from his chair. He didn't want this to be a full-blown confrontation, but at the moment, he had no choice but lay his cards on the table. Things had changed from even a day ago, much less a week ago when he'd first made his deal with her about the book, or all those months ago when they'd first started writing. He knew without a doubt that she had expected his cooperation—and God help him, he wanted to give his consent more than anything in the world.

Mainly because he loved her. He wasn't ready to say it out loud because he was one hundred percent certain she wasn't ready to hear it. But he loved how she turned to ice when she was angry, how her chin turned to stone and her eyes blazed with fire. He loved how she thought alcohol and a sunset would cure all ills and how she could dance the Electric Slide until someone shot a hole in the jukebox. He loved how she stood by her wacky friends and how she would move heaven and earth to help those few and cherished people who'd proved their loyalty in the weirdest, but most clever of ways.

He loved how she fed the dogs scraps from the table, how she thought fresh fish was fine to serve for dinner every night of the week and how she slept in a room that looked like a sultan's harem.

He loved her sun-streaked hair. Her slightly crooked eyetooth. The fact that she could change the timing on a complicated boat engine, but hadn't driven a car in almost a year.

And yet, no matter how his love stretched into every aspect and facet of her life, he had to keep his emotional revelation to himself. First, they had to figure out the business side of their relationship. Only then could they concentrate on the personal side in the way it deserved.

"Not what you meant?" she asked, not bothering to turn around and face him. "Then why don't you do a quick revision? Sounds to me like you're jumping ship because the engine fire is about to burn your award-winning, respected journalistic ass."

He smiled at her choice of words and he was very glad she wasn't facing him. Truth was, he didn't care all that much for his clout in journalism, not when compared to what he felt for this woman who'd clammed up tighter than a dead scallop in a stew.

God, he even thought like she did now. He'd never cooked a scallop in his life.

"I only mean that you shouldn't need my name on the book," he explained. "You can write the rest without me and market it without me. You'll have huge success and accolades. Your readers are going to love this story. You proved that this morning."

She twisted around, her eyes narrow and sharp. Did her lips really quiver or was he imagining the vulnerable signal?

"This is all about the scene, isn't it?" she asked. "I was pretty sure you hated it since you haven't said a word since I left it on your pillow, but I didn't think you'd bail on me just because I took the story in another direction."

"I'm not bailing on you," he said, standing. "I'm in this for the long haul, Tessa. I'll do whatever it takes to help you and *Son of the Siren* succeed. But you don't need my name on the cover to be successful."

She lifted her chin a little higher. "Audrey says I do."

"Audrey's right, but only to a point. I understand that I'll need to vouch for you, share our e-mails, provide whatever I can to verify that you wrote the vast majority of the book. I can write letters, glad-hand industry bigwigs—you name it and I'll do it. Although…"

"What?" she snapped.

"People may not believe me. We are, after all, lovers. They might assume that I'm just using my clout to help you because you give good head."

For a moment, the righteous indignation and anger on her face disappeared. She snorted a laugh and then turned away again. He knew the last thing she wanted to do right now was find humor in any of this. The book and her success meant too much to her. But they had a rhythm, he and Tessa. One that defied propriety and expectations. He had to hold on to that for as long as he could.

With her hands on the window, Tessa leaned her forehead

on the glass. "If you'll just put your name on the cover with mine, we'll be set. You did write half. It's only fair."

"I've never really written half," he said, moving closer now that her anger had decreased from boil to simmer. "More like a quarter, perhaps a third."

"You hated that scene," she said.

"Yes, I did."

"Because I wrote it?"

"No."

"Because it was a Reides scene? You always wrote those."

"We didn't have any agreement. Things just sort of fell into a pattern. But if you count the scenes from Alina's point of view and the ones from Aphrodite, you've written more of the book than I have. And you also wrote the outline on your own. You're an amazing writer, Tessa. You don't need me to make this book a success."

"You're wrong. I never would have written a word if not for you."

He nodded, closed the rest of the distance between them and slipped his hands around her waist. "You would have, eventually. I just kicked you in the butt and got you started. We'll do what it takes to make sure Audrey can market the book, okay? But I think we have something much more important to pursue."

Tessa glanced over her shoulder, a sultry look darkening her eyes to deep, emerald green.

"Okay, two things," he replied. "But first things first. I have every confidence that Audrey and Karen can handle the situation here, don't you?"

She leaned her head back against his shoulder. "Yes, I do. I hope to hell you're suggesting we go back to Key West because now I remember why I hate New York so much. I hate the buildings, so tall and all sharp glass and concrete. Not a tiki hut in sight."

Colton winced. "That's not exactly good news."

She twisted around in his arms. "Why not?"

"Because where I think we should head next has the tallest building in the Western hemisphere."

She eyed him skeptically. "You want to go to Chicago? Do you have something you need to take care of?"

"Absolutely. Tessa, we've explored every possibility of who might have wanted to screw up your career. I think we both agree that Cynthia is too sincere, literal and efficient to lie about sending the proposal to the wrong editor, right?"

"Right."

"And Martin Reese probably hasn't thought about you in months with the grand jury meeting. And Daniel, well, you said yourself you didn't think he gave enough of a damn about you to go to the trouble of finding an old work of erotica, having someone type it up and submit it to eight major publishers in your name just to ruin your reputation again. Who else is there?"

Tessa shook her head. "I had a lot of people turn against me in West Palm Beach, but I was old news five minutes after the network trucks pulled out of town. I haven't published a book in over two years, so professional rivals are out, unless I have some crazy stalker I don't know about. I hate to say something as arrogant as I don't have any enemies, but Colton, I really don't think I do."

Colton nodded. He agreed on every point. "That's why I want to go to Chicago."

Her eyebrows disappeared into her bangs. "To bait Martin?"

Colton shrugged. "I can't rule out Martin Reese anymore, Tessa. He's a powerful man. He even owns a good deal of stock in the computer company that runs my e-mail server. I checked. There is a very slim chance he could have somehow accessed my files."

"But you don't think he's the one?"

"Not exactly. Look, I have no proof, but what if *you* aren't the target of this craziness? What if I'm the one this person is after?"

Tessa pressed her lips together tightly and after a moment of quiet concentration, sat on the low credenza beneath Audrey's window. "I hadn't thought about that."

Colton cleared a space and eased down beside her. "I know, neither had I. Everything happened while we were on your turf and since it all connected to you and your agent, I never really thought to look down other avenues. But I think it's time we did."

Her hands locked tight on the edge of the bookshelf, Tessa leaned over and pressed her head on his shoulder. "I've always heard Lake Michigan was a beautiful shade of turquoise."

He laughed. "I've seen it rival any ocean on the right summer day. I promise, Tessa, you'll enjoy the view from my condo. And a whole lot more."

FIVE MINUTES into the flight, Tessa fell asleep. Colton politely waved away the flight attendant passing out warm towels and adjusted the blanket around Tessa's shoulders. The longer he looked at her, the more the deep, heavy feeling melted away— a feeling that had sat in the middle of his chest since their discussion in Audrey's office. They'd come to no clear conclusion about the book and his name and reputation or her future in publishing, but they'd made a few interim decisions. First, Karen and Audrey were going to continue to concentrate on damage control in New York, keeping the incident out of the press. Second, he and Tessa were going to explore the possibility that Colton had been the object of this smear campaign, and that Tessa had suffered only collateral damage.

The possibility had caught her off guard and she'd spent

the entire drive to the airport badgering him about who would want to ruin him this way. Unlike Tessa, his list could go on for days. As a political columnist, he had no shortage of enemies who understood the power of a good scandal. He also had more than his fair share of professional rivals who might have the investigative skills to delve into the secret life he and Tessa shared.

Then there was Martin Reese. If the old man had caught wind of his interactions with Tessa, the rich son of a bitch could have made it his mission to destroy them both. Even before the messy Palm Beach divorce, he'd hated Colton intensely for not buying into his noble intentions of redeveloping the depressed neighborhoods of Chicago. And he harbored no love for his ex-daughter-in-law because she hadn't rolled over for his attorneys like a good, obedient little girl, signing the divorce papers and disappearing without a cent to her name. Together, Tessa and Colton gave Martin Reese a lot of reasons to hate them. His troubles with the grand jury might keep him from pursuing Tessa for revenge, but Colton was damned certain Reese would make time for retribution if he knew Colton and Tessa were lovers. Especially if the case against him currently being heard by the Cook County grand jury resulted in indictments. He'd have nothing to lose.

Colton had tried to reassure Tessa that they'd get to the bottom of the trouble before sunset the next day, but as the soft hum of the flight lulled him into quiet thought, Colton wasn't so sure.

If Reese was behind this, the situation could get very complicated and very ugly. Both of them could easily lose everything they'd worked for. She, her self-respect and desire to write. He, his reputation as a proponent of truth. In the beginning, he'd justified his secret project with Tessa as being personal, a part of his private life he didn't have to share with his readers. But if things went badly, he wasn't sure his readers—or the advertisers, and therefore, his bosses—would be so quick to understand.

All this weighed too heavily on his mind to allow him to sleep, so he decided to use this red-eye flight from New York to Chicago to accomplish a few important tasks. So much was at stake. In his love life, in his career, in his very existence. His and Tessa's relationship might have started with no strings attached, but they were now connected in ways he couldn't completely comprehend. And untangling was not an option. What he had to do, he was sure, was weave those links together to form a bond neither of them would ever want to escape.

First, he unpacked his BlackBerry from his duffel and established a wireless connection to the Internet. From there, he sent a few e-mails to his editor, his assistant and some of his colleagues at the paper. He checked in with a researcher on a column he'd been working on, then hooked in his expanded keyboard and, certain Tessa was trapped in her exhaustion, began to type.

The arrow sliced through the air and found its mark. Warm, sticky, icy ooze slid against Alina's skin, breaking the spell that entranced her. In moments, her eyes focused, as much as they could from the bottom of the fountain. Submerged deep beneath the water, her lungs instantly squeezed hot and tight with the intense need for air.

She kicked her legs wildly, her arms and hands clawing up from the deep pool. She burst through the surface and gulped air, choking on the sultry night wind that tossed through the olive trees planted near the marble ledge. Water rained down her face, filling her mouth with a bitter flavor that made her gag. She lifted her hand to her face and felt the gelatinous remnants of the creature clinging to her skin. The slime coated her, dripping into her ears, seeping out from between her legs.

She dived furiously back into the water, and desperately washed herself clean. As she scrubbed her limbs, she found the arrow that had sliced the life out of the creature and yet had barely pricked her skin.

Screaming, she scrambled to the ledge, stumbled over the side and toppled to the ground with a thump. She was cold, naked, and after a few long moments of lucidity, ashamed. Sensations flooded back at her, at once erotic and forbidden and ugly. The butterfly had been so beautiful, like a blooming ocean flower undulating in the water, reflecting the sparkle of the stars, glowing with colors her eyes had never seen. She couldn't resist it, not when her mind had been so instantly flooded with promises of pleasures never experienced by mortal woman.

She dropped to her knees. The creature had fulfilled the promise, melding around her body, introducing sensations that were at once delicious and terrifying. She'd been lost in the stirrings, intoxicated by the pure, irresistible assault. Her mind had swirled with nothing but the joys of intense sexual release.

She covered her face with her hands and sank lower to the ground, her body spent, her soul empty. Good gods of Olympus! What had she done?

"Weep not, Alina," a husky female voice said. "By my hand, you are free of the siren's psyche. Vile creatures. Created by the sirens to torture women the way their voices torture men."

Alina struggled to find the strength to lift herself off the ground. She managed to raise her head high enough to squint against the golden light surrounding the warrior standing in front of her. Dressed in the skin of a great golden stag, a gilded bow in her hand and silver-tipped arrows pointing toward the sky in an argent arc behind her head, Alina knew in an instant who had come for her.

All strength deserted her. She slid prostate onto the damp tile. "Artemis, great goddess of the hunt, forgive me."

Alina fought with every fiber of her being not to weep. Artemis had once been her great protector, the deity of Olympus who'd come to the rescue of her betrayed and abused sisters by offering them sanctuary from the world of traitorous men. But had Alina appreciated her generosity? Had she understood the kindness of the goddess before she set out on her quest to meet her secret lover? No. She'd considered nothing but her intense desires, planted in her mind by Morpheus but fueled by her own selfish needs. Reides' heartfelt promises still rang in her ears, but where was he now? Why hadn't he rescued her from the curse of the psyche?

She'd broken the trust of a goddess, and for this, she expected to die.

Though her eyes were downcast, Alina heard the slide of the silver arrow as Artemis removed it from her quiver, followed by the melodious twang of the bow and the swish and thud of the weapon hitting its mark. Yet Alina felt nothing. She looked up to find the arrow just inches from her face.

"Stand, Alina. Take my arrow."

"I don't deserve your benevolence, great goddess. I betrayed your trust."

"You were tricked," Artemis said, striding forward.

The air seemed to fill with incredible warmth as she reached down and took Alina's hand. "Fret not, child. The forces that worked against you were beyond your resistance. Morpheus, Poseidon, Aphrodite all conspired to bring you to this end."

Alina stood, but her knees quaked so that Artemis aided her to the side of the fountain. Once she sat, she found the courage to ask Artemis what she meant.

"Why have the gods turned their attention to me?"

"Because you pose a threat, of course. When you were but a child, Morpheus and Poseidon quarreled over a vision the god of dreams planted into the god of the sea's brain, a dream that prophesied that a son of Poseidon would someday rule a powerful realm of mortals and would effectively destroy the need for those of us on Olympus, particularly the gods of the sea and oceans. Such a dream, if delivered to the other gods of Olympus, would mark Poseidon's son for death. Poseidon challenged Morpheus to admit the dream was naught but fancy, yet Morpheus insisted he'd been told by the Oracle at Delphi of this coming to pass. Poseidon summoned the Oracle and learned that his son, Reides, born of the siren, Cyestra, would fall slave in his adulthood to a mortal woman and their union would upset the balance of all we know."

Alina struggled to breathe. Was she this woman? Reides and she had shared an interlude of great passion, but he'd not fallen slave to her. If anything, she'd become his helot, his servant, bound by the intensity of his gaze, the power of his carnality. How could she be the woman in the prophecy?

"I do not understand."

Artemis's smile was gentle. Alina managed to keep

her gaze on the goddess and listen, despite her fascination with the deity's remarkable beauty. Her mane of dark hair glistened in the moonlight and her eyes, as silver as the tips of her arrows, shone with cool, unstoppable power.

"I do not expect you to understand, Alina. You have become a woman, but you do not know the ways of men or gods. Poseidon, determined to waylay this sequence of events, banished Reides to this island and forbade him to take a mortal lover. Poseidon chose the servants here for their simplemindedness, certain that any mortal woman with an ounce of cunning could destroy him. But Poseidon never thanked Morpheus for his prediction and this angered the sleep god. So when Reides reached his amorous peak, he implanted him with dreams that showed him the woman he'd been destined to love. That was you. Morpheus knew that if he stirred Reides to the point of madness, he'd search for you but never find you, as Morpheus knew you were under my protection. He hoped Reides would die in his quest and thus Morpheus would have his revenge on Poseidon for his lack of gratitude."

"But I had the dreams, too," Alina said, her voice betraying her confusion. She slid her fingers into her wet hair and tugged, hoping the pain would clear her mind so she could understand. "I did nothing to offend Morpheus. Why would he torture me so?"

"He did not. Morpheus is a proud god, as most are. He could not bear to keep his clever revenge secret. He shared his plan with Aphrodite, his lover. Once she saw Reides, she wanted him for herself and plotted a scheme of her own. You were the key to that scheme. She convinced Morpheus to torture you with the dreams, as

well, and then she provided Reides with the map to our hidden island. It was she who brought you and Reides together."

Alina's stomach twisted in fire-hot knots. *"She's the goddess of love. Is this not her lot? To bring mortals together in true love?"*

Artemis's laugh vibrated against the marble all around them. *"Be not fooled, child. Aphrodite cares not for the hearts of mortals. She toys with the affections of the Earth dwellers for her own amusement. She plotted to have Reides for her own and to destroy you in the process to thwart the prophecy and keep her station safe. She sent the psyche to you. She intended for the creature to drown you in sexual pleasure—and she would have if not for my bow."*

"Do you not care about the prophecy?" Alina asked.

Artemis shrugged and smiled. *"I am confident in my place, Alina. If mortals forsake me, I'll have more time to hunt. Aphrodite, on the other hand, feeds off the adoration of mortals. She cannot exist without it."*

"And now she has Reides?"

"She does."

Alina shot to her feet. *"Where?"*

Artemis frowned. *"What does this matter to you? You cannot fight her, Alina. I should have intervened sooner, but you deserved punishment for defying my protection. Now, I will return you to your sisters. You will not be tortured by that son of a siren any longer. Let Aphrodite have her diversion. When she tires of him, he'll receive the retribution he deserves."*

"No!"

Alina fell to her knees and in a burst of impudence, grabbed the hem of Artemis's tunic and buried her face in the magically soft hide.

"I beg of you, great Artemis. Reides was a victim of the gods as much as I. Save him."

Artemis rose to her feet and pushed Alina aside. "Woman, you are mad. The man has betrayed you. Even now, he licks at the treacherous folds between Aphrodite's thighs, drinking her essence, gorging himself on the orgasmic moans he evokes from her lips. He's her servant, Alina. He cares nothing for you. He left you here to die. Reides knew the psyche would drown you, both in sexual ecstasy and in the water that gives him life."

Alina's vision shook, her balance upended so that she had to grab the ground to keep from crumbling into a defeated heap. "I cannot accept this. Reides fought the Hydra to find me; he gave me life when the ocean stole the breath from my lungs. When I begged to go to the surface, he brought me here. How could he so easily toss me aside?"

Artemis sat down and stroked Alina's hair as she would the pelt of a beloved pet. "He's a man, Alina. And Aphrodite is a powerful and vengeful goddess. Forget him or you will die."

Rearing backward, Alina dragged herself to her feet. Leaving the warmth that surrounded Artemis left her chilled, naked, and open to the elements, much as she'd been that first night on the lookout, when she'd spotted Reides' glistening body floating in the wind-ravaged sea. She'd survived a battle with the gods then, hadn't she? Could she abandon Reides now, when his own nature dragged him into a fate of doom?

"He's not a man. He's the son of a siren and a god. The prophecy said he would do great things. I cannot leave him."

"You're a fool," Artemis announced, pithily.

"No, I'm a woman who has known love."

"Love is fleeting, Alina. This is the truth I tried to protect you and your sisters from."

"Love is what makes mortals breathe. It is what makes us willing to go into battle and face our mortality. Please, Artemis," Alina begged, once again dropping to the ground, her knees hitting hard on the cold marble stone. She paused, trying to think, knowing that although Artemis seemed like a wise and benevolent woman—she was a goddess, just like vain Aphrodite, jealous Poseidon and vengeful Morpheus.

"You are the great huntress, my protector. Aphrodite spited you when she gave Reides the map to your island."

Alina then stood tall, ignoring her lack of clothing, how she'd come to be on Crete and all she'd done to insult the goddess who'd vowed to protect her and her family. With every word, her resolve grew and her strength chased away the night chill.

"Because of her, my maidenhood has been taken by a man who has forsaken me." As the goddess had ordered earlier, Alina snatched the arrow still standing between the marble tiles. She held the weapon high in front of her, as if she wielded a magic shield. "Bestow upon me the strength of the huntress and allow me to be the instrument of your revenge. I beg you, Artemis."

Artemis considered Alina's proposition, her eyebrow arched and the stirrings of a smile teasing at the corners of her lush mouth. After what seemed an eternity, the goddess held out her hand.

"Beg me not, child, but let me hear your plan."

CHAPTER NINETEEN

"WELCOME TO CHICAGO."

Though she'd been flirting with the idea of opening her eyes for a good five minutes, Colton's husky voice near her ear gave her the incentive to wake up despite the warm, soft sheets and the undoubtedly early hour. She blinked against the sunny glare in the room, and then realized the bed faced the biggest, clearest window she'd ever seen, with nary a blind nor sheer curtain to hamper her view. She sat up, rubbed her eyes until they teared and then gazed out onto a huge, blue body of water sparkling with sunshine and dappled by the wind.

"That's a lake?"

Colton chuckled, handed her a mug of coffee mixed just the way she liked it and scooted off the mattress. "Pretty impressive, huh?"

"Looks like the ocean," she said, amazed. She might have grown up with a lot of money, but Tessa hadn't traveled much beyond the route between New York state and Key West. Lakes to her were dark and had visible shorelines surrounded by tall trees, with mountains looming in the distance. Here, she could see nothing in the distance but a squat, round structure just off to the left and about two hundred white-sailed boats of various sizes and shapes. She slipped out of bed and walked to the windows, glad she could feel the warm sunshine through the glass.

"Can all journalists afford views like this?" She sipped the coffee, warmed instantly by the slightly sweet, nutty flavor.

"Afraid not. Thank the horse-breeding fortune of the Kentucky state Grangers for this view."

She turned around, surprised. She'd known Colton's family had money, but she'd never guessed he dipped into the coffers. "Trust fund?"

"Inheritance from my grandfather. I guess that's another thing we have in common."

She wouldn't have pegged this hardworking man as a trust fund baby like herself, but at least no one would ever accuse him of being after her money.

"There are worse things to have in common than healthy portfolios."

Tessa strolled down the length of the window, finally glancing straight down and realizing how high they were in the sky. She stepped back, slightly disconcerted by the height. Cars, thousands of them it seemed, snaked down the paved road beside the waterfront. She glanced north and noticed the tall line of buildings that made up Chicago proper and picked out the few famous structures she knew on sight—the Sears Tower, the monolithic Aon Center, the diamond-shaped Smurfit-Stone Building. She breathed in the crisp, air-conditioned air and realized as much as she wanted to hate this big, burgeoning city simply because it wasn't Key West, her curiosity had been piqued. She was hit by the unbidden desire to explore the distinct neighborhoods Colton had told her about, shop on Michigan Avenue, taste real Chicago-style pizza, maybe even take in a Cubs game or taste a burger at the Billy Goat Tavern he was always talking about.

Didn't mean she wanted to stay. Didn't mean she wanted to live here for the rest of her life.

But damn it all to hell, she wanted to understand Colton's world. Could she do that from long distance? Did she have to decide today?

"You don't ever have to apologize to me for having money, Colton," she said, preferring to talk about their finances rather than grapple with emotions. "If you've got it, you might as well put it to good use. And this—" she toasted the view with her cup "—this is a good use."

Colton smiled and Tessa watched his face, so relaxed, so handsome and so comfortable with who he was, a rich guy with a powerful job, who could sway public opinion and influence public policy with his words. Sometimes, she forgot that the columns he'd written about her divorce had been few and far between. For the most part, he spent his time taking to task the people elected to power, like the mayor or city councilmen, or the people who bought power where they could—like Martin Reese. His job, unlike hers, shaped the way government agencies were run. And yet, he respected her writing and had taken great pleasure in being a part of it—even when someone had tried to turn her professional comeback on its ear.

She ran her hand through her hair and then searched around for her suitcase, which she found on a love seat in the corner of Colton's spacious bedroom. She'd been so exhausted last night, she could barely remember the taxi from the airport, the ride up the elevator, the changing of clothes, brushing of teeth and falling into bed. This morning, dressed in her coziest pajamas, a cup of coffee in her hand, and the sun shining outside in a cloudless sky reflecting off the amazingly dark turquoise water of Lake Michigan, Tessa was starting to feel

more than ready to take on what she knew would be a difficult day.

"So, what's the plan?" she asked, sipping at her drink.

"For this morning?" Colton asked, poking around in his
closet and extracting a pair of jeans, a burgundy polo shirt and
an incredibly soft-looking camel hair sport coat. "We're going
to try and find our old friend, Martin."

"God, how can you mention his name before I've finished
my first coffee?"

He looked at her with a slightly repentant smile. "As if you
weren't thinking about him."

Tessa sat down beside her suitcase. "You know me too well."

Luckily for her, he let that one go. "I know Martin too well.
He despises both of us. He's the only common link we have
and he has the money to hire the right people to screw us over.
I shouldn't have dismissed his involvement before."

Tessa put the mug down on a side table. "I'm not so sure.
Wouldn't Martin Reese be more overt? I was in that family
for ten years. When he took revenge, his targets knew he was
the one on the giving end of trouble. He isn't a man I'd call
subtle, except when he's breaking the law, of course."

Colton scoffed and tore off his loose T-shirt.

Tessa folded her lips together to keep from whistling.

Luckily, Colton didn't notice as he worked through their
situation, his brow furrowed. "Even then Martin isn't good at
being secretive. Hence the grand jury. Let's get dressed, stop
by my office, get an update on the case against Reese and then
try and catch up with him at the courthouse. Maybe if we confront him together, his legendary temper will get the best of
him and we'll find out the truth for certain."

Tessa pawed through the clothes in the suitcase beside her
and found a breezy sundress and sweater that was as close as
she was going to get to business casual. "And then what?"

Colton crossed the room where she toyed with the spaghetti straps of her dress, twisting them tightly around her finger. He sat on the arm of the love seat and Tessa couldn't resist leaning her head on his lap.

He grinned down at her. "Then we move on."

"Seems so easy."

"You finally moved on from Daniel, didn't you?"

"That wasn't easy. Took three tries."

"He was drunk and obnoxious the first two attempts."

"Yeah, and only obnoxious on the third. You do realize that once this whole mess is over, I'll have used up my entire allotment of time for discussing that whole insane family?"

Colton cursed with humorous exaggeration. "And I haven't even heard about the mother yet."

Tessa winced. God, she definitely was not going down that road. "Suffice it to say that she made my agoraphobic mother look like Carol Brady. But enough about the Reese family before I've had a bagel to settle my stomach. I have a more important question for you."

Colton slid down onto the seat beside her, his eyes glittering. "Do we have time for a quickie? Yes."

She placed her hand flat on his chest, stopping his forward momentum, even if his suggestion wasn't such a bad one. "That wasn't my question."

"But it's generally a good, all-purpose question for most occasions, don't you think?"

"Is sex all you ever have on your mind?"

"Am I male?"

"Point taken," she said with a chuckle. "But first I want to know what you were typing last night."

"Typing?"

"Yes."

"When?"

"Last night, on the plane. Am I speaking another language?"

"No, just asking me something I don't want to answer."

"Clearly. Fess up, Granger. You were writing."

"I'm a writer, so you can see where this is going."

"You were writing a column?"

"No."

"The next scene in the book?"

He stood and paced away.

Bingo.

"Let me read it," she insisted.

"It's not ready."

"I think I can suffer through comma splices and misplaced modifiers."

"I mean, it's not what you wanted. I just had an inspiration and I followed it. Call it a fun exercise. Kept my mind off the turbulence."

"Interesting since that flight was smooth as silk. Come on, Colton. This has been our project, together, from the start. I understand if you don't want to put your name on the book with all the plagiarism allegations, but that doesn't mean I don't want your input."

He grabbed his jeans and slipped into the bathroom to put them on. As if she'd never seen his naked ass before. Well, considering her usual response to him when he was undressed, maybe his ducking into the john wasn't such a bad idea.

"I don't think this is the direction you intended for the story," he said, his voice echoing against the polished bathroom tile.

"Because of the outline? I abandoned that already, remember? Come on, Colton. I'm curious. You hated the scene I wrote. I want to see how you got your revenge."

He came out, an electric razor clutched in his hand. "I did hate the scene, but do you know why?"

Tessa sat back in the love seat and hoped he wasn't going to shave away the stubble he'd been nurturing since his trip to the Keys. A permanent five o'clock shadow looked good on him. Better than good. Damned delicious.

"Tessa?"

She sat up straighter. "What?"

He glared at her. "Why did I hate that scene?"

They hadn't discussed this in any detail, but Tessa knew the answer. She'd anticipated this very response. "Because Reides cheats. He abandons the woman he claims to love with all his heart and soul."

He tossed the shaver from hand to hand. "That's not how you usually tell a story. Your heroes are not always right, but they are always loyal."

Tessa groaned. "Those were fairy tales, Colton. This story needed something less simplified, with its complex characters and interrelationships. You and I both know that Reides doesn't have the depth of character to love Alina the way she deserves."

Colton crossed his arms and nodded, as if agreeing with some argument raging in his head. "For a long time, I thought I was a lot like Reides. Sexual, determined, willing to fight the very fabric of his world to get what he wants. But in that scene you wrote, I realized he wasn't anything like me at all."

"I didn't want him to be," she admitted. "I just wanted him to be real, and that means flawed. Reides had to reflect the best and the worst of the gods who spawned him. He had to make the wrong choice."

"You expect the same from me, don't you?"

"No!" She stood, realizing she had an innate talent for making a mess out of things, even when she wasn't trying. "It was time for us to separate the fantasies we had about each other from the story we were trying to tell. I know you would never betray me like Daniel did or hell, like my father, who frankly could have fought a little harder to keep me around."

Colton's eyes widened. "That's the first negative thing I've ever heard you say about dear, old Rip."

She rolled her eyes, pushing back the emotions welling in her chest like a bottomless whirlpool. "I've never been the kind of woman who dwelled on her disappointments. Maybe if I did more often, I wouldn't be so screwed up."

"You're not screwed up, Tessa. You're human. You've had painful things happen to you, but you've found your ways to cope."

She retrieved her coffee, disappointed when she discovered the drink had already cooled. "Including cutting myself off from people, trying to have my emotional needs met through fictional characters in stories of my own design rather than in the unpredictable world of real life."

She slammed the cup down and took a deep breath, knowing she couldn't pull back now, no matter how much she wanted to. Colton needed to hear this. She needed to say it.

"After the divorce, I couldn't even manage filling the emptiness with fiction anymore. I was blank. I think it was kismet that I met you around the same time I moved to the Keys, reconnected with Brew and hooked up with Willa. In a way, they are the reason why I had the energy and courage to think about you and eventually, e-mail you my work. Emotions are so easy with them. They put no demands on me, let me live the way I want. They respect that same independent spirit that my mother always squelched and that my father didn't take the time to nurture. But now look what's happened. I've become so self-contained, I can't even let you in."

Colton put down the shaver, crossed the room and dropped to his knees in front of her. Tessa leaned back, overwhelmed by the intense look in his gray eyes. So full of hope and possibilities.

"You *have* let me in," he claimed.

"But not the way you want." She couldn't resist the urge to press her hands to his cheeks. The sensation was at once rough and warm. "I care about you so deeply, Colton, it hurts. And the pain is because I know I can't be the woman you deserve, the woman willing to uproot her life to move to Chicago so you can keep your career going, the woman who will alter her appearance and her attitudes to please your family. You deserve someone who fits into your world, who isn't going to be hounded by notoriety for the rest of her life."

Colton sat back on his heels. "You've thought about moving here?"

She chuckled. He would focus on that part, wouldn't he?

"I've thought about doing whatever I could to keep us from being apart. But even if I did come here, Colton, it wouldn't last."

"Why not?"

"Let's start with the plagiarism."

"Old news. We'll handle that one later. Give me another reason."

"Your parents."

"How do you know my parents won't love you?"

"Because you've told me about them at length," she said with an ironic laugh. "They'll hate me and you know it."

Colton opened his mouth to argue, but the truth caught up with him before any denials spilled out. "You're right. They'll hate you. At first. But you have a lot in common with them, Tessa, beyond the privileged upbringing."

"Name one thing."

"Me."

"Name another."

"Your love for life. The fact that you work hard in your chosen career, even when you don't have to. You care about people. I'm not saying it'll be easy to win them over, but I know you will. Eventually. And I'll be there, by your side. Besides, I only visit them about four times a year. What's a dozen days in parental hell compared to three hundred and fifty-three days of paradise with me?"

She sighed. It was so tempting. Tempting, but not irresistible. "But we wouldn't be in paradise. I live in paradise, remember? You live in Chicago."

"You like the lake."

She giggled, God help her. "The lake is nice. But this is still summer. How do you think I'm going to feel about the wind that cuts over that water come, oh, let's say, January?"

He made a pshaw sound, but didn't bother to argue the fact that some of the cruelest winter weather passed through this very city.

"You're going to cut me out of your life because of the weather?"

She threw her head back. "No! I mean, yes. I mean, God, Colton! Do you see what I mean? This is hard."

"Yes, it is. Love is hard. It can be ugly and frustrating and downright gut-wrenching. But we're worth it, don't you think? Tessa, stay with me."

The doorbell rang. Tessa wasn't sure who was on the other side of the door and despite that the one and only person she knew in Chicago was kneeling right in front of her, she was going to kiss whomever had interrupted them as a reward for perfect timing.

Colton cursed, ordered her to get dressed and then left the bedroom. Tessa slipped on her dress and scurried into the bathroom, her mind swimming from all they'd said to each other. And all they hadn't said. Still, she'd managed to push more heartfelt honesty out of her mouth than she'd ever thought possible.

She brushed her teeth and dusted her face with a little

makeup, used the blow-dryer to fluff her hair. After pushing her feet into a pair of strappy sandals, she exited the bedroom and stopped dead at the sight of the man she'd thought she'd want to kiss.

Martin Reese.

He looked exactly the same as he had a year ago—same slicked-back snow-white hair, same three-thousand-dollar suit, same superior facial expression, only now his frown was just a tad bit more pronounced. She cuffed her fists onto her hips and let out a withering sigh.

"And this before my second cup of coffee?"

Martin sneered. "Coming here wasn't my preference, I assure you."

Colton gestured toward the sitting area of his living room. "Mr. Reese was just explaining that his attorney advised he seek us out, to clear up any misconceptions we might have about his involvement in our current troubles."

Tessa narrowed her eyes at her former father-in-law. "How did you know anything about our current troubles, Martin, unless you caused them?"

Colton grinned. "Funny, that's exactly the same question I asked—though I notice you haven't answered yet," he said to the scowling man.

Stubbornly, Martin marched into the living room, took a seat on Colton's comfy leather couch and then waited with barely checked patience for Colton and Tessa to follow. For an instant, Tessa was stunned in place. Could all this be coming to an end? Colton helped out by cupping her elbow and guiding her into the room.

"Where's your attorney?" she asked.

"Downstairs. I thought we could handle this better without benefit of counsel."

Tessa lowered herself into a sleek leather easy chair and

Colton took a spot standing immediately behind her. "That doesn't sound like you, Marty," Colton said. "Seems to me you don't go anywhere without a contingent from Zinberg, Spiridon and Tomlin."

Martin took a deep breath and though his hard gaze shot sparks in their direction, his response was oddly even-toned. "I'm a big boy. Did business for years without a mouthpiece."

"And what business are you here to do now?"

Martin leaned forward on his elbows, watching them both with keen consideration. If Tessa didn't know better, she'd think they had something on him instead of the other way around.

"I hear you're in some sort of trouble."

Tessa glanced up at Colton before leveling her most unbelieving stare at Martin. "Don't try and convince us you're here to help. You hate my guts and Colton at least bugs the crap out of you."

"You have a foul mouth."

"Thanks, I try."

He opted to ignore her sarcasm. "I don't really give a damn what happens to either of you, but my sources say you're barking up my tree, blaming me for whatever situation you've created for yourself."

Colton stepped forward. "What sources?"

Martin grinned as if he'd been waiting for Colton to ask that question for a very long time. "I'm not at liberty to reveal my source, Mr. Granger. Rest assured, my information is reliable. Bottom line is, your integrity may soon come into question because of your association with my former daughter-in-law. You should have checked with me before you unzipped your pants, boy. I could have saved you some trouble."

Colton's fists clenched. Tessa reached out and grabbed him by the wrist. Daniel might have been too drunk and outnumbered to press charges in Key West, but Martin was stone-cold sober and likely itching to call the police, if for no other reason than to take the focus off his own possible indictments.

"Don't bother, Colton. He's just baiting you. What he says can't hurt me. What he does can't hurt me." She turned her gaze on Martin and relaxed into the chair. "A year ago, you spent hundreds of thousands of dollars just to ruin me as retribution for telling your spoiled brat son to leave me the hell alone. Aren't you done burning your hard-earned cash on me yet? And why go after Colton? When the truth comes out, you're going to look more like a criminal thug than you already do, attacking the private life and reputation of a journalist who has called you out in his columns, not to mention continuing a vendetta against your former daughter-in-law who is just trying to get her career back on track."

Martin stood, smoothed his slacks and jacket and adjusted his tie. "Clearly, you grew a brain since we last met." He turned to Colton. "She's right. Any connection between me and any attack against you is not in my best interest. Grand juries are not sequestered. They are barred from reading the news, but who knows what they'll find out anyway? Even a hint that I've sought retribution against a journalist who has been following the investigation against me would cause me more trouble than it's worth. Of course, some other people might think it's worth doing for me. They might believe taking the two of you down would make me…grateful."

With a slight nod, he moved toward the door. Then he stopped and removed a white envelope from his jacket pocket and placed it on the table beside the door. "You might want to do a more internal investigation, Granger. Sometimes enemies can be so close, we don't see them until it's too late."

And with that, he was gone.

Tessa stood, took two steps toward the door, then spun

around and faced Colton, who was deep in thought. "What did he mean by that? Was he trying to point the finger at me?"

Colton stalked to the door and retrieved the papers Martin had left. "No, I don't think so. Martin Reese may be a lot of distasteful things, but stupid isn't one them. He wouldn't come here himself, sans lawyers, unless he had a lot to lose if he were implicated in trying to set us up. He's right. If the grand jury gets wind of this kind of coercion, he's cooked."

He tore the envelope open and slid the papers out, his gaze scanning at a rapid rate. Suddenly, Colton's eyes widened. He ran his hand through his hair, then across his chin and mouth. When he pointed toward the bedroom, Tessa had no idea what he was trying to convey with his silent gesture.

"Get your stuff. We're going to the paper," he said, his tone rushed.

Tessa took a few steps back, certain she was missing something important. Before Martin had showed up, they'd planned to go to the newspaper. What had Martin left them?

"Colton? What's going on?"

Colton's laugh could best be described as ironic, definitely enigmatic and clearly absent of humor of any kind. He handed her the papers, which looked to her like the draft of a newspaper article.

"I don't think Martin Reese had anything to do with the missent proposal or the plagiarism setup, but he just told us who did—his so-called source. And that son of a bitch is going to pay."

CHAPTER TWENTY

IN THE CAB ON THE WAY to the new *Sun-Times* building, Tessa reread the column, still in manuscript form, that Reese had given them. She hadn't recognized the byline. Colton had had to tell her who the guy was. She'd never met him, never crossed paths with him—and yet, he'd been willing to sell her out in order to get brownie points with her ex-father-in-law.

That pissed her off, but *stunned* best described Tessa's emotions as they wove through the heavy traffic. In fact, she was so stunned that she forgot to look outside the glass and catch all the sites she'd been so anxious to see this morning. By the time she thought to glance up from her lap, the cab driver had pulled in front of the building and Colton had disconnected his wireless Internet connection and stored his BlackBerry.

He tossed the cabbie a few bills. "Here we go."

Together, he and Tessa looked up at the tall glass-and-tan brick building. The end to their troubles resided somewhere inside. Still, Tessa couldn't muster the confidence that they'd get out of this unscathed. Someone was going to get hurt and she couldn't shake the dread that the person with the most to lose was Colton.

Silently, she followed him through the security in the lobby, where she signed in and attached a visitor's badge to the collar of her sweater. They rode the elevator in silence, but Tessa could see rage building in Colton's eyes, their gray irises brimming with cold, steely anger. She'd known from the night at the Paradise Club that there was a limit to Colton's patience and unruffled demeanor—and this morning, that capacity had not only been reached, but surpassed.

A pretty blonde in a short, swishy skirt greeted them as they stepped off the lift.

"Hey, Colton. I know you called ahead, but Frank said—"

Colton grabbed Tessa's hand and without as much as a nod in the woman's direction, tugged Tessa to whatever destination he'd determined was important. She stumbled as she attempted to glance over her shoulder to see if the woman protested or followed. She looked forward again just as Colton slammed through a closed conference room door and brought them to a halt in the midst of a meeting, which included five very startled men.

"Colton!"

A man about Martin Reese's age, with similarly silver hair but by no means as expensive a suit, jumped to his feet and pounded his palms on the tabletop. "I told Rhonda to tell you to meet me in my office."

Colton released Tessa's hand. She stepped to the side so that even though she was still behind Colt, she could see the increasingly enraged look on his face.

"I don't give a damn what you told Rhonda. I've worked for this paper a long time, Frank. I won't be railroaded by some fame-hungry weasel who needs a refresher course in why journalists shouldn't break privacy laws to get a story."

As he spoke, Colton pointed at a man cowering in his seat. Tessa'd best describe him as a pretty boy. A terrified pretty boy—so she concluded he was John Nichols, the local issue columnist Colton had told her he never would have suspected of such down and dirty dealings. He didn't think the guy had the cojones or the smarts to pull off something so devious. He'd actually respected the guy's ethics.

How wrong he'd been.

"You need to calm down," Frank insisted. "I'm not going to tolerate a brawl in my newsroom."

Colton's volume lowered, but the icy evenness of his tone packed just as much punch. "Then let's take it outside. You game, Nichols?"

The man, visibly shaking, forced himself to sit up straighter. "I'm just doing my job, Granger. Reporting the truth. Nothing I've written about you is a lie. Nothing."

"Written?" Frank repeated, his bushy eyebrows arched. "About Granger? What the hell are you talking about?"

John leaned over the side of his chair and extracted a file folder from his briefcase. With only a moment's hesitation, he slapped the folder on the table in front of Frank, the editor-in-chief, and then glared at Colton with pure defiance.

"I wasn't going to go to Frank with this today, Granger. I was going to give you a chance to tell your side."

Tessa stepped forward and wrapped her hand around Colton's arm. The tight, bulging muscles of his biceps, once simply a turn-on, now imbued her with strength. So the guy wasn't just going to 'fess up? He was going to turn this around and blame Colton for the story coming out?

Frank took glasses out of his shirt pocket, slipped them on and started to read. Only a few sentences in, he looked up at Colton, clearly shocked.

"This true?"

Colton shrugged. "For the most part, yes. I have been using my *personal* and *private* time to conduct a seduction of Martin Reese's former daughter-in-law and yes, this seduction resulted in a book entitled *Son of the Siren* that we wrote together and are currently preparing to market to the major

New York publishers. That any of this is the business of the people of Chicago is ridiculous."

Frank flopped back into his chair. The other three men whispered to each other while they stared at her with expressions Tessa didn't want to take the time to read. She simply stared back. Hard. At each and every one of them. To their credit, they had the decency to look away—even John Nichols, who'd yet to make eye contact with her, now that she thought about it.

"What I do on my own time is my business, Frank."

John scoffed. "You used *Sun-Times* equipment."

At that accusation, Colton merely raised his eyebrows. "Really, John? How would you know that?"

Though he was wearing a polo shirt with no tie, John tugged at the collar as if it were choking him. "Accidentally, of course. I needed a phone number one day when you were out. You'd left your BlackBerry in its cradle to charge and I took a look. I stumbled on an e-mail between you and Mrs. Reese. Her name caught my eye."

Tessa opened her mouth to protest the use of her married name, but after a second of consideration, popped her lips together. How he referred to her in this office didn't matter. Now, if the faux pas made it into the paper, she was going to sue his tailored pants off.

Colton stepped forward and leaned his hands on the table. "Funny, my phone numbers and my e-mail aren't accessed the same way. You'd have no reason to see my e-mail if you were just looking for a phone number. Don't play games, Nichols. You've been caught and the time has come to lay your cards down and tell me what you want."

Nichols's blue eyes narrowed. "As if you don't know what I want. It's not complicated, Colton. I want your job. I'm not the only person in this building who could say that on a polygraph and pass. But unlike the mealymouthed jerks around here, I was willing to do something to ensure my success."

He turned to Frank. "Everything in my column can be verified by two sources, both of whom are standing in this room. How many years has Colton been taking up space in your paper, spouting off about how politicians have no right to privacy if their actions affect their constituencies? This is no different. This man who has taken the moral high road to the people of Chicago on a daily basis for years is now spending his time writing smut with some slut from West Palm Beach."

Colton lunged forward, but Tessa grabbed his arm before he could smash John Nichols through the nearest plate-glass window. She didn't appreciate the man's insult any more than Colton did, but she'd been called a hell of a lot worse than a slut. So far as epithets went, that was chump change.

Tessa sneered in the man's direction. "Is that the best you can do? Slut? You clearly didn't read the tabloids around the time of my divorce or you'd be a little more creative."

"I'll leave the wordsmithery to Granger," Nichols spat back. "I've written a column here that is going to call into question a man who has become synonymous in this town with truth and integrity. Not so much anymore, eh, Colton?"

By this time, Frank had finished reading the article and had passed it along to the salt-and-pepper-haired man to his left. Frank leaned forward and entwined his fingers, staring at Colton and Tessa, clearly disturbed by what he'd read.

"Did you use *Sun-Times* equipment to carry on this affair with Mrs. Reese?"

"Ms. Dalton," she corrected, unable to stand the misnomer for another second.

Frank nodded, his gaze clearly apologetic, though he said nothing to that end.

"No," Colton said. "I worked from home on my personal

PC. And I bought the BlackBerry with my own money when the gadget first came out. I'm sure I can produce the receipt."

Nichols pursed his lips. "But the *Sun-Times* pays for your e-mail service."

Frank frowned. "Actually, no we don't. Haven't for over two years. During our last contract negotiation Colton gave that up in exchange for a bigger office. Unless you've got something better than that, John, I'd keep my mouth shut for a few minutes."

John turned away, staring out the window, silenced. As the article made its way around the table, each man looked up with dismayed surprise.

"You admit you wrote the book with Ms. Dalton," Frank asked, coolly clarifying the situation.

"Yes," Colton replied. "On my own time."

"And this was before or after you wrote columns reporting on the state of her divorce?"

"Several months after," Tessa answered. "Colton and I met only one time, on the night before the judge made a ruling in my divorce countersuit against my husband."

Frank rubbed his chin, then gestured for Tessa and Colton to sit. Both of them silently declined.

With a sniff, Frank continued. "So you knew Colton wrote not-so-flattering articles about your former father-in-law?"

"Colton told me himself that night that he and Martin Reese were not friends. We bonded over it. Does any of this truly matter? The part Mr. Nichols isn't telling you is much more interesting, like how he decided to turn Colton's secret into more than just a way to discredit a colleague. He wanted to ruin Colton, but frankly, so far, only I've been attacked. He's trying to create a scandal about me."

"You?" Nichols said, protesting a little too loudly for Tessa's taste. "Why would I care about a woman I've never met?"

"You don't," Colton supplied, "which is why it was so easy for you to use your knowledge about my project with Tessa in order to ruin her career. If you had access to my BlackBerry, then you could have gotten the passwords to my home PC—you must have. Only someone who has read at least part of the book could have drawn the conclusions you did in your article. You probably figured if you outed us, you could not only ruin my reputation, you could buy points with Reese."

This deepened Frank's frown.

John shook his head, but without much of the shock someone falsely accused might possess. "Why would I do that? Reese and I are not friends. I've been just as critical of him as you have been, Granger."

Colton's smile bordered on a sneer. "I'll admit, you started off that way. But over the course of the last year, you've softened your stance on Reese, balancing all your reporting on him so that his admirable renovation projects outshone the accusations of neighborhood and community destruction. That article you had me proof for you a week ago had a hint of your revised opinion of Reese. A few sentences here and there implied that you'd gone sentimental on the man because he'd donated liberally to charities. I pointed that out to you, remember? Was that a slip, John? Or were you trying to warn me?"

John lifted his chin. "I didn't want to show you that piece and you know it. I didn't give a damn about your opinion. I stand by what I wrote then and now. Every word."

Colton nodded. "I'm sure you do. Opinions like that could get you on Reese's good side, couldn't they? Maybe you're banking on Reese beating the grand jury investigation. Maybe you're thinking having a friend like Reese wouldn't be such a bad thing, especially since one of his holding companies bought the *Palm Beach Post* three weeks ago. Thinking about a more temperate climate, John?"

In seconds, John Nichols's face flushed from pink to scarlet.

Colton leveled his gaze on Frank. "One of our investigative guys has been working with me on following the Reese grand jury. I checked with him on the way here. He discovered the highly covered-up purchase, but was holding on to the news until he could tie it to the indictment if it ever came down."

"I knew about the media purchase," Frank said. "I am the editor-in-chief of this paper, Colton. I usually know what the staff is up to."

Colton grinned. "Yeah, Frank, but you can't be everywhere all the time. If you were, you'd also know that John's known about the purchase for quite some time, just as he knew about my project with Tessa. He laid the groundwork to kiss up to Reese by working Reese's philanthropic projects into his columns. He was sly about it, but now I see he was just biding his time. Then a week ago, someone sent a few stolen chapters from our book to Tessa's former publisher, I'm guessing in an attempt to out me as her coauthor and to discredit Tessa. When that didn't work, he set Tessa up to look like she'd plagiarized her newest book, knowing I'd have to step forward as her partner in order to clear her name."

Colton filled them in on all the details. Tessa knew they had no proof, nothing but supposition and clues they'd strung together. Colton had told her earlier that with the help of a good hacker, who were a dime a dozen in a metropolis like Chicago, John might have easily tapped into Colton's e-mail server and lifted the work they'd shared exclusively on the Net.

They had nothing to back up their claims except the incredibly guilty expression on John Nichols's face.

"You can't prove any of this," John said.

"Not at the moment, but proving your guilt doesn't really matter." Colton said. "The damage is done."

John sat up, his spine straight, his eyes finally meeting Tessa's straight on. "Will be, once Frank runs my column."

Colton reached for Tessa and she slipped close against his side, his arm hooked possessively across the small of her back.

"Frank?"

The column had made the complete round of the room. The editorial board looked at each other, at Colton, then at John.

"This is crap," Frank said. "I don't give a damn what my reporters do on their own time."

"But he's a hypocrite!" John said, jumping to his feet. "His columns are all about honesty and character." He said the last three words with mocking exaggeration. "And here he is writing smut so he can get into that slut's pants!"

One slut she'd give him. Two sluts pushed her over the line. Tessa shoved away from Colton and before any of the men in the room could react, she'd backhanded Nichols and sent his glasses flying. Her hand stung, but so much adrenaline surged through her veins, she was quite certain she could beat the crap out of him.

Luckily for Nichols, she wasn't a violent woman. One good lick had served its purpose.

"I'll sue you for assault!" John said, clutching his cheek.

"Go ahead," Tessa taunted. "You think Reese is rich? Check out my bank account. You keep screwing with us and I'll sue and countersue you until you have to live in a cardboard box. How hard do you think it will be to trace that plagiarism scam to you? How much money do you think it will take for me to get the hacker you used to hand you to us on a silver platter? Besides, I'm about certain the real men in this room will agree that my physical response to your taunt was completely justified."

Colton came up behind her. "I'll testify for you, sweetheart."

Frank grumbled, "So will I. Nichols, I think you need to take a little break from the grind for a few days."

"I'm suspended?" He slammed to his feet so fast, his chair went flying behind him.

"For the time being." Frank's tone was even and brooked no argument. Tessa could see why he was the guy in charge.

"But don't touch a thing on your desk or your laptop," Frank ordered. "Hacking into another reporter's computer, implicating a fellow journalist in plagiarism, that's serious shit the editorial board is going to have to think hard about."

Colton watched the scene without any of the smugness Tessa would surely have shown.

"What about him?" Nichols cried, pointing frantically at Colton.

Colton stepped forward. "I'll take a suspension while you investigate, chief." He glanced down at Tessa and she was thrilled to see that hot look back in his eyes.

Oh, yeah. They could definitely make use of more free time.

"Jasper," Frank said to a colleague sitting on his left, "go with Nichols. Make sure he doesn't take anything. The rest of you clear out."

The men left the room. When they were alone, Frank gestured for Tessa and Colton to sit down and this time they did. He asked a few questions for clarification, reviewed how Colton had come to the conclusion that Nichols had been behind the smear campaign and then, finally, asked Colton about the book.

"Nichols has a point, Granger. Your writing this book could be seen as a conflict of interest."

Colton nodded. "So run Nichols's piece."

"What?" Tessa turned, shocked that Colton would make such a request after what they'd just gone through.

He shrugged, a mysterious smile curving his lips. "Nichols did have a point. What he's said in his column about the public having a right to the truth is valid. But I feel what I do in my private life is none of anyone's business and I wouldn't mind a chance to respond to that rather than cover it up."

Tessa grabbed Colton's hand and swiveled in her chair, ignoring the fact that Frank was in the room. "Colton, you'll ruin your career."

He shook his head. "I'd like to think I've established a little more clout than that, Tessa. Yeah, I'll take a hit. But the truth about you and the book and how we worked on it together will be out—soon and in a big way, too. At least here in Chicago."

"Hell, boy," Frank said, chuckling. "Didn't you pay attention to the scandals at the *New York Times?* Journalists who screw up are big news all over the country."

Again, Colton's grin curled enigmatically. "I guess you're right, chief. Imagine the publicity."

He raised his eyebrows, Frank cursed under his breath, said something mildly polite to Tessa about taking pleasure in meeting her, and then stalked to the door. "You working on anything important?" he asked, turning back.

Colton leaned closer to Tessa. "Incredibly important, Frank."

The man groaned. "I meant with your column."

"Nope. I finished off a few extras before my vacation. We're good to go."

With a nod, the editor left the room.

"You're going to put your career on the line for me?" Tessa asked.

Colton whipped out his cell phone and made a call to Audrey. He filled her in, then suggested she use the upcoming publicity to up the price of their advance. As he pushed the end button, Tessa could hear Audrey gleefully whooping on the other end of the line.

"Lemons to lemonade, babe," he said, taking both her hands and leaning as close to her as the conference table and chairs would allow. "Maybe trying to keep my professional life separate from my private life was a mistake. I'm not ashamed of our work together. I'm not ashamed of us."

"I never thought you were. But I know how hard it is to face people's perception of you when it undergoes a radical change."

"You survived. So will I. Besides, I'll have you and that hefty advance Audrey's going to get us to heal my wounds. Yesterday, I really believed you should write the rest of the book on your own, but after working on that scene last night, I realized, I really care about the story, Tessa. I like writing. I like writing with you. Hell, let's just say I like you and leave it at that."

"You *like* me?" she asked, suddenly willing to push her luck. Today was, after all, turning out to be one hell of a day.

His grin was so sheepish, she blushed for him.

"Well, it goes a little deeper than that. Has for a long time. But I haven't said it. I don't want to spook you."

She managed a nonchalant shrug, despite that she was shivering inside. "I don't really spook that easily."

He sat forward and grabbed her hands. "No, you don't. Not anymore. What the hell, I've risked everything that means something to me today. Might as well go for broke. I love you, Tessa. I've probably loved you since that first night in Karen's backyard, but now that I really know you, I'm one majorly whipped puppy."

She laughed, mainly because it was easier to do than cry. "You are the most amazing man I've ever met. You've turned my world upside down. I love you, too, Colton. Now what the hell are we going to do?"

Colton glanced at the window that opened onto the newsroom, which bustled with loud, quick-paced activity. He dashed up from the chair, closed the blinds, locked the door, and then pulled Tessa into his arms.

"First, I'm going to kiss you until you faint. Then we'll figure out the rest."

EPILOGUE

COLTON TOOK A LONG SWIG from his daiquiri and let the rum and fruit juices slide down his throat as he glanced around the crowd. Willa and Brew had created a dance floor in the middle of the room, swaying to the easy rhythms of Jimmy Buffet's "Come Monday" while other couples followed their lead. Heather was holding court to a gaggle of wide-eyed men Colton recognized from the paper's tech department and though she looked slightly discomfited by the attention, was holding her own. In the corner by the bar, Karen, Frank and Frank's wife were having a discussion too serious for this gathering and Audrey was working the room like the pro she was, shaking hands and handing out business cards. Even Colton's sister, Grace, had joined in on the fun, talking shop while she sipped a margarita with the editor of the soon-to-be publisher of *Son of the Siren*. Not surprisingly, considering his sister's tastes, he had four earrings and a tattoo.

When Tessa sidled up behind Colton and smoothed her hands beneath his loose-fitting, untucked Hawaiian-print shirt, the temperature in the room rose at least ten degrees.

"You throw one heck of a party," she said, kissing his shoulder.

The sensation of her lips against his muscle buzzed through him. He and Tessa had been together for three months solid and the thrill still hadn't abated. Having her close, catching a whiff of her scent, feeling her hair against his skin. Man, he was the luckiest man on earth. He twisted around and snared her in his arms.

"We, my darling, *we* throw one heck of a party. I still don't know how you managed to get Brew to leave Key West."

She laughed. "Well, we basically transformed your condo into his pub, for one. Then there was Willa. She dangled a pretty amazing carrot."

Colton watched the couple, who were now dancing with just about every body part touching. "What was that?"

"She agreed to move in with him."

"No kidding?" Colton asked, surprised by this turn of events. "I thought she was convinced their relationship was doomed, what with Brew's commitment phobia and the age difference."

Tessa snuggled in closer. "I think Brew figured if I could overcome my fear of commitment, so could he. He was married once, you know."

"No, I didn't know."

"Yeah, happened in Tijuana. Didn't last more than a few months, but the whole ordeal shook him up. Of course, when you finally find someone worth fighting for, you'll take on even the most formidable fears. I know this all firsthand."

Her choice of words invited Colton to slide his hand down her arm and take her palm in his. He really loved how the two-carat blue diamond he'd chosen for her reflected the color of both the ocean and the lake, but mostly, he loved how the symbol of their soon-to-be vows looked on her hand. Call him a Neanderthal, but the ring branded her as his with such brilliance, no one could ignore that she belonged to him—and vice versa.

"Then again," she added, "so do you."

He kissed her lightly and the mere brushing of their lips injected him with as much desire and need as ripping each other's clothes off right in the middle of the party would have. He wasn't disappointed, however, when she winked and led him through the crowd. He'd hired party planners to transform every room in his condo into a Key West hideaway, complete with sand on the floor and palm fronds on the wall, grilled mahimahi and grouper sizzling on an electric grill set up in his kitchen and umbrella drinks flowing by the pitcherful. They'd flown in Tessa's friends from the Keys and his parents were set to arrive from Kentucky in about half an hour. Technically, they were celebrating the upcoming release of their book, but everyone knew the party was more about the fact that they'd beaten the odds and fallen helplessly and hopelessly in love.

The past three months had been filled with ups and downs. Only his sense of humor and coming home to Tessa in his bed had gotten him through the countless interviews and attacks he'd endured. This week was the first time he'd turned in a column that dealt only with his view on politics and not on his personal exposure to the dark side of the press and public interest.

Over that time, Tessa had concentrated on finishing the book and traveling to and from Key West and to New York, where she'd helped Audrey aggressively market their novel. But mainly, she'd remained at his side. That she'd agreed to leave the home that had become such an integral part of her, even for a short time, touched him deeply. They'd weathered this storm together and after this party was over, they were headed out of the Chicago cold to the temperate climate of Key West, at least until summer. The publicity over the book had brought Colton the opportunity for syndication, so with his topics now focusing more on national interest, he could write from just about anywhere.

All because of Tessa and her penchant for making waves.

When Tessa twisted open the doorknob to his bedroom, a jolt of fire-hot lust surged through him. When she shut the door and locked it behind them, then treated him to a look so sultry, he was about sure several body parts were going to melt, he pulled her roughly to him and made quick work of tasting the sweet, scented flesh on her neck. This woman was exactly the kind of trouble he needed in his life.

"Oh, my," she said, feigning surprise. "You still only have one thing on your mind."

He yanked the top strap of her sundress down and blazed a fiery path of kisses across her shoulder. "So do you or you wouldn't have led me in here."

She pulled away, laughing, but didn't bother to straighten her top as she moved around him, and he caught a flash of bare breast that made his mouth water.

"That's not true. I have something to show you."

As she approached the bed, she grabbed the fabric of her skirt and slowly scrunched it up higher and higher until her bare bottom peaked from beneath the hem. When she climbed onto the mattress, he caught the flash of silk. He forgot to breathe. Even after all these months together, knowing she was wearing nothing but a thong beneath her clothes drove him insane with need.

She reached beneath the pillows and pulled something out. Turning, she situated herself seductively in the middle of the mattress, then thrust the pages toward him.

"What is it?" he asked.

She licked her lips. "Something we've both been waiting for."

He arched a brow. "The prenups from the attorney?"

She clucked her tongue. "Colton, be a little more creative. What was I doing in here, at your computer, all alone, while you were bossing the caterers around?"

Colton's chest tightened. "The final scene?"

She nodded, and her pouty frown was a seductive contrast to her amorous eyes. She spread the papers out in front of her like a winning poker hand, then leaned ever so slightly forward so that her nipples fairly spilled from her loosened top.

"I wrote the entire scene all alone, wondering if it was hot enough, sexy enough, erotic enough to fulfill our promise to the readers. I mean, it got me pretty steamed up, but maybe I'm just too close to the material, you know?"

Without any further urging necessary, Colton unbuttoned his shirt and joined her on the bed. He gathered the pages and handed them to her, then wrapped his arms around her and started working on the zipper that was holding her dress stubbornly in place. "Why don't you read it to me? Aloud. Then we'll know if the scene has what it takes."

She laughed, but when his lips locked around her breast, she cooed. "You certainly have what it takes to turn me on, Colton. You always have and you always will."

He looked up, caught the intense expression in her green eyes and grew all the more hard from knowing how badly she wanted him. "Right back at you, babe. Now, read. I want to know how the story ends."

She smeared her tongue over her lips, then leaned forward and did the same to him. "Didn't I tell you? It doesn't end. Theirs is a desire that lasts forever. A hunger that can't be sated."

He cupped her cheek, knowing with all his being that what she'd described applied to them even more than to the fictional characters on the page. "Poor Reides. He's a doomed man, isn't he?"

She grinned. "No more than Alina. Doomed to love for a lifetime."

Exerting more than his fair share of restraint, he ignored his own need and leaned down to situate his head in the vicinity of her lap while she continued to organize the pages. "And we know exactly how they feel."

Bonus Features:

Everything you love about romance...
and more!

Please turn the page for Signature Select™
Bonus Features.

BONUS FEATURES

Making Waves

A conversation with
Julie Elizabeth Leto

The questions you know you want to ask about *Making Waves*.

Why is there mythology in this book?
I've had a fascination with these ancient stories for years. At first, Tessa only had dogs named Artemis and Apollo—she was their "mother"—sort of an inside joke because of my last name. Then I came up with the story of Alina and Reides and surprise, surprise, Aphrodite showed up in one of my scenes, totally uninvited (just like the goddess she is.) From there, other mythological creatures made the scene, from Poseidon to Morpheus to the elusive sirens. I thought the mythological story gave the book a sort of added depth, since many of the emotions felt by Reides and Alina are mirrored by the relationship between Colt and Tessa, though not in an obvious way.

Is it true this book was rejected many times before Harlequin bought it for Signature?
Actually, yes. I came up with a version of this story in 1998, shortly after the birth of my daughter. It

would have been my third book, rather than my twentieth! But I'm actually thankful that things didn't work out back then. I wasn't really ready to write the book. The story line was much simpler, the characters less affected by all the people around them. In other words, the original plot was too linear and the secondary characters, except for Willa, were nonexistent. Time is a great teacher, and in all the years that followed, the story never left my mind like other rejected story ideas often do. This one stuck with me and grew. I knew that meant something.

When my editor called about Signature, I knew the story was finally going to find the right home. The emphasis on the bonus features alone was perfect since the new version had the story within a story, which can be a risky venture with readers.

How often have you visited Key West?
I live in Florida, but Key West isn't a quick drive, so I've been about four times. The first time was a real disaster! I went with my husband, who was there for business. We had our daughter with us, who was very young, and the hotel was not child-friendly at all. We didn't have a car, I didn't know the island and there was a festival going on that wasn't exactly the kind of atmosphere a good parent would choose for a child. I swore I'd never go back! Then the second time, we went during a slow time of year and stayed closer to the action. That was the trip where I fell in love. I actually started doing research

on that trip and then followed up every time we went back.

Tessa is a writer who struggles with the fact that what she puts on the page reflects on her as a person. Do you struggle with that, as well?
I think all writers struggle with this to some degree, contemporary writers moreso than historical or fantasy writers though, where the settings and atmospheres are so different from real life. I'm constantly asked if I've done all the things my heroines have done and the answer is a resounding no. The act of vicariously living lives I'd never actually have the opportunity (and in some cases, desire) to live myself is what draws me to fiction. If I wanted to write real life, I'd write nonfiction. I like to play "what if" with my characters and see where it takes me.

That said, there is a little bit of me in every character I write, the heroines most of all. Tessa, for instance, has my smart mouth. But her family experience and her experience with her writing are completely the opposites of mine. I've never had to hide what I do. Everyone in my life, from friends to family, is very supportive of my career.

You often write about wealthy characters. Is that part of your vicarious living thing?
Absolutely! For the most part, I do write about characters who are financially stable, even if they aren't rich—though rich people make great fodder for the mill. Especially in this story, where money

acts as yet another wall that keeps Tessa from forming lasting relationships. Finally, in Key West, she's able to transcend that, which makes her much more connected to Willa, Heather and Brew, because they don't hold her wealth against her—nor do they covet what she has. They ignore her money, which means a lot to her because in her childhood and her life with Daniel, that was never the case.

Colton is a journalist. Is it risky to focus a book on two writers, on a profession that a lot of people don't really understand?
There is a lot of misconception about the writing career, so I guess it was risky to make both my hero and my heroine have this rather odd job. It's a job a lot of people want to try, but they have no concept of how isolating it can be, Tessa's moreso than Colt. A journalist depends on getting out, doing interviews, staying in touch with society around them in order to do their job. A fiction writer is the opposite. They live in their head. Most writers I know have to struggle to remind themselves to get out and interact with people on a regular basis! So putting Tessa and Colton together is almost like opposites attract. I hope readers will appreciate their differences as well as what they have in common.

Tessa and Colton begin their relationship with fantasy role-playing. Isn't this kind of kinky?
Sure! That's sort of the point. Daniel hurt Tessa very badly. Her humiliation was not only personal, but it was very public. Tessa was so blocked off from the

idea of having a real relationship with a man again, I felt that Colt had to really shove her out of her comfort zone in order to break through her defenses.

Marsha Zinberg, Executive Editor,
Signature Select Program, spoke with
Julie Elizabeth Leto in the fall of 2004.

Julie's TOP TEN

Key West Attractions
by Julie Elizabeth Leto

I'm by no means a Key West expert, but here are ten places I like to visit when I'm down on the island. All of them are kid-friendly if you go at the right time, except for the winery. Well, actually, the winery is in a cute little shop, so if I remember correctly, my daughter looked around at the souvenirs while my husband and I tasted wine. So in case you get a chance to visit Key West, here are my recommendations for must-stop sites!

1 Key West Aquarium
1 Whitehead Street at Mallory Square

Don't be deceived by the size.... This small aquarium package packs a lot of oceanic punch! With amazing tour guides giving regular tours, you can't go wrong checking out the sharks, stingrays, barracuda and tarpon that are housed in this wonderful collection. There are creatures to touch, habitats to visit and tons of stuff to learn. I've been more than once and am never disappointed.

2 Mallory Square

1 Whitehead Street

You've heard about the famous sunset celebration
in Key West, right? Well, this is the place for the daily
gathering. It also has one of the most convenient
parking lots on the island if you want to walk around
Old Town. Come early, though...but stay late and
enjoy the street musicians, food vendors and
carnival performers who make the event
unforgettable, no matter how many times you go.

3 The Coral Reef

*Extends from Fowey Rocks near Miami to the Dry
Tortugas*

No, this isn't the name of a restaurant—I'm talking
about a real, *live* coral reef, the only one in the
continental United States. If you're not afraid of a
few barracuda swimming beneath you, be sure and
take a snorkeling tour of the reef. We did so with my
then-three-year-old, who I should probably mention
is part fish. But she floated on a raft with her father,
snorkeling over the side. I swam around too, and
frankly, the rafts provided by the charter sailboat
were fabulous. Make sure you have one when you
go! Gives you more time to focus on what's beneath
you than on staying afloat and not touching the
coral with your fins (this actually kills the coral).

4 Jimmy Buffett's Margaritaville Café
500 Duval Street

Okay, here's my confession—I've never really eaten here. Okay, I've eaten at the one in New Orleans, so I figure it counts since it was delicious with great service. There are always so many amazing culinary choices on the island that it's hard to get to all of them—but here's a place you shouldn't miss if you're a newcomer. Jimmy Buffett is an icon in Key West and well, where else can you go to get a genuine "cheeseburger in Paradise?" Plus, there's live music. I swear, next time, I'm there.

5 Turtle Kraals Waterfront Seafood Grill and Bar
1 Lands End Village

This one I've been to! And it's wonderful food and great atmosphere. This turtle cannery turned restaurant is one of the hot spots on the island at nighttime with live music and billiards, so if you want a quieter experience, go for lunch. Some of the menu has a Cuban flair, with a delicious roast pork sandwich—besides all the seafood, of course. Amazing frozen margaritas, too. Don't miss it!

6 Key West Shipwreck Historium
1 Whitehead Street

This one is part museum, part live performance where an actor playing the role of Asa Tift, one of the many wreckers who made his fortune saving the cargo of floundering ships, tells the story of an amazing industry unique to Key West. This place is perfect for children, of course, but the salvaged pieces and recreations from the SS *Isaac Allerton* will intrigue adults, as well. And for those of you who don't suffer from vertigo, you can climb up to the top of the lookout and get an amazing view of the island. Or so I'm told.

7 Mel Fisher Maritime Museum
200 Greene Street

Mel Fisher, another Key West icon, is the explorer and treasure hunter who discovered the wreck of the Spanish galleon *Nuestra Señora de Atocha*. Real artifacts from the wreck are housed here, including amazing jewelry, bars of silver and gold (you'll even get a chance to try and lift one!) as well as guns and cannons to entertain the boys, young and old. The museum changes, too, so you'll want to come back every time you visit. And the gift shop is amazing, if you're interested in that sort of thing...which I am!

8 Key West Winery
103 Simonton Street

Okay, it's not really a winery, but a very cute little shop that sells wine that is made...in other parts of Florida. But if you want to taste the Key Lime wine that Tessa and Colton drank after their midnight rendezvous, this is the place to get it. It's where I got mine! They have amazing blended wines with such flavors as blueberry, chocolate and currant. I had a blast tasting the offerings and if you like fruity wine, you will, too.

9 Key West Lighthouse
938 Whitehead Street

Built in 1847, this lighthouse, just across the street from the famous Hemingway House, offers you a chance to step into the past. It's reportedly eighty-eight steps to the top of the ninety-foot tower, which is about seventy-eight steps too much for me, but my husband and daughter traversed to the top and reportedly enjoyed the experience. I stuck around in the museum, where you can read from the journals of the lighthouse keepers and their families, as well as check out wonderful artifacts from that era. Oh, and in case you're wondering why the lighthouse is so far inland? Can you say hurricanes?

10 Blond Giraffe Key Lime Pie Factory
Multiple locations, including 629 Duval Street

Recipient of the Best Key Lime Pie Award from several sources, this is the place to go to try this Key West delicacy. They even have the tourist favorite, key lime pie on a stick. With several locations, you can make sure not to miss this creamy, tangy treat...and best of all, they have a wonderful Web site (www.blondgiraffe.com) where you can order dessert, even if you can't make it to the Keys. Trust me, one taste and you'll be joining the crowds soon enough!

Special thanks to Janet Ware, a friend and fellow author, who with her associate, Victoria Shearer, wrote a marvelous book called THE INSIDER'S GUIDE: THE FLORIDA KEYS AND KEY WEST, *5th Edition. Janet sent me a copy to make sure I had my places and names straight...and I am very appreciative! Thank you, Janet!*

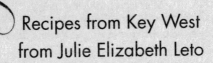

Recipes from Key West
from Julie Elizabeth Leto

I *love* to cook! But more than that, I love to eat! One
of my favorite things to do in Key West is troll the many
restaurants and bars, looking for irresistible foods and
drinks I can bring home and make myself. Here are a
few of my favorites.

MOJITO

Thanks to the popularity of all things Hispanic, this
drink is gaining in popularity. It's sometimes hard to
find bars that have fresh mint, but you can always go
to Sloppy Joe's in Key West like Ernest Hemingway did.
Or you could, like me, make them myself! I've planted
my own mint, which even the most black-thumbed
person can grow. In fact, keep it in its own planter or it
will choke out other plants.

The Mojito has been called the Cuban cousin to
the Southern Mint Julep. I agree!

INGREDIENTS

Simple syrup
Mint leaves (about 8 sprigs)
2? oz. light rum
1 lime
Ice
Club soda
Tall glass

First, make your simple syrup by heating equal parts of granulated sugar and water in a saucepan until just before boiling. Stir a lot to make sure the sugar is dissolved. This mixture will keep in the refrigerator (I put it in a Mason jar) for a few weeks and can be used to sweeten all manner of drinks, including lemonade.

Next, place your mint leaves and at least a tablespoon of simple syrup in the glass, then smash and squish with the spoon for a good thirty seconds, until you've bruised the mint and released all the flavor. I like mine "extra sweet" and usually put in about four tablespoons!

Juice the lime (removing all seeds) and add it to the mix. You can drop in one half of the squeezed lime if you wish. The mojito is a very trashy-looking drink.

Pour in the rum and stir.

Add lots of ice then top with the club soda. Garnish with more mint, a thin slice of lime and enjoy!

CONCH FRITTERS

Conch is pronounced "Konk." It is a mollusk. In fact,
it's the second most popular edible mollusk, after
escargot, of course. Conch is also the name for native
Key Westers, but in this recipe, stick to the snail. It's not
cheap, but it is yummy. You should be able to get it by
special ordering it through a specialty seafood shop...or
just go to the Bahamas and catch some! It is currently
illegal to take conch from U.S. waters.

INGREDIENTS

1 cup conch
2 tbsp Key lime juice
2 tbsp tomato paste
1 yellow bell pepper
1 medium onion
1 big garlic clove
1 tbsp thyme
1 tbsp parsley
1 tbsp oregano
1 tbsp celery seed
1 tbsp hot sauce
3/4 tbsp salt
1/2 tbsp basil
1/2 tbsp cumin powder
1/2 tsp black pepper
2 eggs
1 cup flour (not self-rising)
2 tbsp baking powder
some milk (just in case)

Pound conch with a rolling pin until it has flattened out (especially the thick and hard "foot"), then dice into small pieces and place in a small bowl. Mix in lime juice and tomato paste. Dice the pepper, onion and garlic and place in a separate large bowl. Mix in spices, then conch mixture, followed by the flour, baking powder and eggs.

The batter should be thick enough that if you take a spoonful of it and turn it upside down, it'll stick to the spoon for a few seconds. If too thin, add more flour. If too thick, add a little milk. You could also substitute a little beer for the milk.

Get a couple of plates with paper towels handy, as well as a tablespoon, a teaspoon, a fork and a metal device for scooping stuff out of hot oil.

Heat a pot of about 2 inches of cooking oil on medium heat. Stir after a few minutes. Oil should be ready after 7 or 8 minutes. Don't heat too fast or oil and fritters will burn.

Scoop up 1 tablespoon of fritter mixture, scrape it into oil with teaspoon. Let cook for about 2 minutes, then roll it over with fork (they float) and let cook on other side for about 2 minutes or until lightly browned. Scoop out with scooper and let drain on napkin plate. Let cool a bit and then taste. Adjust the spices until you have the flavor you like—don't be afraid to kick it up a notch, as Emeril would say!

Serve with lemon or lime wedges, some more hot sauce and plenty of cold drinks!

AUTHENTIC KEY LIME PIE

First of all, the most important rule—key lime pie is not green. Key limes are not green. They are yellow. They are small and potent and alas, hard to find as they don't grow well in cold weather. I can't even grow them in Tampa! The best bottled stuff is by Nellie & Joe's—you can order it online, though it's carried in some grocery stores.

Also, authentic Key Lime Pie is not baked—so use pasteurized eggs to avoid salmonella. Your grocer should be able to get these for you. Or you can go online and look up a recipe that calls for baking.

INGREDIENTS

3 egg yolks
1 14-oz can sweetened
condensed milk
1/2 cup Key lime juice
1 9-inch graham cracker
baked pie shell

> If you make any of these recipes and like them, please let me know!

Whisk the egg yolks into the condensed milk. Add the lime juice little by little, stirring until mixture starts to thicken. Scrape into the pie shell and let it chill and set up.

You can use the leftover egg whites to whip up a meringue—3 egg whites with 6 tablespoons of sugar, beaten to stiff peaks and then piped onto the pie. Put in the oven and bake until just barely brown on the tips. Or you can dollop on some good, sweet whipped cream to offset the tanginess of the lime. Serve with *cafe con leche* and you've got one delicious Key West dessert!

Only in Key West
by Julie Elizabeth Leto

One of the most enjoyable parts of researching this book was reading Gregory King's The Conch That Roared (Weston & Wright Press, 1997). The book is readily available, less than one hundred pages long and funny as all get-out. It was my main research source (though I consulted a few others, just because I could) for the famed 1982 secession of Key West from the United States of America—and the subsequent declaration of war—that Tessa's father, Rip Dalton, had become famous for. Well, that and his speedboats.

To understand exactly how this very real event came to pass, you have to study a little geography. Don't worry—it's easy. If you look at a map of Florida, you'll see a bunch of little islands extending from the southeast tip of the peninsula to the west. Key West is at the end of that line. Highway 1 runs the length of the Keys and ends at mile marker 0 (a designation tourists celebrate by purchasing cute, green refrigerator magnets that look like mile marker signs). There are only a few ways to get into Key West: on a boat, on a plane or drive the one and only highway—a great deal of it a two-lane bridge—that connects the islands to mainland Florida. It is approximately 150 miles of road.

I'd say that a good number of people go to Key West in their cars. More so in the past, too, before the cruise ships started making Key West a regular stop. So now that you know how things are laid out, you'll understand why the federal government caused such an uproar when on Sunday, April 18, 1982, they set up a roadblock that brought the drivers returning to the mainland from the Keys to a screeching halt for hours in the heat with no water, no bathrooms, no food—all so they could check for illegal aliens.

Illegal aliens? Well, that was the official story, of course. The U.S. Border Patrol was running the roadblock, with some help from the highway patrol and, most importantly, the DEA. They were really looking for drugs.

But I don't want to dwell on the politics, because really, what fun is that? (For more on the politics, do consult King's book. He explains all of the players and motivations with wit and clarity.) What impressed me was the way that rebellious, outrageous, infinitely fun Key West decided to respond to the fact that the U.S. government had essentially established a blockade on US 1. Anyone leaving the Keys had to submit to a search of their cars, which slowed traffic to a standstill. So, led by a group of businessmen who had been struggling to establish Key West as a tourist destination, the people of Key West revolted à la South Carolina just before the War Between the States. They seceded and established their own independent nation, The Conch Republic, then declared war on the United States.

And they were only halfway kidding because you see, once they surrendered, they planned to apply to the United Nations for $1 billion dollars in foreign aid. Okay, I said no politics. But darn, I think the irony is priceless.

No one really knows whose idea it was to secede, but there are plenty of people who want to take credit. That's part of the charm of Key West—the pride with which the locals defend their way of life. They established a new government, a military force, filed all the right paperwork and most importantly, called in the press. They wanted to make Key West a tourist destination, and thanks to a political gaffe by the feds, they did just that.

Conch Republic flags still fly high and proudly in Key West.

24

SON OF THE SIREN

*Just exactly how did Alina and Reides'
story end? Read the final scene!*

CHAPTER 1

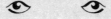

WITH ONE LAST BURST *of strength, Alina raised Artemis's arrow over her head and then drove the silver point deep into the siren's chest. The creature screamed, reared back onto its razor sharp tail, claws slashing the ashen sky above her. Despite the wax Alina had jammed into her ears, the edges of the virulent cry seeped into her brain. Excruciating pain threatened to overwhelm her, so she struck again. And again.*

Then, the once-beautiful face of the siren, splattered with blood, twisted into a frozen mask of pain and defeat and fell cold to the ground.

Alina stumbled to the side, praying to the goddess that this was the last of them. For what seemed like an endless succession of bloody days and terror-filled nights, Alina had searched for her lover. She'd solved riddles, sailed angry oceans and battled with every ounce of strength and cunning lent to her by Artemis, her patron. And now she knew with all her soul that despite her victory, her life was nearly spent. Though not foolish enough to curse her aloud, Alina thought silently that Aphrodite deserved whatever punishment Artemis meted out to her.

They'd forged that bond, she and the goddess of the hunt. Alina would spite Aphrodite by stealing Reides back, but Artemis would deal with the goddess of love herself and end the cycle of retribution.

Bleeding profusely from a wound to her shoulder inflicted by the last clawed siren she'd battled, Alina felt her life spilling from her body as she unplugged the wax from her ears. Though the siren's cry would not affect a woman the same way as a man, Alina had been unwilling to take any chances. She dragged herself away from the carcass of the siren, searching the beach beyond for any sign of her lover. Months and months of tracking led her to the place of his birth, where Poseidon had spirited him. Artemis had told her Poseidon wanted his son to live, but could not risk that a reunion with Alina would bring about the prophecy. He'd ordered the sirens to fight to the death, but neither the god of the ocean nor the cruel, clawed creatures of the deep anticipated the fury of Alina's passion.

She'd won, but as a reward, she'd die. And yet she had to see him one more time. She had to know, before she slipped away into the underworld, if all had been for naught.

Finally she spotted him, lashed to a slim marble column in the middle of a ring of tall spires decorated with treasures of the sea—shells, corals, the fins of mighty fish. Determined, she gulped in the air and forced herself to stand, stanching the wound with her hand. She dragged herself closer and closer to the shrine, urged forward by the fact that Reides, while still as stone, was even more beautiful than she remembered. Beautiful, but broken.

Above him, a shell the size of a chariot wheel gurgled with seawater from an unseen source. When the water filled the shell completely, it tipped, streaming Reides with his life-sustaining liquid from the sea. He was saturated, glistening, and Alina realized with a strangled cry, warm to the touch.

"You live, my love," she whispered, invigorated by knowing she had not fought for nothing. She stared into his passionless eyes and forbade herself to lose hope. "See me, Reides. Know that your betrayal did not destroy me, as Aphrodite threatened. She tricked you. She tempted you in ways no mortal or god could counter. I know that now. I'm stronger for her duplicity, for yours. I can stand now and say I want you, fight for you. Take you."

She kissed him hard, molding her wind-cracked and bloodstained lips against his smooth, moist flesh. She ran her one, uncut hand across his chest, down his arms, around his hips, feeling him, learning him all over again. The shell tipped, bathing them in a shower of warm seawater. The salt splashed against her wounds, and though the pain made her knees buckle, she wrapped strong arms around his neck and held herself against him. Her breasts filled as his warmth reached her. Her body throbbed to know his hardness inside her again.

She would die in his arms, if need be, for all she'd endured to find him, but she prayed to Poseidon and

Artemis to bring him back, even for an instant, before she slipped away.

When the water stopped, Alina felt Reides' lips move beneath hers. She pressed her tongue into his mouth and he responded. The flavors of the sweet sea filled her senses so that she imagined if she submerged beneath the water now, she'd still be able to breathe.

She flashed her eyes open and watched as life slowly seeped back into his gaze.

"Reides?"

She'd known he was alive, but she'd thought the spell Aphrodite had cast on him would imprison him forever. Emboldened by the blaze of awareness in his eyes, Alina spun around him and untied the bindings lashing him to the spire. He dropped to his knees just as the shell tipped again, splashing them both and making Alina laugh aloud as she washed away the grime and gore of her battle.

This time, the pain in her arm abated and she watched the wound close to the point where no more blood oozed down her tunic. The water in the shell must have been enchanted by the sirens to keep Reides alive, no matter how the battle raged.

Had they known they were doomed to be vanquished by a love stronger than even creatures of the sea?

Weakened by the sight of her lover, by the magnitude of the battle she'd fought and won, Alina dropped down beside him and grabbed his face in her hands, forcing his ocean-green eyes on her.

"Reides, do you know me?"

28

He swallowed hard, his lashes fluttering against the water and the sunlight streaming from high above.

"Alina?"

"Yes!"

"Aphrodite…said you…died."

"She lied to you, Reides. She manipulated you, made you her slave. She would have killed you if not for your father, who interceded on your behalf and had you transported to the land of the sirens. They would not release you to me."

Though the action cost him, he struggled to wrap his arm around her. "I will protect you."

She smiled and tenderly stroked his cheek. "There is no need. With Artemis's help, I defeated them. The island is ours now. You are free."

He shook his head, not in denial, but in deep despair. Her chest ached for the sadness in his face.

"I betrayed you," he said.

She cupped his chin, and then slid her hand up through his hair, relishing the feel of his flesh against hers. "Yes, but not of your own choice. In order to entice you, Aphrodite enslaved you with spells and potions, the smoke from a fire burning with the magic of the gods. Had she left you to your own heart, you would not have left me."

Reides looked aside and Alina's heart wept. She said the words, wanted desperately to believe her own hopes and dreams, but doubts remained. What if what Artemis had claimed was true? What if men had not the capability to love selflessly? To sacrifice all for the happiness of their mate?

When he turned back to her, the devotion in his eyes brought tears to hers.

"I would not have abandoned you, Alina. I did not know love until you. You sacrificed all for me, including your life that first night, when I foolishly fought the Hydra in order to sate my lust. I could see nothing but my own desire then. Now I know love. Because of you. How can I repay such a debt?"

Alina stood, ripped away her battle-torn garment then reached up and waiting for the shell to tip once more. The water splashed down her body, invigorating her, refilling her with the power she'd lost in the fight, in the loneliness since Reides's abduction. Artemis had sent her lovers to ease the pain, but none had touched her soul.

When she glanced down at Reides, she did not see lust in his eyes as she had before. She saw adoration. Love. Desire, yes, but his need sprang from deep within his heart just as this rejuvenating water spilled from the heart of the sea.

"Make love to me, Reides. Not as we have in the past, but as we will now, two souls intertwined by fate and destiny."

With the sun gilding his skin, Reides stood, tall and proud and strong. He tore away his garment as she had and Alina's mouth watered at the sight of his sex jutting toward the sky. He circled her and without touching her, adored her with his eyes. When the shell tipped again, he splashed the water over every inch of his skin, bathing away the last remnants of what had transpired in the past.

Twining Alina's fingers in his, he led her to the

shore. Hand in hand, they walked waist-deep into the water. The waves raged and pushed at them, knocking them with their majesty, until Reides dipped his palm into the ocean and calmed the seas.

Alina gasped.

Reides smiled and cupped her chin. "Fear me not, Alina. I have only now understood the powers I possess over the ocean of my birth. I am not just the son of a siren, but the son of the god of the sea. But born to the sea, my strength is in the depths, in the currents. I learned as much from the sirens before they took me captive, to protect me from my destiny."

"What is your destiny, Reides?"

His smile brimmed with pride, but also with joy. "To create a new civilization, starting here. I will move this great island beneath the ocean, to protect it from the vagaries of the Olympians."

Alina's heart sank. The sadness must have reflected in her eyes, because instantly Reides brought her close to him. "You will come with me, Alina. You will be my queen. Though our life will be beneath the sea, the air you require will sustain us. You can bring your family. We will pick and choose among the brightest and best of the mortals and create a utopia more brilliant than even Olympus."

Alina watched the sky, waiting for a thunderbolt from Zeus, yet none came.

"The gods will be furious," she warned.

Reides looked entirely undeterred. "They have no choice. The fate is theirs, they knew this. They conspired to keep us apart so that our progeny would not build the land I plan to call Atlantis."

With this declaration, he kissed her. All of his strength returned and Alina's blood instantly pumped hard through her veins, matching the rhythm she could feel surging through him. Suddenly a whirlpool swirled around them, splashing their bodies and pressing them closer together.

Reides motioned with his hands, inviting fingers of water to tease and tantalize them from all directions. Alina's heart hammered in her chest. She thought of the horrible psyche that had nearly drowned her in the pool on Crete, but Reides anchored her face with his hands and looked warmly into her eyes.

"Fear not the sea, Alina. Nothing will ever hurt you again. The water will bring you only rapture."

She captured his hands in hers, kissed his knuckles, then guided one palm onto her breast and the other between her legs. "Only you can bring me true ecstasy, love. Only you."

And so Reides complied. In the swirl of the waves, Alina and her dream lover discovered their destiny of pleasure, together, for all eternity.

THE END

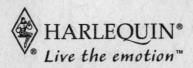

LAUNCHING AUGUST

Fall in love all over again with classic stories
by *New York Times* and *USA TODAY*
bestselling authors.

Fantasy by Lori Foster
Available August 2005

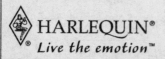

SAGA

Coming in August…

**A dramatic new story in
The Bachelors of Blair Memorial saga…**

USA TODAY bestselling author

Marie Ferrarella

SEARCHING
FOR CATE

A widower for three years, Dr. Christian Graywolf
knows his life is his work at Blair Memorial Hospital.
But when he meets FBI special agent Cate Kowalski—
a woman searching for her birth mother—the attraction
is intense and immediate. And the truth is something
neither Christian nor Cate expects—that all his life
Christian has been searching for Cate.

> **Bonus Features,
> including:**
>
> **Sneak Peek,
> The Writing Life
> and Family Tree**

Where love comes alive™

MINISERIES

Coming in August…

USA TODAY bestselling author

Dixie Browning

LAWLESS LOVERS

**Two complete novels from
The Lawless Heirs saga.**

Daniel Lyon Lawless and Harrison Lawless are two
successful, sexy and very sought after bachelors.
But their worlds are about to be rocked by the
love of two headstrong, beautiful women!

**Bonus Features,
including:**

The Writing Life,

Family Tree

and Sneak Peek
from a NEW Lawless
Heirs title coming
in September!

Where love comes alive™

SPOTLIGHT

The exciting and always powerful Fortune family is back in a brand-new continuity series!

THE
F RTUNES
OF TEXAS:
Reunion

In August look for...

In the Arms of the Law

by *USA TODAY* bestselling author

PEGGY MORELAND

Detective Andrea Matthews was known for storming through investigations, not letting herself lose control or become attached to the wrong man. But when she's assigned to work with Officer Gabe Thunderhawk on a murder involving a lost Fortune, she has trouble controlling both her excitement and her emotions!

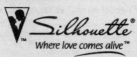

Where love comes alive™